BEYOND

REVELATION

A FRANCINE VEGA INVESTIGATIVE THRILLER : BOOK 3

JOHN HAZEN

Black Rose Writing | Texas

Third printing

ISBN: 978-1-68433-605-0
PUBLISHED BY BLACK ROSE WRITING
www.blackrosewriting.com

Printed in the United States of America
Suggested Retail Price (SRP) $19.95

Beyond Revelation is printed in Cambria

*As a planet-friendly publisher, Black Rose Writing does its best to eliminate
unnecessary waste to reduce paper usage and energy costs, while never compromising
the reading experience. As a result, the final word count vs. page count may not meet
common expectations.

This book is dedicated to my wife, Lynn and also to those journalists who search for truth and hold our leaders accountable.

Also by John Hazen

Fava

Zyklon

Journey of an American Son

Aceldama

Dear Dad

BEYOND
REVELATION

The truth is incontrovertible. Malice may attack it and ignorance may deride it, but in the end, there it is.

—Winston Churchill

1

My phone buzzed.

After spending a much-needed long weekend with Will and the kids at Disney World, I was up to my neck in pending deadlines. Westbrook Broadcasting Corporation, the WBC, was only three months old, and we needed to get stories on the air. WBC hoped to be a breath of fresh air in an already crowded world of cable news, but so far we hadn't found a niche that would set us apart. We hadn't yet gotten to where we could fill up our 24/7 schedule. If you were to turn on our channel at 3:00 AM, you'd more likely find an infomercial about the latest herbal supplement to stop hair loss or weight gain than you would an actual news story.

I am Chief Executive Officer of WBC. I'll get into how that happened soon. When we first started up the WBC, I wanted to do everything and, as CEO, I thought I could do everything. I anchored the nightly prime-time news hour. I was one of our four field investigative reporters. I hosted our weekly public affairs and opinion hour. That's besides doing whatever a CEO does.

It took me less than a week to conclude that I was a damn fool thinking I could perform all these functions, leastwise perform them professionally. I had to jettison something.

I had no choice in being CEO, but hopefully I could delegate much of those duties to people I trusted who knew what they were doing in running a company. My passion has always been investigative journalism. I love digging up stories, interviewing people and getting to the truth. It came down to choosing between my weekly show and my anchor duties. There was no contest. I would no longer be an anchor.

Even with this voluntary cutback, I had lots on my plate. My job was to think up, write, investigate, produce, approve and present new stories. One story I was working on—an analysis of rampant favoritism by the New York City Mayor's Office in awarding construction contracts—should have run the previous night, but I wasn't ready. Luckily, missing one day was not a tragedy, but it was not a habit I wanted to get into.

I was also busy prepping for my weekly opinion show, *Back at Ya!*, where I moderated a discussion amongst groups of experts on an important topic of the day. This week's edition was airing this very evening so, unlike the construction contract story, I couldn't procrastinate. I had to be ready for the evening broadcast; it was only a couple hours away.

There are times I wished I listened to various advisors who told me I shouldn't do this show live. In a live broadcast there is so much room for mistakes and gaffes that could backfire. I just loved the spontaneity that live television brings.

The last thing I needed right now was to invest time to talk to anybody, but I'm a creature of habit. I couldn't help myself and glanced at my phone. Jonas was calling. There is a small cadre of people for whom I would drop what I'm doing at a moment's notice to do whatever they asked. Jonas Clarke—my longtime friend, cameraman and someone who once took a bullet for me—is part of that cadre. I answered the call.

"Hey, J. What's up?"

"Frannie, I need your help."

"You're off today, aren't you? Where are you?"

"I'm in Massachusetts."

"What are you doing up there?"

"I'll get to that in a minute but what I'm calling you for is because I'm in jail."

"You're what? What happened?"

"Eunice left on Saturday to come up here to help her cousin and his wife move into their new house. That was the last I've heard from her. I came up here to find her."

"J., why did you run up there after what, six days? It's not unusual for Eunice to disappear for days or even weeks at a time, is it?"

"In the old days, yeah, but ever since my car blew up, and I nearly died, she's been on me like white on rice."

I always found it somewhat amusing when this big Black man used this expression. Oh, I mentioned that he once took a bullet for me. I should also say that his car blew up due to mistaken placement of C-4 in his car, not mine. He continued.

"She should have called me when she arrived and a couple times since then. I tried her phone, and it went immediately to voicemail. When I tried calling her cousin, I got a recording that the number had been disconnected. I called the local cops up there. The cop I spoke to never saw or heard of Eunice. He said her family moved away this week with no info on where they moved to. He was very unhelpful and got me off the line as fast as they could. That's when I sent you the text I'd be out today and drove up here."

"You still haven't told me how you ended up in jail."

"I went to her cousin's house. It was empty with a For Sale sign out front. I then went to the lawyer who Eunice told me had helped them buy the house. He lives in the middle of town. There was no one at home. When I went around the side to see if there was a separate entrance to his office, a cop showed up and arrested me for attempted robbery. I tried explaining what I was doing, but he didn't want to hear it. He put me in the holding cell at the police department in the town hall. They'll transfer me to a real jail in a different town in the county. Since we're coming into the weekend, I won't get to see a judge until Monday. I can't even get bail until then."

"Where exactly are you and what's the name of the lawyer?"

"Little town called Fairbrook. The attorney's name is John Foster."

I jotted this information down and plugged Fairbrook into the map program on the computer. It's between Worcester and Springfield, about a four to five-hour drive, depending on traffic.

"What's Eunice's cousin's name?"

"Rutledge, Lynn, and Carl Rutledge. Carl is Eunice's cousin."

"Oh, what's the policeman's name?"

"Sykes, Andrew Sykes."

"I'll come up and get you out of there."

I looked at my watch. It was after four. I would have to get someone to host my nine o'clock show, go home to pick up the car (which undoubtedly needed gas, adding more time), pack and make arrangements for someone to take care of the kids since Will was out of town. I wouldn't be able to leave New York until seven or later. In addition, there was Friday night rush hour traffic to consider. As a result, I probably wouldn't get to Massachusetts until midnight or later. I was thinking of several candidates to take over my show when Jonas spoke up. It was as if he was reading my mind.

"Frannie, don't even think of coming up tonight. You'll be exhausted and couldn't do anything because it'll be so late. Do your show and come up tomorrow."

"You sure?"

"Yeah, I'll be okay. I have to go now. They're coming to take my phone away."

"And once I'm up there, we'll find out what happened to Eunice. Don't worry, we'll find her. She probably is off doing something. I'm sure it's something we'll all laugh about later."

"Thanks, Frannie. See you tomorrow."

2

After I hung up, it was tough focusing, but I went back to work. I put the finishing touches on the Mayor's Office piece. This was one of those cases where procrastination paid off. I had that morning received a call from my confidential source, a close aide to the Mayor that I've known for years, who confirmed some details of contractor corruption on which I was reporting. If I had completed the story on schedule the day before, I would have reported the findings as "alleged" but now, with this confirmation, I could report it with more certainty.

I was happy my research indicated the Mayor himself was not involved in the corruption. He'd only been in office less than a year and I liked him, the things he stood for and the positions he took. Perhaps he should have known that the corruption was happening under his nose by a trusted member of his administration, but at least he wasn't directly implicated. If this piece had any legs, a lot would depend on how he responded. Many elected leaders claim that the buck stops with them but have an innate ability to convince people that the buck stopped somewhere else. I wasn't sure whether this mayor had that ability or whether the stink would stick to him. Only time would tell.

I finished the piece and reviewed the film footage that would accompany the story on the 7:00 news hour. Everything seemed polished, so it was time to move on. Next, I had to review the lineup for the news hour. Everything seemed in order. Frank McDermott, our News Director, had done his usual complete job. I knew I was ready to go.

After that, I needed to concentrate on our 9:00 talk show, which I hosted. This was where I focused most of my work, and consequently most of my job satisfaction. It wasn't until I officially became a "talking head" last year on my previous job with Allied Broadcasting's acclaimed program *Issues and Answers* that I came to realize how much work goes into these weekly news programs. I had a fine mentor in the host of this show, Richard Leitz, who had earned a national reputation as a hard-hitting, fair and informed journalist. One of the proudest days of my life was when

Richard called me within an hour after the first edition of *Back at Ya!* aired to tell me how great the show was.

Whenever I was preparing for *Issues and Answers*, I always felt so inadequate. Richard was an Ivy League and Oxford trained economist who could keep up with any expert he may have had on any given Sunday. In fact, Richard put many of the inadequately prepared "experts" in their places as he picked their arguments apart bit by bit, fact by fact. There were some people who vowed never to return after Richard publicly humiliated them. He was fine with that because there were scores of people who clamored to be on his highly-rated show.

I came to Richard's attention first from a story I did on a terroristic threat to destroy the City of Mecca. Luckily, my efforts were instrumental in thwarting that threat. I personally thought I should have received the Pulitzer Prize. Not to worry, though, I'm not bitter... much. My stock rose even further in his eyes with my work on last year's Presidential campaign, and he asked me to be a regular on his show.

Unlike most of his guests, I did not bring a wealth of expertise to the show. Hence, I had these feelings of inadequacy. I raised my lack of qualifications to him before my first appearance. His answer was succinct. "I didn't want you on the show because of your in-depth knowledge; I want you because you're one of the best journalists I've ever seen in action." I knew that, on the one hand, he'd just called me a dummy (he said it in a very nice way, but the message was clear) but, in the next breath, he gave me the highest compliment I'd ever received.

I worked closely with Richard for about eight months, and they were probably the most rewarding eight months of my professional life. Like I said, I got a newfound appreciation for the intense amount of work that goes into producing a show like *Issues and Answers*. The behind-the-scenes effort makes the show come off seamlessly. Once I left Allied Broadcasting, I knew that I was one day going to be part of a show like *Issues and Answers* again. I just didn't know when.

"Good morning. I'm Francine Vega and welcome to this evening's edition of *Back at Ya!* seen here exclusively on Westbrook Broadcasting. Today we will discuss White Privilege: Fact or Myth? To assist me today, I'm joined by William Prescott, Founder and President of the National Association for the Advancement of White Culture, Reverend Malcolm

McKenzie, the former presidential candidate and now a syndicated talk show host discussing issues of our day, and Cornell Abernathy, President of the New York MultiEthnic Exchange. Thank you all for joining me today."

I had always envisioned taking part in a weekly show different from what you can normally find on your typical news channel. All too often on the various news programs, you'll find groupings of people who agree with each other, talking with each other to reinforce the strongly felt shared beliefs they arrived with. Many of the people on these shows are experts in their fields and bring a lot to the table because of his or her respective expertise. However, they rarely get pushback or are even challenged. With my show and the whole network, I was hoping to provide a forum where people at the opposite ends of the spectrum can present their views, argue, disagree, agree to disagree and perhaps occasionally find a bit of common ground.

Growing up, my mother tried to limit my television watching. She did not want me wasting my time watching frivolous things. She didn't totally ban these shows, but she made it clear she'd prefer me not to watch them and the one thing I always wanted to do was please my mother (and still want to even though she passed away years ago). As a result, I'm probably the only person in America who didn't watch cartoons as a kid. While it gave me time to pursue more serious matters, I sometimes miss out on references to pop culture that might be useful to know in my line of work as a journalist. A recent interaction with Jonas provides a case in point.

We were driving to a location to film some background on a story I was doing when we passed an Acme Supermarket in Clifton, New Jersey. Jonas wondered whether we could pick up an anvil or some sticks of dynamite there.

"Why would you expect to get things like that in a supermarket?" I asked.

"You know, Acme?"

"So?"

"Roadrunner? Wiley Coyote? You never heard of them?"

"I've heard of them but I still don't know what Acme has to do with them."

Jonas just shook his head in wonder. Later that day I plugged these terms into my search engine and came up with the cartoon he was referring to. I learned how the coyote was always trying to trap or kill the poor roadrunner bird using Acme products such as anvils and dynamite. I suppose these are things I should have learned before the ripe old age of thirty, but what can you do?

The one program my mother would always let me watch was any news program that we could get on our ancient Admiral television. I suppose that's where my love for journalism was first nurtured. Anyway, I was a strange kid and at some point I fell in love with the McLaughlin Group. I loved the back and forth and the different viewpoints of the journalists who represented both ends of the spectrum, liberal and conservative. I loved the final word when John McLaughlin would make the pronouncement "and the answer is..." regardless of what the panel had said previously. What I liked most was that the panelists, who ranged from extremely liberal to ultra-conservative, could discuss things without rancor or recrimination. Neither accused the other side of hating America or being an "enemy of the people" or acting in bad faith. They disagreed. Occasionally, they would agree on some point or other, but often they gave their points of view and opinions. The viewer received a range of viewpoints on a subject and could come to their own conclusion, but after watching this show, no one could say it was an uninformed conclusion.

My mother's mastery of English was not the greatest. Often she would get lost as we watched the show together, but she knew enough to know that the pundits were saying something important. She would jot down things she didn't understand. Then, during commercial breaks and after the show, we would go over what she didn't understand. Sometimes her notes were comical because she was writing what she thought she heard in a language she was only just learning. Looking at her notes, which were her phonetic guesses of the English she heard, it could be a bit of a challenge trying to figure out what the pundit had said. Usually, though, my memory was enough to recall what he or she said.

I would then explain the word or phrase to her. Sometimes it would take a couple attempts because she would not allow me to take the easy way out to tell her what the word meant in Spanish. I would have to explain it solely in English, using words in her vocabulary that she would understand. From the viewpoint of learning English in an English-speaking country, this was a beneficial process for both of us. My mother was determined that my accent or insufficient English skills not hold me back.

One drawback is that my Spanish skills are definitely lacking. My mother was a Cuban immigrant, so I'm a first-generation American. Many people therefore assume that I have a greater fluency in Spanish than I do. Sometimes I have to tell fellow Latinos to switch to English so I can understand them.

I apologize for this digression, but whenever I talk about my mother I have a tendency to go on and on. Her passing away from cancer left me devastated and rudderless. Thank heavens Will came along. He became my rock.

Even the name of my show, *Back at Ya!*, is a tribute to my mother. She was buying groceries in a local bodega. After she paid, she said in her broken English that the clerk should have a nice day. The clerk, a pleasant middle-aged Black man who later became one of my mother's closest friends, responded by saying "Back at ya!"

My mother came home shaken, not understanding what the clerk said to her. She was unsure whether he'd insulted or complimented her. I was doing my homework at the kitchen table when she came into our apartment.

"Mama, what's wrong?" I asked.

"Fava," she said using the pet name for me she adopted when, as a toddler, I mixed up my name, "please tell what means 'back at ya!' Someone told me this and I don't know what he means."

"Mama, it's a good thing. It's a way of him saying the same thing you just said to him. What did you tell him?"

"I say 'have a good day'."

"Then that's what he was telling you. It's a friendly way of telling you to have a nice day, too."

I'll always remember the way the tension in her body dissolved away and a warm smile emerged on her face. I think she was a little embarrassed that she assumed the worst but, in her defense, she was in the middle of organizing a rent strike in our building because the landlord had ceased any repairs nor would he do anything to evict drug dealers on the first floor. She was on edge much of the time during that period.

From then on, 'back at ya!' became a regular expression of hers. As her mastery of English improved, so did her use of 'back at ya'. Sometimes, she would use it ironically. It became her version of the Southern expression 'bless your heart', which could literally mean 'bless your heart' or could be a genteel way of saying 'f*** you'.

When it came time for me to develop my talk show, there was no doubt in my mind that I would call it *Back at Ya!*. Several people told me it wasn't a good name for my program. The name was too colloquial: it wouldn't be taken seriously. I didn't care. It said exactly what I wanted it to say, both good and bad.

After only a few months, our email and social media chatter has shown *Back at Ya!* to be amassing a small but steadily growing loyal following. People seem to like the format of freewheeling open dialogue. It's my job to keep the show from devolving into a shouting match. It's not always easy. A few weeks earlier, we had a forum on 'Government Regulation: How much is too much?' and my guests included a member of the American Libertarian Party on the one side and a member of Green Action on the other that nearly resulted in a fistfight. Eventually, cooler heads prevailed, and the situation calmed down.

One effect that the histrionics and near fisticuffs had was a significant bump in the show's ratings. I'd have wished people would watch my show because of the information and substance we offered but, in this business, you take what you can get, especially with a new start-up. I didn't want an updated version of Jerry Springer, but I wanted an audience. Keeping them watching would result from good solid journalism, or at least I hoped it would be.

Returning to today's show, the subject of white privilege and white supremacy had the potential to be even more volatile. I knew it would not be easy keeping the two sides from getting violent and I needed help, so I called an old friend/foe: the former candidate for President of the United States, Reverend Malcolm McKenzie.

I went to my contacts list on my phone. It'd been nearly a year since I'd last spoken with him, so I hoped Reverend McKenzie hadn't changed his number. The last time we talked was the day after the presidential election that he nearly pulled off. He came within percentage points of becoming President of the United States. My efforts in broadcasting the sordid truth about his opponent, Governor—now President—Peter Kent contributed to the closeness.

After the election, The Reverend tried to resume being a simple minister, but that proved impossible. He was in too great a demand as a pundit and forecaster on the national scene. As such, he worked right here in New York for a rival network with his own show called *Truth to Power*, which aired at three every weekday afternoon. I called four days ahead of my show, but I was skeptical he'd agree to come on. If nothing else, I didn't know what his contractual restrictions were. He could tell me there was nothing he could do; his contract precluded him from appearing on a rival network's show. I understood, but it was worth a shot.

I called at around one in the afternoon. He would be deep into preparation for his afternoon show and I assumed he wouldn't be able to talk to me but I called anyway figuring I could leave a message to get the ball rolling. I was shocked when he took my call but then I was even more shocked when he suggested getting together for lunch at a small Moroccan restaurant near his studio.

I thought it ironic that he suggested a Moroccan restaurant since it was his anti-Muslim and anti-immigrant polemics that brought us together to being with. He realized a story I was working on about a plot to destroy Mecca with the express intention of bringing down the Islam religion. Instead of being appalled by such a thought, he thought it a great idea and ran with it. He was such an articulate spokesman that he would eventually ride it all the way to a Presidential nomination.

Two things made him back off his anti-Muslim stance. First, he softened after his brother reconciled with his Muslim wife. She had initially fled to Jordan, taking their children with her. After a few months, she called and begged for him to take her back. Whether she missed her husband or the children missed their father or they all missed their American way of life or some combination thereof is unclear. Whatever the reason, he gladly accepted her back. For his brother's sake, The Reverend toned down, but didn't entirely suspend, his anti-Muslim rhetoric.

He stopped this crusade completely when he received word about the fire-bombing of a mosque and Islamic Center in Ohio shortly after one of his speeches. His aides and spokesman argued that he was not responsible for such a horrific act, but he knew better. He demanded to see pictures of the damaged center and a report on the casualties and injuries. They said he nearly collapsed from grief after viewing the corpse of a baby girl who had died in the blast.

"Francine," he bellowed out from the booth where he was waiting when I walked in, "it's wonderful to see you. First, how have you been doing? How's that little daughter Rosa doing and how's that FBI Agent husband of yours?"

"All are well. You have quite a terrific memory there, Reverend."

"One of God's gifts to me. How's the new network coming along?"

"Slowly, I'm sad to say. We still have to find our niche and build our audience. We'll get there but it'll take some time."

We talked about politics and the new Kent Administration. Apart from the new President's vendetta against me, I thought he'd make a good President. The Reverend agreed.

"It's been great catching up but let's get down to the reason for the pleasure of hearing from you again."

"I'm not sure if you're aware I have my own talk show now."

"Yes, of course I'm aware. I've set my DVR to record it every week."

"I thank you for that. I know you have your own show, but I was wondering if you'd consider appearing on my show."

"Tell me when and where."

"You don't even know what we'll be talking about?"

"Doesn't matter. I trust you. That's all that matters."

"You don't have issues with your network? I'd have thought they'd have built in an exclusivity clause in your contract."

"I'm sure there is but I really don't care. They need me more than I need them. But while we're on the topic, what will we be talking about?"

"White privilege and whether it's real or myth. William Prescott, President of the National Association for the Advancement of White Culture and Cornell Abernathy, President of the New York MultiEthic Exchange, will both be there. Do you know either of them?"

"I know Cornell rather well. A good man. I met Prescott at a conference a few years back. He's very intelligent and articulate. Both are committed to their respective causes. You've covered both ends of the spectrum. It could make for a spirited show."

"That's kinda why I'd like you there. You'd provide a moderating, middle-of-the-road perspective."

"Funny, there was a time when I don't think you would have labeled me 'middle-of-the-road'."

"We've all grown up a little since those days, haven't we?"

"Yes, we have."

"I don't know if you caught my show a couple weeks ago on regulation that almost ended in a barroom brawl."

"Yes, that was exciting."

"And it didn't hurt ratings-wise. I got quite a few new viewers the following week, but it's not the type of show I want to be known for."

"Understood. I'll be glad to play referee and send the combatants to neutral corners if need be. When and where do you want me?"

"As you know, we air Friday at nine. It would be great if you could show up around 7:30 to do any make-up and to chat ahead of time with the other panelists. Here's a card with our address. It will help you get through security downstairs."

"Great. See you then."

The Reverend and Cornell Abernathy arrived at the requested time, but William Prescott arrived only fifteen minutes before airtime. When he arrived, he offered no explanation, nor did he apologize for his tardiness. The one thing I learned from Richard was that you needed to go with the flow and always have a Plan B. My Plan B was to call my friend, newspaper reporter Anson Phipps, to come and fill in. He lived about five blocks from our studio and he'd said he could be ready at a moment's notice.

I haven't had to use Anson yet, but I've already taken to calling him Reilly. I'd read that in the old days of the Tonight Show, if a guest had cancelled out at the last minute, the producers would call Charles Nelson Reilly. He lived near the NBC studios and would hurry over to fill in with very little need for preparation. He was quick and sharp and entertaining and could talk for hours on any subject. He always had a story at the ready. Anson is like this. Anson could also play devil's advocate, taking a position he didn't especially support, but one would never know it from the arguments he put forward. I knew the show wouldn't lag if he were on the panel.

The one advantage Johnny Carson had was that he could juggle the schedule of guests to give Reilly time to get there. Since my show was a live hour-long discussion with the same panel throughout, I couldn't exactly do any shuffling. The entire panel had to be there from the opening of the show. So, about a half hour before airtime, I gave Anson a call to see if he was available. He was home and said he could be at the studio in ten minutes if needed. I gave him a rundown of the show. He groaned a bit when I advised him he'd have to take the role of a white supremacist, but he was game and would come up with his patter on the way over.

Luckily, Prescott showed up with about fifteen minutes to spare. I called Anson and told him to stand down. I would not require his services after all. I could hear the relief in his voice. While he would do it, he didn't relish the potential hit to his image playing this role.

The show began and I gave Prescott the opportunity to make an opening statement. He was into his second sentence when the fireworks began erupting.

"Thank you, Ms. Vega, for having me on your show this evening. I start off by refuting the title of this show, White Privilege: Fact or Myth? It should be: White Privilege: A Well-Deserved Fact. Whites have earned this privilege by being the authors of every worthwhile advancement of the civilized world since the recording of history."

"Any advancements made by whites were made on the backs of the other races," countered Cornell Abernathy.

"Whites civilized the other races. They'd be living in mud huts or pueblos if it weren't for whites."

"Which part do you believe to be more civilized? Capturing other human beings to enslave them and steal their labor or the genocide of entire peoples?"

"Those are unfortunate incidents in our history but that's what they are, history. The past. These events pale compared to all that the white race has contributed to the world in terms of science, the arts, music, industry, you name it."

"Incidents? Incidents? That's what you call slavery, the mark that will forever stain this country? An incident?"

"Well, we had it once upon a time but now it's gone, isn't it?"

"Only to be replaced by Jim Crow, lynching, segregation, redlining, poor schools, poor economic opportunity, voter suppression, mass incarceration, you name it. White America's great contribution to the world has been racism and oppression."

This could spiral out of control in the first five minutes if I didn't exert control. However, The Reverend beat me to it.

"Gentlemen, maybe we should take a step back and appreciate everybody's contributions, whether it was voluntary, coerced or stolen. Now, I believe the topic for today's discussion is whether white privilege is real, not whether it is deserved. I'm guessing by your opening, Mr. Prescott, that you believe it to be real. Mr. Abernathy, I sense that you believe it's real, as do I and Ms. Vega. So, we could all come to this conclusion and end the show now, but I don't think Ms. Vega's advertisers would appreciate that approach since people would stop watching and we'd have fifty minutes of dead air. Or, we could do something productive like discuss whether white privilege is beneficial to the American society or whether it is something that's only beneficial to one particular segment of our society. Let me turn this show back over to our host and see if we can make some lemonade here."

With that, The Reverend turned to me and gave me a smile and a wink. I smiled back and from there we had a productive show. There was still the occasional digression about white supremacy that had the potential to derail the show and have one or more of the panelists storm off the set, but Reverend McKenzie had set the stage for the discussion. He made it possible to rein the participants back in. As a result, we finished the hour intact. Nobody changed their minds, but they came away a little better informed. I hoped my viewers also left the show better informed.

3

I went to Frank to fill him in on Jonas. I'd be up there until at least through Monday in order to help free Jonas. For the past eight years, I would have had to ask Frank for permission to take a day off, but the situation has changed and now I simply had to advise him. I'm not exactly sure what Frank's and my working relationship was at this point in time. Let me explain.

Frank had been my boss and mentor for over eight years. Straight out of New York University, I went to work for him at Action 6 News, the Allied Broadcasting New York affiliate. I worked my way up from intern to production assistant to reporter to morning anchor and even had a regular spot on Allied Broadcasting's acclaimed nationally syndicated *Issues and Answers* weekly program. Along the way, I covered several stories that gave me national and even international prominence.

I could not ask for anything more professionally. Then, within a space of two months, it all unraveled. It started when I exposed on national television that the father of New York Governor and presidential candidate Peter Kent had been a war criminal, a Nazi SS Officer at the infamous Buchenwald Concentration Camp. Not only that, I revealed that the governor knew that his son, Alexander, was a notorious serial killer, but he did nothing to stop him. He didn't even speak up when the State of Texas executed an innocent man for Alexander's crimes.

Once I made these revelations, Kent's double-digit lead over his opponent, Reverend Malcolm McKenzie, shrank to a statistical tie. It was so close that the results didn't become official for two whole days after the election. Governor Kent held on and became President Kent.

After Kent was declared the winner, Frank predicted that the new president would exact revenge, making things ugly not only for me but for anyone involved in the broadcast. That included the host of *Issues and Answers*, Richard Leitz, NYPD Detective Jane Kelly, my husband, FBI Special Agent Will Allen and Frank himself. I tried taking a more optimistic view of the world, arguing that this was America and we still had a First

Amendment. Everything I said on the air was true and documented. I always believed that truth was a journalist's best ally.

It didn't take long for me to realize that I was being naively optimistic. By the end of November, the NYPD had demoted Jane Kelly to street cop, pending a disciplinary hearing on her actions. Kent's Deputy Director appointment to the FBI tried to torment Will, hoping he would resign. However, the FBI Director would have none of it and shielded Will from the abuse. While he appreciated the Director's support, Will is a stubborn man and he would not back down in the face of any assaults. In addition, he was approaching a pension milestone. He would not give anybody the satisfaction of leaving before being totally vested.

To attack me, and the network, Kent would have to wait until he became President. Starting on January 20, Frank's prediction was borne out. First, the White House denied credentials to reporters from Allied Broadcasting. Then the Administration called into question licenses for various affiliate stations. It was one thing after another until ultimately the network buckled and fired me.

To her credit, Network President Janet Kahn called me directly to advise me they had no choice but to can me. The pressure was too great. The network couldn't afford to be on the outs with the new Administration. I had to go.

Without even telling me, Frank submitted his resignation immediately upon hearing of my firing. I tried talking him out of quitting. He had two boys in college and could hardly afford an extended period of unemployment. He responded that he could no longer work for such a gutless organization and walked away.

It didn't take long for me to realize that I was a pariah in the news industry. News had traveled quickly how toxic I was. No other network would even interview me for a position, despite my credentials.

It was my husband, Will, who came up with the alternative: Start my own news station or network.

I was sitting in the kitchen feeling sorry for myself when he walked in and brought up the possibility.

"Fava," he said, (he and my kids are the only people other than my mother who I've ever allowed to use that pet name for me), "you do remember that we have in excess of $200 million dollars at our disposal, don't you?"

Of course, I remembered that, before he was killed, our friend Alan Westbrook had bequeathed us $200 million. It's not exactly something one forgets. This was the amount from his lottery jackpot winnings that was left over after he helped finance a plot to destroy Mecca, a plot he eventually helped us to thwart. He had no family and we were practically his only friends on earth.

We had this money, but it somehow never seemed appropriate to access it. Even after Alan's murder, we were reticent to touch it. As a result, it sat in an account accumulating interest while we went about our lives. Now that the powers-that-be had interrupted my life the way it had, Will was proposing we use these funds.

"Alan told you in his final note to continue on as a journalist. You were put on this earth to be a journalist, he said. I can't imagine he would suggest a better use of his money than this."

"A new network?"

"You've said many times how much the entertainment divisions at all the networks control and ruin the news operations and content. Allied is no different. So, start your own all-news network. Give the people a fresh alternative. Make it a hybrid broadcast slash social media outlet slash whatever else you want it to be."

"I know nothing about starting up let alone running a new network."

"Well, it just so happens that a person with a lot of experience and contacts became available at the same time you did."

"Frank?"

"You bet. He's worked in the field for over twenty years, much of that time in management at both the station and network level. He hasn't found anything new yet, has he?"

"No, he's had a few nibbles but nothing he's jumped at. I guess I could talk with him to feel him out."

When I called Frank, I intrigued him with the possibility of starting up a new network. We met to talk about it.

"This won't be easy, you know. There's so much competition. It will take a long time to get a viewership. Don't expect to turn a profit for at least three years."

"Frank, are you trying to talk me into doing this or out of it?"

He laughed.

"Most definitely into it, but we have to go into it with our eyes wide open. We have to anticipate what's ahead. I know of a couple stations that are looking to sell off their licenses. They're rather low on the cable spectrum, but they still could be profitable. If so, we can expand from there. We need to decide on a niche, some aspect of news that viewers aren't getting now but would want to tune into.

"I know a few of our colleagues who have been looking for a change and would consider joining us. A few may even be willing to provide some upfront investment if they can get in on the ground floor. You mind if I talk with them?"

"By all means. In terms of other investors, I'm not so sure."

"Francine, you may think $200 million sounds like a lot of money—and to most people it is—but owning a station is a lot like the adage of owning racehorses."

My blank stare told him I wasn't aware of the adage.

"The way to become a millionaire owning horses is to start off as a billionaire. We can purchase the rights to a station for a lot less than $200 million, but then you're going to eat away at it bit by bit. Just hiring the talent we need and the capital investment required to start up will cost us dear. It's always wise to get other investors involved."

I reluctantly agreed, but I made it clear I wanted to maintain control.

"You'll be in total control."

Six months later, Westbrook Broadcasting was born. It was to be an all-news station, focusing primarily on New York politics, current events and culture with an occasional foray into national affairs.

Mercifully, I trusted Frank enough that my involvement in the business aspects of the new start-up was limited to signing checks and nodding knowingly when he made suggestions. I'm always amazed at his expertise in the nuts and bolts of news broadcasting, but I'd only seen him in action regarding the content and programming aspects. Now I was seeing him in full glory on the business and operational facets, and it was impressive.

So, my relationship with Frank had become somewhat complicated. While I technically paid his salary, especially in the early days before we started building up our advertising base, I reported to him on all other matters. I've got a substantial ego, but I also have a decent awareness of my strengths and weaknesses. In the decade that I've worked under Frank, he let my strengths come forward and be on display. It would have been foolhardy to mess with success by introducing a new dynamic into the mix.

Before leaving for the night, I again punched Fairbrook, Massachusetts into a map program on my iPad to get the exact route. It's in the west-central part of the state near Springfield, near the Connecticut border, about a four-hour drive from New York City. I could leave our home in Queens first thing in the morning, get Jonas out of jail, figure out where Eunice was, and be back that same evening or the following morning at the latest. I'd want a second driver, so I asked my assistant, Heather, to accompany me.

It's always a great feeling when you see someone blossom and reach his or her potential right before your eyes. Heather Abernathy is such a person.

Heather came to Action 6 News as an intern. She was one of the few interns at the station who was there on merit, not because she was somebody's daughter or niece. She came to us with unbelievable research and computer skills. In fact, these skills helped me to uncover the Nazi lineage of now-President Kent. However, she lacked confidence in herself, which manifested itself in a clumsy, mousy appearance. She wanted to be a journalist but, when I first met her, I could not see that happening. Although she had the drive, ambition and intellect, she just did not have the personality or skill set to be a successful journalist. She would accompany me on interviews, but there was no way I could see her conducting a successful interview on her own.

Over the few months we worked together, we became very close. I'd long thought of Frank as being my mentor. She was my opportunity to pay it forward.

Heather was like a sponge, absorbing anything I could impart to her. She kept a journal, scratching down everything I said, and I mean everything. It was embarrassing how she hung on my every word, preserving it for posterity like I was the Dalai Lama or somebody like that.

I worked late one evening and, as I headed out, I passed by her cube and saw that she was still there. She didn't notice me behind her and I glanced at her computer screen. She was transcribing her notes from the day to a computer file. She took such good notes that I could recognize my phrasing and word choice. I thought I'd embarrassed her that I caught her doing this, so I departed without saying a word.

She was more upset when I got sacked than I was. She felt like she was losing her best friend. Perhaps she was. We cried and said our goodbyes. But before I left, I told her how proud I was of her and I wanted her to keep growing and developing. You could see how much she had matured just in her appearance and in her confidence. She carried herself more erect. She dressed much more fashionably. She got a new haircut. I was very pleased.

I'd call on her every week and we'd get together for lunch every month. I progressively sensed she was losing confidence in herself and was slipping back into old habits. She was folding back into herself. She was still a brilliant researcher and had much to contribute to the station, but her personal development was being stifled.

I was at a loss, but I didn't know what to do. I was at loose ends myself, trying to figure out what to do with my life. At least I had a strong support network in Will and my kids, Frank and Jonas. Heather had no boyfriend or significant other. Her parents had broken off relations with her.

When Will first came up with the crazy idea of starting my station, I immediately thought of stealing Heather. However, I didn't want to say or do anything prematurely until I knew the station/network was a viable possibility. I did not want to raise her hopes only to cast them down. When our new venture became real, I gave Heather a call to ask her out for lunch. She was one of the three people from Action 6 News I asked to come with me over to the new venture—Frank and Jonas were the other two.

She cried anew when I offered her the job. She said she was ready to join me that day, that minute. I told her to do it the proper way and give Action 6 News the obligatory two-week notice. In this industry, it's never wise to burn bridges. You'll never know who you may need for references or when covering a story.

I put her in charge of our nascent research and social media department, but I made it clear that I did not want her to work only on whatever Frank or I fed her. I wanted her to take initiative and look for stories on her own. If she developed a story idea, she should present it to us. If we approved, the story was hers. This would include having airtime of her own. However, her research and follow-up duties couldn't suffer.

Verification and collaboration are crucial in our industry. Our new venture could topple in an instant if facts did not back up our stories.

It was always fun whenever I asked Heather to help me or accompany me in the field. Her immediate enthusiasm at being included was so over the top that it could not help buoying my enthusiasm. Such was the case when I asked her to go with me up to Massachusetts. I told her we would try to do it all in one day, but she should pack an overnight bag just in case.

My plan was to leave our home in Queens at four-thirty in the morning, swing through Brooklyn to pick her up and then be on our way, hoping to avoid New York rush hour traffic. However, Heather insisted that she come to me and be at our house by four thirty. She promised me she'd take a cab so she wasn't riding the subways alone at that ungodly hour. I'm not sure she kept that promise, but she arrived safely at twenty after.

Will, who agreed to take the day off to take care of the kids, was groggy but awake. I kissed him goodbye, and we were on our way.

It was early October. I was looking forward to seeing some brilliant New England foliage. I'd never traveled through New England in the autumn, so this would be a treat. However, leaving so early in the morning, we would have to wait a couple hours before it got light enough to see the colors.

Heather would never be confused with a super conversationalist so I made sure I loaded my iPhone with plenty of music playlists to pass the time. I'd just put on the Sergio Mendes *Fool on a Hill* album, one of my mother's all-time favorites, when Heather spoke up.

"My mom called me the other day."

"She did?" I responded, knowing full well of her estrangement from her parents. They practically disowned her because she pursued journalism rather than medicine as a career. They thought she was throwing her life away, and they didn't want to be any part of it.

"Yeah, my Uncle Steve, my father's brother, passed away. She thought I should know. It was rather perfunctory, but then at the end I said, 'I miss you, Mom. Dad, too.' There was a pause. Then she said, 'I miss you too, Picky'. Then we hung up."

"Picky?"

"It was a childhood nickname. I used to pick out tunes on the piano and my Dad came up with that name. It wasn't one that I wanted used outside of the family. Anyway, it was nice hearing from her."

"Sounds like an opening, anyway."

"Who knows?"

We continued our trip, mostly in our own thoughts. I mentally contrasted her life with mine. I never knew my father; he abandoned my mother and me shortly after I was born. I'd always assumed he went back to the Caribbean, but I can't say for sure. Nor do I really care. But I was always close with my mother. We'd talk at least once a day until cancer took her a few years back. She had no qualms about me going into journalism. In fact, she would have supported me in whatever I did with my life. The only thing she would never accept was if I did not do my best.

Heather's situation is much more painful. Having parents that you were close to turn on you must be devastating. Hopefully, this was in fact an opening.

We hit some rush hour traffic around Hartford but we still made it to Fairbrook, Massachusetts in under four hours. By the time we got in the area, the foliage was in full glory. A painter's palate of reds, oranges and yellows was on display everywhere you looked. It seemed every house had an assortment of fifty-year-old oaks, maples, poplars and other trees.

After weaving through some back roads, we entered Fairbrook. As is the case all over Massachusetts, a huge sign with the town name and the year it was settled—1664—told us we had arrived but we still had about three miles before we'd get to the town center. Shortly after this sign we drove beside a ten-foot high chain-link fence topped with rolls of razor wire. On the other side of the fence was a lush, thick forest. The fence ran alongside the road for at least a mile.

"What do you think? A prison?" I asked.

Heather shrugged.

"Have you ever heard of the terms LULU and NIMBY?"

"I've heard of NIMBY but I don't know what it means."

"LULU is a 'locally unwanted land use' and NIMBY is 'not in my backyard,'" I explained as Heather pulled out her pen and pad.

"People don't want to live next to a sewerage treatment plant or a prison, even if their community needs one. They'll pressure or pay off local leaders to put these facilities somewhere else, as long as it's out of sight and the town residents can't smell it. My guess is that Worcester or Springfield needed more prison space and could get it located here out in the boonies. They probably bought off a few local politicians to do it."

We continued our way into town as the forest and an occasional farm gave way to an increased number of white clapboard residences. I got a kick out of the 'Thickly Settled' sign just before the final curve leading into town.

The dominant feature as you drove into the town center was its Common, an expansive park area bounded by the roads leading in and out. The Common was home to large field areas, its own assortment of majestic trees, a baseball field and band pavilion on one end, a large fountain in the middle and a couple war veteran monuments at the end closest to the town center.

There was a large white town hall with a towering cupola in the center of town. Around the town hall was a small grocery store, a brick town library that dated back to 1880, a pizza parlor and a couple other small businesses. There was one traffic light in the very center of town, which blinked yellow for Main Street and red for Central Street that crossed it. I guessed the lights would be entirely red if a pedestrian wanted to cross.

We'd made good time on our trip and arrived in Fairbrook before eight in the morning. I parked in front of the town hall. We climbed the impressive set of marble steps up to the front door, which we found locked. We then walked around the side of the building and saw a sign 'Police' at a side entrance. I tried that door, but it was also locked.

"I guess on a weekend they get little in the way of walk-in traffic."

"They probably rely on 911," Heather noted. I nodded in agreement. I pulled out my phone and tried Jonas's number, but I got no answer.

"They probably confiscated his phone after he called me. Let's swing by the Rutledge's house and then find this lawyer, Foster."

We proceeded through the intersection and headed west to locate Eunice's relatives' house. The Rutledge's house was about two miles away, close to the boundary with the next town. It was a modest one-story home, probably two bedrooms at most. I could see it as a starter home for a young couple, but not a couple comfortable with other people. The next closest house was at least a quarter mile away.

The house was empty and, as Jonas had noted, there was a For Sale sign on the front lawn. I jotted down the name and number of the realtor, Sheila Higdon, and then we drove back into town.

John Foster's office was on High Street, a block away from the town center. I looked at the address I'd jotted down and it read 7 High Street, but the house that would have logically been that address had a painted over '3' on the front door. It was a two-story structure with weathered natural shingle siding. In front was a sign that read: John Foster, Esq., Attorney at Law.

We parked and went to the front door, which we found locked. We waited on the front doorstep after ringing the doorbell. Less than a minute later the door opened to reveal a gray-haired man in his late sixties or early seventies. He was of average height and build. He looked like he had once been fit but had of late put on a few pounds.

"Mr. Foster?"

"Yes."

"My name is Francine Vega, and this is Heather Abernathy, we're journalists from New York."

"The Francine Vega who used to be on *Issues and Answers*?"

"Yes, sir." I answered with some trepidation. I couldn't sense whether he was a fan or whether I was about to receive a tongue-lashing about my liberal views.

"That was some bombshell you dropped last November. It sure made a stir of things." He chuckled a bit, so I felt at ease. "Please come in and tell me what brings you all the way up here to our little backwater."

Unlike a typical office where you would enter a reception area We walked into his modestly appointed office. After offering us some refreshments, we told him why we were there.

"Mr. Foster, we're here to get my friend out of jail."

"I'm afraid I do little in the way of criminal law. I can give you the number of a friend who might be better able to help you."

"We don't need your services as a lawyer, although your friend's services as a criminal defense attorney might at some point prove useful. The reason we came to you is that my friend, Jonas Clarke, was up here trying to track down his girlfriend, Eunice Williams, who's gone missing.

She came here to help Lynn and Carl Rutledge move into their new home, but we've lost track of her."

"Rutledge? Yes, I helped Lynn and Carl buy a house out on Route 9. The sale closed about a month ago."

"Well, Jonas went to the Rutledge's house, but it was vacant. There's a For Sale sign out front. Then he came here to see you. You weren't here. He walked around the side to see if you had an office. That's when a cop showed up. He arrested Jonas for attempting to rob your place. I can assure you, Jonas had no intention of robbery or committing any other crime. He just wants to find Eunice."

"I believe you."

"I stopped at the town hall and the police department. They were locked tight."

"Welcome to Saturday morning in small-town New England."

"After that, we went by the Rutledge's house and verified a For Sale sign on the front lawn."

"There is? Well, that's sure a surprise. I've been away a few weeks and just got back first thing this morning."

"Eunice told Jonas that you were very helpful to the Rutledges in getting their home."

"Lynn's grandfather worked for a close friend of mine, Terrance Rogers. He's an old army buddy. When Lynn and Carl decided they wanted to move out of the city, they started contacting realtors in the area to look at houses. Let's just say they weren't having a lot of luck on their own. They expressed their frustration to her grandfather who told Terrance who called me. I cut through the red tape so they could get their home. It was a fixer upper, but it thrilled them to finally get their own place, so it's a big surprise they've moved out. Do you know the name of the officer that arrested your friend?"

I looked at my notes. "Sykes, Andrew Sykes."

"Figures."

"You're not a fan."

"Not particularly. Could you please excuse me for a few minutes?"

He left us in his office. We weren't sure if he had to go to the bathroom, was getting us some coffee or what he was doing, but we didn't have much choice in the matter. We sat quietly and waited. Ten minutes later, he returned.

"Your friend, Jonas, is free to go, or at least he will be once the paperwork gets processed, which may take an hour or two. It is a weekend."

"He is? That's wonderful! How'd you manage it?"

"First, I called our police chief, Harry Dumont, to explain the situation to him. He's not a big fan of Sykes, either. Harry agreed the charges were bogus. Then I called Superior Court Judge Sam Farrell. I told him that Jonas was here to see me on business—which he was—and it was a big misunderstanding. Sam's the chief judge in this circuit and he also agreed the charges were baseless. It didn't hurt my cause that we played tennis for over twenty years until he tore up his knee. Jonas is being held in the cell at the State Police barracks in East Fairbrook, so that's more paperwork. Harry said he'd let me know when he gets word Jonas is ready to go. We can drive there."

"I don't know how I can thank you."

"We have an hour or two to kill so maybe we should look into the disappearance of, what did you her name is?"

"Eunice Williams."

"Right. Did you happen to notice the realtor's name on the sign?"

"Sheila Higdon."

He shook his head. "Great."

"Is there a problem with Sheila Higdon?"

Before he could answer, the door to his office/parlor burst open as a lanky eleven-year-old boy with a mop of curly dark brown hair on his head burst in. He stopped in his tracks, obviously intimidated by the two strangers in the house.

"Marcus," Foster patiently said, "say hello to our guests, Ms. Vega and Ms. Abernathy."

The boy mumbled his hellos to us. We greeted him back.

"This is my grandson, Marcus Foster. Now, you seem to have something very urgent on your mind. What is it you want, Marcus?"

"I'm hungry."

"You know what? I am too and I bet Ms. Vega and Ms. Abernathy are as well after their long drive. Unfortunately, I don't have a thing in the house.

How about if we all head uptown to the Top Hat Restaurant for some breakfast? I think they may be able to pull together a grilled cheese sandwich, which if I remember correctly is your favorite?"

The boy smiled a broad grin and nodded vigorously.

"Go round up your sister then."

The boy ran out as boisterously as he entered.

"You will join us, won't you?"

I wanted to keep moving but we had a couple hours to kill before they released Jonas. Plus, I was hungry, and most likely Heather was as well.

"In addition," Foster spoke up, "the police department should be manned by now, but Harry won't be there for forty-five minutes. I'd like him to be there when we go."

A few minutes later, Marcus reappeared with his six-year-old sister, Sara, in tow. She was a cute little thing who reminded me a bit of Stella. Off we went for the seven to eight-minute walk up to the restaurant. The kids streamed on ahead of us but stayed sufficiently close for Foster to keep an eye on them.

We had just turned the corner onto Central Street when Foster asked a curious question.

"Do either of you believe in love at first sight?"

The question came so much from left field that I hesitated answering. Heather spoke up.

"Yes, I do. I haven't found him—or her—yet, but I'll know it when I see it."

I had to conceal my astonishment at the 'or her' in her answer. It wasn't something I ever considered about Heather.

"And you, Ms. Vega?"

"I used to. But I guess you could say I wised up after a failed marriage I was in because love blinded me. I didn't realize Eddie was an alcoholic until after we were married. We divorced after only a couple years. Love at first sight definitely wasn't the case with my current husband, Will. My first introduction to him was when he interrogated me as part of a terrorist investigation. I was a suspect."

He laughed.

"I know it's a rather personal question from someone you met just ten minutes ago but Marcus and Sara's parents' meeting was such a sweet story I can't resist telling everyone I meet. I mentioned my war buddy, Terrance. Well, we were out visiting him and his family in St. Louis when Nathan, my son, was fifteen. We had just arrived and were standing in the living room when Terrance's daughter, Tracy, came bounding down the stairs like a gazelle. She stopped short when she saw we were there but, in that instant, Nathan's and Tracy's eyes locked. They were in love, just like that.

"I expected it to pass; their love would fade away. They were fifteen and they lived a thousand miles apart. But my son is a determined young man. He wrote Tracy letter after letter and called her when he could. He wouldn't let the love die. Seven years later they married."

"That's a nice story. And you? Were you and Mrs. Foster the victims of love at first sight?"

A soft smile bent his mouth. It was a fond smile, but one that showed he longed for something he lost.

"Well, it was for me anyway. Sara and I were classmates since third grade. I was always fond of her but I fell head over heels in love with her in junior high. Unfortunately, she set her sights elsewhere through high school and college. She didn't fall in love with me until I was in a coma."

"In a coma?"

"Yes, I was severely injured in Vietnam and they shipped me back to the VA hospital to either recuperate or die. Sara worked as a social worker at the hospital and she ran into my father, who told her what happened to me. She knew my father from church and school events, so it surprised her to see him there and that I was a patient in the hospital.

"My father would come to see me nearly every day and he and Sara would often have lunch together. My dad would read her the letters I had written him from Nam and through him, she fell in love with me. Well, after two years I finally woke up and the first thing I saw was her face looking down on me, like an angel. Since I sort of count that as a second first day of my life, I guess you could say that it was love at first sight."

"Wow, that's amazing. I can't think of a lovelier story."

Since Sara wasn't joining us I was hesitant to ask about her.

"Cancer took my Sara five years ago. She was so happy to hold her namesake in her arms before she passed away." He paused. None of us knew what to say, so he resumed. "Before we get too maudlin, let's order our food and then get back to the reason you're here in our lovely town."

The Top Hat Restaurant was a standard luncheonette with a counter and six booths. It was fine for standard breakfast and lunch fare. The waitress, a skinny teenager with a streak of iridescent blue hair bisecting her blond scalp, advised us they wouldn't be serving the lunch menu for another couple hours and therefore Marcus couldn't have his beloved grilled cheese. I was expecting a replay of the scene from *Five Easy Pieces* but all Foster had to do was shoot a glance over to Madge, the restaurant owner standing behind the counter. Grilled cheese magically was added to the breakfast menu.

Foster had helped Madge navigate through a messy divorce a few years back, allowing her to keep Top Hat, which her family had owned for nearly fifty years. After he had helped her, if John Foster wanted to dine on lobster thermidor in this simple luncheonette, Madge would drive to Gloucester to get the best lobsters and then figure out how to cook it for him. Luckily, the most complicated dish any of us ordered was eggs over easy, bacon and whole wheat toast.

"Mr. Foster,"

"John, please."

"OK, John, you were about to tell us about Sheila Higdon before we headed out."

"Ah yes. You should definitely talk with Mrs. Higdon, but it'd probably be best if you didn't involve me. We have a bit of a history. More exact, I had a bit of a run in with her mother, who was also a realtor, and that family holds a grudge."

"Well, I'm intrigued."

"It was a couple days before Sara's and my wedding. Terrance was in town and we played a practical joke on Sheila's mother. Before Terrence arrived, I went to look at a few houses with her. I told her I really liked this one house but I wanted my "partner" to look at it before I committed to buying it. The next day, I showed up early and was chatting with Sheila's mother, Frances Wright was her name, when Terrance drove up and I introduced him as my partner. The look on her face was priceless. I imagine she was thinking about her reputation if she sold a house in the middle of town to a gay African American man. Instead of trying her best to sell the house, she described all the negative aspects of the property, trying to talk us out of buying it.

"My father was livid when he found out what we did and made me apologize to Mrs. Wright. The family has hated me ever since. As a lawyer who deals in real estate deals, I've had to deal with Sheila over the years, but it's never comfortable."

"Why did you play this practical joke?"

"It was a battlefield promise. I was a medic, and Terrance was severely injured. He was slipping away, and I had to think of a way to keep him awake so he wouldn't go into shock. I concocted this plan for him to come visit me and live in this town, breaking the color barrier. I kept embellishing it so that, despite excruciating pain, Terrance was laughing his head off. Regardless of how juvenile the promise was, I felt obliged to fulfill the promise when he came to town. My father was a former GI, so he understood, but he was still pissed with me."

I was enjoying Foster's stories so much that I was losing track of my main purpose for being there. Luckily, he didn't.

"You should go and see Sheila. She's a nice person; we just don't get along. But first, we should stop by the police department. Harry should be there by now."

To increase our efficiency, I asked Heather to track down Sheila Higdon to see if she could shed any light on the Rutledge's mysterious departure from Fairbrook. Foster, his grandkids and I went over to the police station in the town hall.

I was used to police precincts in New York. I could walk into any precinct at any hour of the day or night and it would be a hive of activity. There would be numerous cops, police personnel, perps and members of the public all busily milling about, carrying on various law enforcement functions. Here, we walked in and there were only two men, one in uniform and the other in casual street clothes. The one who wasn't in uniform was an older gentleman who appeared to be about Foster's age. He had his feet up on his desk talking on the phone in what was obviously a personal call. The uniformed guy was a much younger man with a sandy-colored buzz cut. He was talking over the police radio with someone that I assumed was another officer. A game of solitaire was visible on his computer screen as he chatted.

"Hi, Andy," we overheard on the police radio.

"Hey Greg, what's up?"

"Karen Gagnon flagged me down," was the response from the voice on the radio.

"What's Crazy Karen want this time?"

The older officer, who I assumed to be Chief Dumont, shot the other officer a nasty look over the use of this derogatory nickname. The officer, Andy, didn't pay him any mind as the voice on the radio responded.

"More of the same, but she seemed even more agitated than usual. She kept carrying on about something she saw up near Indian Rock. I'll take a ride over there to check it out."

"One of these days we should tell her to pound salt."

"Ah, she's harmless enough and means well."

"Did you say near Indian Rock? I'll be heading in that direction at lunchtime. I can handle it."

"I'm not doing much right now so what can it hurt to take a ride out there."

"I said I'd handle it!" he responded angrily.

"Okay, okay. You don't have to take my head off."

"Just continue your patrol. Out."

Andy, the younger officer, went back to his solitaire game, but something bothered him. The older officer ended his phone call and headed our way.

"John! Welcome. These your grandkids? They seem a little young for a 'scared straight' session, but I'll do my best."

Foster laughed.

"Hi, Harry. Yes, this is Marcus and Sara. I'm worried about her. She's a mean one."

"Grandpa," she said in her most exasperated tone.

"Say hi to the Police Chief, kids."

I could see a hint of sadness on the Chief's face when John introduced his granddaughter. I took it to mean that he knew Foster's wife, Sara, who died a few years earlier. They had all grown up together.

"Police Chief Harry Dumont, I'd like to introduce Francine Vega. She's a reporter out of New York. Francine, this is Chief Dumont."

I took note that Foster didn't bother to introduce me to Officer Sykes.

"*Issues & Answers*, that Francine Vega?" Dumont asked.

"The same," I responded. I always assumed that our show was geared toward more urban and suburban demographics, but I made an impression out here in the rural hinterland.

"You haven't been on the show for a while now."

"No, let's just say there'd been developments."

He seemed to understand what I was saying.

"Well, the show isn't as good without you."

Foster looked at Sykes and then back at Dumont. "Harry, can we talk? Confidentially?"

We walked into a conference room.

"Chief," I said, "John told me how you helped in getting Jonas released. Thank you very much."

"It was nothing. Sykes never should have made that arrest. I'll call when we're done to see when they'll cut him loose." Dumont replied.

John got down to business.

"Ms. Vega here is trying to track down a friend of hers, an African-American woman named Eunice Williams, who came up here to help her cousins, the Rutledges, move into their house out on Route 9. That's the reason Jonas Clarke had come to see me."

"I met Mr. Rutledge a week ago at their house. He was working out in the yard and said his wife would arrive the next day. He was a little leery of me at first. Can't say I blame him. But he was at ease once he understood I really was there to welcome them to Fairbrook. He seemed to be looking forward to moving into their new home. I was surprised yesterday when I drove by and saw a For Sale sign."

"My friend, Jonas Clarke," I interjected, "is Eunice's boyfriend. He saw her off last Thursday when she left New York to come up here. That's the last he'd heard from her. He's tried her cell several times with no luck. He came up here to find out what was going on."

"Do you have a picture of Eunice?"

I dug out my cellphone and scrolled through the pictures until I found the one I took of Jonas and Eunice at a picnic last summer. I showed it to the Chief.

"I haven't seen her but I can check around. Can you email the picture to me?" He asked as he handed me his card.

As I was entering the email address, there was a loud shout from the main office.

"God damn you, Greg. I told you I would handle it."

Startled and concerned, Chief Dumont opened the door and rushed out of the conference room.

"What the hell is going on out here?"

Before Sykes could respond, the voice on the radio spoke up.

"Harry, is that you? Get out here right away."

"First, where is here? Second, why is it so important I get out there in such a goddamn hurry?"

"I'm in the woods about one hundred yards north of Indian Rock. There's a dead body here. An African American female, age in the upper twenties, lower thirties."

My stomach immediately knotted as Chief Dumont looked over my way.

"I'll be right there. Do nothing."

4

Chief Dumont and Officer Sykes left without a word, leaving Foster, me and the kids standing there, wondering what we should do. We decided the best thing would be to go back to Foster's house. At least the kids would be comfortable.

I called Heather. She hadn't yet been able to meet with Sheila Higdon but they'd probably get together in a half hour. I told Heather to meet us at John's house when she was done.

Foster had explained that he was looking after the kids for a week. Foster's son's employer, a major pharmaceutical firm, had transferred him to Singapore for two years. Once he and his wife located a home, Foster would fly there with the kids. They would attend an English school there, but for the present, they would be out of school. However, Foster would not let them off easy. He had contacted the school they'd attended to find out what they had been learning, and he took over their lessons.

It was touching watching him teach the kids. He was gentle but firm. They enjoyed their lessons, and being taught by their grandfather. It made me resolve that I would be more diligent about interacting with my kids.

An hour and a half after we left the police station, Heather showed up to fill us in on her meeting with Higdon. Sheila told Heather that she had never met with the Rutledges. Rather, she got a phone call asking her to handle the sale and then the next day a money order for $5,000, an advance on her commission, arrived at her office. Even though this was the first time something like this had ever happened, she had no reason to have any doubts, so she started the sale process.

We settled in, waiting for news from the chief. I was hoping he didn't forget about Jonas. Chief Dumont probably did not have to handle many homicides in a small town like this and his hands would be full. Finally, he called. He told John that, based on the photo I had provided, the deceased woman did not resemble Eunice. Given the paucity of African-Americans in Fairbrook, he suspected the body may be that of Lynn Rutledge. He requested that Foster, the only person in town that the chief could think of who had met Mrs. Rutledge, come to the local funeral home to make an identification.

I could only hear Foster's end of the conversation. It's sad to say, but I found myself relieved to hear that the woman was not Eunice. The death of anyone is tragic but when it turns out not be someone you know and care about, naturally a wave of relief washes over you.

"I'd be glad to help," Foster said, "I just have to figure someone to watch the kids."

I was about to speak up, but Heather beat me to it.

"I'll be happy to stay with them while you're away."

"I appreciate that, but I can't impose."

"No imposition. I love kids. I'm sure we'll be fine."

He looked at her and me, deciding whether to entrust his grandchildren to someone he met a scant three hours earlier. Deciding she looked reputable enough, he told the police chief he'd be right over. He was about to hang up when the chief added one more thing.

"Harry said they still haven't set Jonas free. They need one more sign-off. He dispatched Greg Davis, the officer you heard on the phone, to make himself a pest at the State Police barracks until Jonas is released. Greg will then drive Jonas back here. I'm so sorry it's taken so long."

It was frustrating, I said nothing.

Before he left, I contemplated asking him if he knew where Karen Gagnon, the woman the cops jokingly referred to as *Crazy Karen*, lived. If she was the one who had found the body, she may have other information about the status and location of Eunice. I stopped from asking him, however, knowing that, as an attorney, he might feel obliged to advise me that this was now an active investigation and the police would probably want to interview Karen first.

I couldn't sit around and do nothing, however. Instead, I waited until Foster departed and then I asked Heather to fire up her computer and find out where Ms. Gagnon lived. Forty-five seconds later I had her address, which was down by the railroad tracks, less than a ten-minute walk away.

Karen Gagnon's house was a converted mobile home with a small porch attached. I knocked on her door and it wasn't long before a middle-aged woman with long unkempt gray hair and a lined, worried face soon answered.

"Who the hell are you?" she asked.

"My name is Francine Vega. I'm a television reporter from New York."

I saw a glimmer in her eyes, excitement at speaking with a New York City reporter. Her excitement did not last long, however, as she went on the attack once again.

"A reporter? From New York? Let's see some ID."

I handed my press identification to her. She inspected it thoroughly, raising her eyes to me several times to make sure the face matched the ID.

"What do you want with me?"

"I'm working on a story on people of color who move into mostly white towns. I asked around, and I was told you were someone who kept her eyes on things."

"Who told you that?"

I didn't want to let on that I overheard her name on the police radio, so I white-lied a bit.

"John Foster."

"John told you that? He's one of the few people in town who doesn't call me 'Crazy Karen'. He never has, and I've known him since we were kids."

I was wondering if there was anybody in this whole town that Foster didn't know since childhood.

"I had the hots for him back in junior high but he only had eyes for Sara Smith. The only one who didn't know it at the time was Sara. It wasn't until after he came back from the war that he and Sara hooked up. He never looked down on me, though, even with the problems I've had over the years. Anyway, why don't we sit down and chat for a bit."

She stepped out the front door and we sat on the chairs on the makeshift front porch. It was a rather chilly fall day and I would have preferred the warmth of indoors but the shabbiness of her home undoubtedly embarrassed her.

"Can I offer you anything?"

"No, that's all right."

"So, what do you want to know?"

"Well, I've noticed very few people of color in this town. What do you attribute that to?"

"They just prefer to live elsewhere."

"Are they welcome here?"

"They're not unwelcome, if you know what I mean."

"John said he helped a young African-American couple, Lynn and Carl Rutledge, buy a house out on Route 9 but he said there was a For Sale sign there, even before they moved in. Did you meet them?"

Karen appeared nervous, looking around to make sure nobody was listening as she leaned over to confide in me.

"I never met them but I saw them late one night. I don't sleep real well and when I can't sleep I like to wander around the woods. Could be why I'm called 'Crazy Karen', I guess. Anyway, three nights ago I was over that way when I heard a scuffle. The moon was out full and I saw about four men pull up to their house. They kicked the door down and a few minutes later they came out. They were carrying what looked like bodies, three of them."

"Did you notify the police?"

"I shoulda, but I figured they wouldn't believe me seein' they think I'm 'Crazy Karen'."

She paused, and then continued.

"Then, this morning I headed back out that way but I only got to Indian Rock before I saw the body of a Black woman partially buried in the leaves. It was way out in the woods. I made my way back to the road and headed toward town. I flagged down Greg—he's a cop here—and told him what I found. He was rather condescending as he took down the info. I came back home and I don't know if Greg ever checked it out."

"Did you recognize anybody you saw that night?"

"No, it was dark. All I saw were shapes. But one guy, he was big, and he walked with a limp. He looked like one of the guys from the other side of the wire."

"Other side of the wire? What does that mean?"

Before Karen could answer, a Fairbrook Police car pulled up in front of the house. Andy Sykes stepped out.

"Ms. Vega. What are you doing here with Craz, with Karen?"

"Ms. Gagnon and I were just chatting."

"About anything in particular?"

"Not overly. I'm trying to get a feeling for the town."

"I hope you're not interfering with an official investigation."

"I don't see how I could be."

"That's good. Now, I have some official questions to ask Karen, if you don't mind."

"Not at all. I better head out anyway. Karen, it's been a real pleasure meeting you and getting to know you. Officer."

I left and walked back to Foster's place. Heather was in the yard playing ball with the kids. I saw no reason to stop her from doing so. When I walked in, John was in his office.

"Any word about Jonas?"

"Nothing yet. Andy Sykes just called, and he was pissed. He's thinking of charging you with hindering a criminal investigation."

"What? For talking with Karen Gagnon?"

"He said when he tried to interview Karen after you left, she wouldn't say a word. She said she told you all she would say. Andy's claiming you inhibited her from cooperating."

"Did Officer Sykes also advise you he started to call her 'Crazy Karen' to her face? He stopped himself, but enough slipped out for her to know where he was going."

Foster shook his head. "What an ass. Anyway, I let him have his say and then I talked with Harry. He won't do anything, and he'll make sure Sykes does nothing. He asked that you relay to him anything Karen may have told you."

"She said she saw the Rutledges and probably Eunice being abducted late at night three days ago. They appeared to be unconscious as four men carried them from the house."

"Why didn't she tell anyone?"

"Well, she was probably drunk or high at the time and was wandering around in the forest because she couldn't sleep. She didn't think they'd believe her. They'd ridicule her. It wasn't something she wanted to go through."

"Poor Karen. She hasn't had an easy time of it over the years, I'm afraid."

"Her face lit up when I mentioned your name. She said she had the hots for you back in junior high, but you only had eyes for Sara Smith."

He smiled at the memory of his deceased wife, but said nothing.

"Did she say anything more? Did she recognize the people who abducted your friend?"

"No, she said that although the moon was bright, the people were only shapes. She said that one man was big and walked with a limp and looked like a person who came from beyond the wire, whatever that means."

"Beyond the wire is what some folks around here call the religious compound called *Beyond Revelation*. You may have noticed the barbed wire rimmed fence on your way into town."

"We did. I thought your town got stuck with a prison of some sort."

"Many people think we did. It's a self-sustaining religious utopian settlement. It's been there for about three years now. When they first arrived, the aldermen—that's what the leaders call themselves—were very open and friendly. They attended local church services to introduce themselves and their new religion. I remember when they came to a service at our church. They made a little presentation about who they were and what they believed. They had a survivalist, waiting-for-the-apocalypse vibe about them. My initial instinct was that they seemed like a modern-day Jonestown.

"They invited the town to tour the facilities and meet the members. Out of curiosity, I tagged along. The compound was impressive. Everything was communal with no ownership of property, not even the clothes on their backs. They were open like this for about two weeks and then the gates closed. To my knowledge, they haven't opened since. Like I said, they're self-sufficient. They raise their own animals and grow their own food. They generate their own power. They even have their own clinic and medical personnel, although I think they adhere to a more holistic and herbal medical practice.

"There's been some questions about them but they're a religious community, and the town officials can't legally walk in to inspect. Since they made the early rounds, I don't remember ever seeing anybody from the compound emerge, but it's not like I keep a close eye out for them. Karen probably knows better than I do."

"So, do you give any credence to Karen's claim that one or more of the guys may be from this cult?"

"I don't know. Karen is often our *Fool on The Hill*. She sees things many of us in town either can't see or don't want to see. But sometimes the things she sees are things only she can see. It's often difficult to separate the wheat from the chaff, and there are many people who only see the chaff."

"So, you identified the body as that of Lynn Rutledge?"

"Yes, it was. They're conducting the autopsy now. There's evidence of a sharp blow to her head and there is some blood at the scene but they're still evaluating to determine what the actual cause of death was."

He paused, probably because of the distraught look on my face.

"I'm sorry. I didn't mean to sound so cold and clinical. I thought as a reporter you'd want all the facts."

"That's okay. I'm just worried about Eunice. No sign of her or Carl Rutledge?"

"No. The police have an alert out for both of them."

Just then the phone and the doorbell rang almost simultaneously. John answered his phone as he headed to the door. I could only hear Foster's side of the conversation. He said things like "Wow, that was quick." and "Any news on her husband or Eunice Williams?" and "I see. Thanks, Harry." Then he opened the door.

I sprung out of my chair like it turned white-hot as I ran to the door. I practically jumped into Jonas' arms. In return, he gave me one of his patented bear hugs.

"J., I'm so glad you're safe."

"I'm fine, Frannie. Not an experience I recommend you try but everyone except the asshole that arrested me treated me well. Any word on Eunice?"

I looked over at John.

"J., this is John Foster, the attorney who helped the Rutledges. He's been very helpful to us."

"Mr. Foster, thank you for everything. Officer Davis told me it was you who got me out and the charges dropped. Much appreciated."

"That was nothing; just a few phone calls. Come on in and sit down. I'll fill you in on what I know. I'm sorry, but there's still no sign of Eunice. I don't know who besides Officer Sykes you dealt with, but I have the personal assurance from Police Chief Dumont that they are taking Eunice's disappearance seriously. He's called the State Police to request their help. I've known Harry Dumont since we were kids. He's a man of his word."

Jonas nodded but said nothing.

"I have some bad news for you. The body of Lynn Rutledge was found a short while ago in the woods. I'm sorry. They have a suspect in custody. A homeless guy living in an abandoned Chevy about a mile away from where they found Mrs. Rutledge. He had her wallet and what appears to be her blood on his clothes. They're confident they got the guy. Sounds like a wrong place, wrong time situation. They're still interrogating him to see what he knows about your friend."

"What about what Karen said?" I asked.

"Who's Karen?" Jonas asked.

John responded. "Karen Gagnon is a friend of mine who has some, let's call them challenges. She has a tendency to wander the woods late at night."

"I just got back from talking to her," I interjected. "She told me she was over near Lynn and Carl's house and she saw four or five men carrying something from the house. It was dark, so she didn't have any details, but the objects looked bulky... like perhaps they were," I hesitated, not wanting to use the word 'bodies', "people."

"I'll pass that info on to Harry. Hopefully, he'll take her seriously and go back and talk with her but I'm not overly optimistic. You heard the cops refer to her as 'Crazy Karen'. They have a witness in custody that wraps everything up nice and neat."

"You don't sound like much of a fan of small-town police work."

"Don't get me wrong. Harry's a good guy. He's very conscientious, honest and well-meaning."

"But?"

"But he's under a lot of pressure to keep this from spiraling out of control. Fairbrook's a nice town with good people, but a lot of these people like to keep to themselves, holding the cruel world away at arm's length. A situation like this can turn ugly quickly as the news trucks and cameras descend on us. He has what he considers a smoking gun with a ribbon wrapped around it and he will not be amenable to alternative theories that may keep the story alive."

"I wouldn't care except that Eunice is still out there somewhere. We have to find her. The cops should at least hear out Karen's story."

I was going to add that I was holding out hope that she's still alive, but I thought better of it. I was sure that was running through Jonas's mind; I didn't need to say it out loud.

Heather rushed in.

"Francine, my mother just called. My father had a stroke. He's asking for me. I have to get back to New York right away."

"Yes, absolutely! I'll stay around for another day, but we'll see if we can't get you on a train back to the city. Would that be okay?"

"That would be great."

"She can go out of Springfield," Foster offered. "Let me go on the computer and see what the schedule is."

He turned to his Mac and started tapping. Two minutes later he turned back to us.

"There's a train leaving in an hour and a quarter. It's about a forty-minute drive, so we should head right out. You can purchase your ticket as we drive. I know the way so I'll drive her if you'll stay with the kids."

"Thank you. In the meantime, I'll call the EconoLodge we saw on the way in to get a couple rooms for us."

"Nonsense, you'll stay here. I have a perfectly good guest room. Room's top of the stairs, first room on the right. Here's a key for the room. The couch in the study opens to a bed. Make yourselves at home. Here's the sign-in for the wi-fi in case you need to do some work on your computer. Help yourself to anything in the fridge or cupboard."

He didn't wait for me to protest as he said: "Let's go!"

And with that, he and Heather were off. I checked on the kids in the family room. Each was perfectly content, playing a game of some sort. I took my bag up to the guest room.

I was curious why a room within the house needed its own key. I opened the door and knew immediately why. The room housed an arsenal. On the walls hung at least thirty vintage firearms, ranging from flintlock muskets through Civil War-era pistols and rifles up to German lugers from World War II. He had bolted each gun to the wall. Even with this precaution, he locked the room because of the kids.

There were also two framed cases on one wall. The first housed two medals: a Bronze Star awarded to Walter Foster for meritorious valor under fire during the Battle of the Bulge and a Purple Heart earned during that battle. In the second was another medal, a Purple Heart, that John had earned during the Vietnam War.

I went back down to John's office and Jonas was sitting there, staring out into space in a catatonic stupor. I sat down beside him and took his hand.

"We'll find her, J. I know we will."

"Thanks, Frannie. I hope so. I just feel so helpless. She must be so scared, wherever she is."

I was glad his mind hadn't landed on the worst outcome, but was entertaining the scenario that she was alive.

"J., why don't you take the guest room and I'll use the sofa bed. I'm sure the sofa bed can't accommodate your size."

"No, I'll be okay on the couch. It wouldn't feel right, me up there and you down here."

"You sure?"

"Yeah, I'm sure. Thanks for thinking of me."

"I'm going to head up and check out some things on the computer if you'll be all right."

"I'm okay. I'm kinda exhausted. I'll just nap here for a bit."

I settled myself into the room to check on my emails and other work-related things. I fired up my laptop and tapped into Foster's wi-fi. On my search engine I typed in *Beyond Revelation*. That gave me a whole range of sites including an Off-Broadway play from the 1970s. I had to narrow my search, so I typed *Beyond Revelation Fairbrook*.

The first hit was a local newspaper article from five years ago heralding the establishment of this retreat. Its founder, Robert Benson, said that the "end of time was at hand". *Beyond Revelation* would help true believers prepare themselves for this eventuality and would help make them acceptable in the eyes of the Lord. Benson noted that the 1,200-acre community was to be self-sufficient, growing its own food, operating its own schools, policing itself. He noted that only rarely would members venture out if there were something they needed.

Overall, the article said the local communities were neutral to the locating of this new settlement in their midst. Construction of *Beyond Revelation* resulted in a boon to local contractors and labor. They made a pledge not to bring in workers from outside of the local communities and to pay union scale wages.

Much of the financing for the community came from Robert Benson himself. The article noted that he was a billionaire whose primary residence was in New York. The reporter was able to speak with only a handful of the compound's residents but those that he spoke to said that, while they were required to pay an annual tithe, it was not an exorbitant amount. It did not appear to be a case where a supposed religious community was bilking the unsuspecting out of their life savings.

The article also repeated what Foster had said about inviting the community in to tour the facilities but then, once it got up and going, the gates shut and nobody had any idea what went on beyond the wire.

I finished the article and then read a few more sites on *Beyond Revelation*, but nothing that removed the shroud that hung over this secretive community. My reporter senses tingled that this on its own would be a good story.

Foster arrived home not long after. Jonas and I met him in the kitchen. We sat and had a drink together.

"Heather's all safely ensconced on the train, hurtling back to the Big City. I hope you don't mind macaroni and cheese for dinner. It's the kids' favorite, and it's not something that overly extends my culinary expertise."

I laughed.

"That'll be fine. Thank you for everything you've done. Can I ask you one question?"

"Sure."

"Why?"

"Why what?"

"You just met Heather and me this morning and Jonas a couple of hours ago yet here you are, opening your home to us, driving two hours to bring Heather to the train station, helping us to get answers to questions regarding Eunice. You could have easily given us token help and sent us on our way, but you didn't. Why?"

"My wife, Sara, spent an entire career doing just that, helping people she didn't know. She'd worked at the VA for thirty years as a social worker and therapist. She'd go the extra mile to help damaged veterans recover from their physical, emotional and mental trauma. Some people would say that it was her job; it was what she was being paid to do. But believe me, the monetary compensation she received was nowhere near the amount she willingly gave. When she passed away, I made a vow to continue her service and selflessness wherever I could. Believe me, I'm a poor substitute for her but we all do what we can."

I understood completely. My mother served others her entire life, often putting her own life in danger as she faced down slumlords, drug dealers, pimps and gangs. When she passed away a few years back, I likewise vowed to carry on her work wherever I could.

"That's quite an arsenal you have in the guest room. There are some great antiques there."

"That was my dad's collection. I never had the heart to get rid of them. I thought my brother, Marty, would take them after Dad passed. They used to shoot together all the time. He was indifferent, though. So here they are. When the kids came to stay, I nailed each one to the wall and put a lock on the door. Plus, there's no ammunition in the house. Still, though, Marcus can be very inquisitive. I should just sell them off and probably will one day, but there's one gun I'll never let go of."

"Which one?"

"The Civil War-era Colt revolver in the center. I was trying to bring a man, Robert Symms, to justice. I witnessed an atrocity he committed in Vietnam. Well, he found out about my efforts. He broke into my home and knocked out Sara and waited for me to come home. He was about to put a bullet in my brain, but he didn't know my Dad was visiting and was down in the basement cleaning his guns. My father burst through that door right there and shot Symms in the back of head. So, I have an attachment to that firearm."

"That's quite a harrowing story."

"It worked out for the best, for everyone but Symms, that is."

He smiled.

"Tomorrow, I'll drop the kids off at the sitter in the morning and then I have a meeting with a client. I'll be back around two so you two will be on your own until then. I hope you have enough of a lay of the land to get some answers."

"I'm sure I'll be fine. I'm a reporter. I'm good at asking questions and annoying people."

"Be careful. You obviously will be watched from now on."

"That's hardly new for me."

"So I gathered."

5

Early the next morning I woke to my phone pinging as a text came in. It was a message from Heather saying that her father was doing well. They caught his stroke early. It did not appear there would be lasting damage. She said she'd be heading to the office right after she went to the hospital.

I wouldn't be able to talk to her until later in the day, but the tone of her text was so upbeat it was obvious she and her parents had greatly mended their relationship. I was so happy for her, but a selfish part of me was even happier that I wouldn't lose her inestimable talents for any significant time period.

While there were still people in town I could ask if they'd seen Eunice, I had another plan for the morning. I wanted to see what I could learn about *Beyond Revelation*. Something about the secretive religious retreat did not ring true. I kept going back to Karen's comment about the man she thought she recognized from 'beyond the wire.'

Jonas and I had some coffee, and then we drove out to the compound. I drove slowly along the full length—all one and a tenth mile of it—of the razor wire topped twelve-foot high fence along the roadway and could not locate a gate or any other entrance. When we reached the end, the fence continued at a right angle into the woods for as far as the eye could see. A gravel path ran along this stretch of fence. I pulled the car as far off the road as I could and we walked up this path.

After walking about a quarter of a mile, still finding no entrance, we heard a rustling in the leaves behind us. I turned around and saw nothing, so we continued on. Until that moment, it hadn't occurred to me we could be confronted by an animal. Bears were plentiful in this part of the world. Jonas is a big guy, but I doubted he'd be a match for a black bear or a mountain lion. All I had in my arsenal was a little can of pepper spray. I could confidently walk on any street in the sketchiest neighborhood of New York, but here, out of my element, I was getting more and more nervous.

We walked on a little further when we heard the rustling once again. This time, two men were standing there when we turned around. One, a hulking bald guy who walked with a limp, fit the description provided by Karen. My hand instinctively slipped into my purse.

"You're that reporter woman who's been snooping around town. What are you doing here?"

"Just out for a walk in this beautiful country of yours."

"It ain't my country. You shouldn't be here. It's private property."

"We must have missed the 'no trespassing' signs."

"There ain't none, but everybody knows not to wander around here."

"Obviously, not everyone knows it. But now that we do, we'll be on our way."

"Not so fast. You're coming with us to answer some questions."

"Thank you for the invitation. As wonderful a conversationalist that you appear to be, we'll have to pass."

Without another word, he reached out, grabbed my arm and pulled me. Jonas instinctively lunged at him. The self-defense training Will insisted I take kicked in. I shifted my weight, pulling him off balance slightly when my left hand shot straight out, driving the heel of my hand into his Adam's apple. He released his grip and sank to his knees as he grasped his throat, struggling to breathe. His partner immediately moved on us. Jonas swung a leg out, tripping him. As he got up on his knees, I had pulled out the pepper spray. I lifted it and squeezed, sending a stream directly into his eyes.

Unfortunately, the bald man had recovered enough to pull out a handgun, which he aimed it at me. Both Jonas and I froze. We had nothing in our repertoire to counter this. I was resigned to either being taken away to who knows where or to being shot. Before I could find out which it would be, a shot rang out from elsewhere in the woods. We all turned in the shot's direction.

"Kurt," a voice called out, "put that damn gun away. You and Freddy get the hell out of here."

I recognized my savior. It was Officer Sykes.

"We seem to keep crossing paths, don't we Officer?"

"We do, Ms. Vega. Mr. Clarke, I so glad to see you're free. That was such a sad misunderstanding."

Jonas merely glared at Sykes.

"Now, what are you two doing up here?"

"We're just out for a walk in your beautiful countryside."

"Looks to me like you're trespassing on private property."

"Trespassing? I didn't see any signs."

"Really? Damn kids must have taken them down again. Well, now you know so I would suggest you get back in your car and drive off."

"Sure must be something very interesting they don't want people to see behind this fence. You wouldn't know what that something is, would you officer?"

"They just want their privacy, that's all. They've asked the police department to keep an eye on things so they can maintain that privacy."

"I'm sure their "asking" wasn't cheap."

He ignored my innuendo.

"All I know is that you are here illegally and, now you know that you're here illegally, you had best move along. In fact, it may be best if you kept driving until you get back to New York."

"Or?"

"Or you could find yourself arrested, or worse. Accidents happen all the time in these woods. Just look at poor Mrs. Rutledge."

I grabbed Jonas's arm to keep him from taking a foolhardy action that could get us hurt or killed. Sykes was trying to goad us into doing something stupid, hoping he could have an excuse.

"Accidents? I thought a homeless guy attacked her."

"Yes, accidents. She was in the wrong place at the wrong time, obviously."

I didn't think I was in any position to argue or banter with him further. I let him escort us back to my car.

Later that afternoon when Foster returned from court, I told him about our encounter with the officer and the threat he made.

"Doesn't surprise me. Andy Sykes came to the Police Department about three years ago. I know about nearly everyone in this town, but he's one nut I've never been able to crack. Sometimes I swear that Chief Dumont works for him, not the other way around. He can be a little off so I'd take any threats he makes—veiled or otherwise—seriously."

"Three years? Wasn't that about the same time that *Beyond Revelation* opened?"

"Yes, I suppose it was."

"Any connection?"

"I'd never thought about it before, but I guess there could be."

"What should I do?"

I don't know why I trusted a man I'd only met one day ago, but I did. Perhaps it was because his manner reminded me somewhat of my husband, Will.

"Perhaps you should go back to New York."

"Without finding Eunice?"

"Francine, I've had doubts about that place since the day it opened. It's always given off a Jim Jones air to it, but they've kept to themselves over the years. Now, I think you hit a nerve poking your nose up there, but I think you'd do better back at your own place where you have much more resources at your disposal. If nothing else, you have Heather. Boy, is she sharp. Get her digging into *Beyond Revelation*. Between the two of you, I'm sure you'll uncover something. In the meantime, I'll do my best to see what I can find out here. Jonas is free to stay here if he so chooses."

"Why would you do this?"

"I grew up in this town. My Dad grew up here as did my kids. It's a good town with good people. If there's a cancer here, I will do my best to root it out and destroy it."

"I don't know. I can't cut and run like that. I think I better stay."

"Suit yourself. I just threw that out as a possibility."

My phone buzzed. It was Emma, our nanny. She was watching the kids through Monday since both Will and I were out of town.

"Hi, Emma. How are the kids?"

"Miss Francine, little Rosa has a very high fever. I called the doctor, but I got the answering service. They said I should bring her to the hospital. I'm driving there now. Albert and Stella are with me."

"Thank you, Emma. Call me as soon as you find out anything. I'm leaving immediately. I should be there in about four hours."

I hung up and explained the situation to Jonas and John.

"I'm sorry, Jonas. I have to run back. Rosa is sick. It's probably a kid thing and she'll be fine in a day or two but I have to be there."

"I understand, Frannie. You need to go."

"I'll continue to do what I can to locate Eunice from New York. John's right about one thing. I am out of my element here. I think this cult is knee-deep in something bad here. Somehow they're involved in Eunice's disappearance. I'll keep digging to find out what gives with *Beyond Revelation* and I think I can do that best from the office."

"That makes sense."

"What are you going to do?"

"I don't know. I probably should stay but I don't know what I'd do except sit around and worry. I can do that back in New York. The one thing I need is a good night's sleep. Perhaps I could stay here tonight and head out in the morning, if that's okay."

"Stay as long as you want," John responded.

"John," I asked, "they wouldn't do anything to you, would they? You said the chief's initial assessment was the coroner should rule Lynn Rutledge's death a homicide, but now it's an accident. Andy Sykes's threat implied the same could happen to me. Are you safe?"

"Safe enough. I'm pretty well known around these parts so it would have to pretty cleverly executed. If something were to happen, well, I'd get to see my Sara that much sooner. I'm not afraid. There's an old saying among Vietnam veterans: When I die I'm going to Heaven because I've spent my time in Hell!"

"I have to go, but I feel funny leaving. I've never been one to cut and run."

"I'll be your eyes and ears here. People know me and will talk with me. If you don't mind me saying, you're a bit of a fish out of water in this small town. You're big city through and through. I think you can be as productive back in your own element than you can here. If anything comes up, I'll contact you. It's not that long a trip back here."

I packed my bag and headed out.

I'd only gotten less than a mile out of town when I kicked myself. If something corrupt was going on in this hick town, why couldn't a prominent citizen such as John Foster, Esq. be in on it? He was awfully eager to get me out of the way. Why was that? He seemed genuinely interested in my safety and welfare, but that all could be an act, couldn't it?

He was very ready to take us in, no questions asked; perhaps it was his best way to keep a close eye on us.

I've always prided myself on being a decent judge of character. I rarely let a charlatan fool me. At most, I'd reserve judgment on a person until he or she proved themselves worthy of my trust. Perhaps that's why I have so few close friends and am missing out on a lot, but it's just the way I am. Yet here I was, trusting a man I met just a day ago. How could I be so stupid!

Because of Rosa, I couldn't turn around to go back to confront Foster, but I was also concerned about Jonas. I pulled over to get my phone to call him. I noticed I was beside the *Beyond Revelation* compound. I cursed the razor wire and the unknown behind it as I leaned over to pull my phone out of my bag. The next thing I knew, glass showered over me. The blast blew out the front passenger side window. My face stung from the glass, but I wasn't seriously wounded. I hit the gas. I had to get out of there before I received another shot.

I did a U-turn and drove back into the town center. I was driving alongside the common and then I saw him. John Foster had just walked out of a hair stylist and was now standing at a telephone pole. He had his two grandkids with him. Sara was carrying a stack of papers. Marcus had a staple gun. When they got to a telephone pole, Sara handed him one of the papers. John lifted Marcus up to staple the paper onto the pole. I slowed down as I approached. I saw what they were putting up.

In the short time that I was away, he had taken a picture of Eunice either I or Jonas had sent him and put it on a poster that asked for information from anybody that may have seen her. He'd given his own number as the contact. I felt so ashamed of myself for doubting this good man.

I was speechless as I sat there watching him go about his business. He was so intent on his task at hand that he didn't notice me. After he put up the poster, he walked into the convenience store on the corner. I could see him through the window, talking to the middle-aged woman behind the counter and an elderly man who was purchasing a half-gallon of milk. He handed each of them a poster and then exited the store. It was only then that he saw me and the blown-out window.

"Oh my God, Francine," he yelled as he rushed over to me. "What happened?"

"A gun. Somebody fired at me. Near the compound."

He opened my door and helped me out.

"My God, Francine. You're bleeding!"

He examined me closer and determined that the wounds weren't too bad. The glass, not ammunition, caused them. But even so, they needed attention.

"Come, let's go back to my house and take a closer look to see whether you need to go to the hospital."

I was compliant as he led me to his car and we drove the few blocks to his house. Jonas came down from upstairs when he heard us come in. He gasped when he saw me. John sat me on a chair at the kitchen table and disappeared into the bathroom. A few minutes later, he reappeared with a basin of soapy water, some antiseptic, some gauze pads and a pair of tweezers.

"The wounds don't seem too bad. There are still a couple small pieces of glass I'll pull out, but nothing major. Don't worry, you'll still look beautiful on TV."

I smiled at his thoughtfulness. "You said you were a medic, right?"

"Yup, I was, a couple of lifetimes ago. After I came back from the wars, I had some thoughts of going into medicine, but I went into law. You don't have to be as antiseptic to be a lawyer. In fact, a little dirt on you is good, if you know what I mean."

He continued on, picking out some glass, mostly in my hair, and cleaning up my face, applying salve in places he thought needed it.

"There, that should about do it. You may still want to go to a doctor to get a more learned eye looking at it to make sure there's no chance of infection."

"I have a feeling I'm in pretty good hands right now. I don't see a need right now. I have to get back to New York. My daughter needs me."

"Let's go back uptown and report this incident to the police first, then you can head out."

"I guess we should."

"I'll watch the kids."

"Thanks, Jonas."

We went back to the station. Only Officer Sykes was there.

"Is Harry around?" Foster asked.

"No, he's off for a few days visiting with his grandkids. What can I do for you?"

"Somebody shot at me."

"I saw you drive in earlier. Is that what happened to your car window? Nasty. You were lucky, I'd say. My guess is that it was a hunter. Season doesn't start for two weeks, but those guys get a little trigger-happy. I'll have Greg go ask around Long Hill Road to see who was up there. We have your contact info. We'll be in touch."

We were about to leave when Foster noticed some posters he had put up on Sykes desk. They'd been torn off the poles. Sykes saw him looking at them.

"I found these around town. Would you know anything about who put these up, Foster? It's a violation of town ordinance 15:203.b to deface public property. A couple hundred dollar fine if I find out who did it."

"I'll ask around," was Foster's reply. We turned to leave.

Once we were back out on the street, I turned to Foster.

"I never mentioned where the shooting occurred. How did he know to send the other officer to Long Hill Road?"

"And I run into Harry at least twice a week. That man was all about his grandkids. He's always showing me pictures or bragging about their exploits. I can't imagine him not telling me if he was going to spend some time with them. He wouldn't have been able to control himself. Something's fishy there, too."

"What now?"

"Well, I still think you should get back to your home turf. You'd be more effective there while I work here. Where exactly was it you got shot at?"

"The shot came from around the *Beyond Revelation* compound."

John nodded.

"John, I have a confession to make. I got it in my head that I didn't trust you. You've been too good to be true and my jaded experience is that I should be on my guard when I come across anything or anybody too good to be true. I thought you maybe were selling me a line to get me out of here, that you could be in on whatever was happening here. I was shot at when I pulled over to call Jonas to warn him about you. Then when I saw you putting up the flyers, I realized how wrong I was. I'm sorry."

"No apologies necessary. It's been a whirlwind and you're under a lot of stress. Let's get to my place. We'll clean your car up and I have some clear plastic we can put over the hole. That should hold you until you get back to New York. Since you've got a target on your back, I'll lead you on a different route out of town and then get you to the Connecticut border. You should be all right after that."

"I don't know how to thank you. You sure you'll be okay?"

"Hey, I've died at least once already. What's one more time?"

When we returned to John's place, Jonas had packed and was ready to go.

"I can't have you drive back alone, Frannie. John, are you okay if I leave my car in your driveway? We'll figure out a way to pick it up later."

"Why don't you leave Francine's car? I know a guy who can replace the window while it's here."

"Thanks, John, for everything."

6

I'd only been away for two days but it seemed like an eternity. I was never so thrilled to see Will and the kids streaming out the front door to greet me as I pulled the car into the driveway. I was especially gratified that Albert was leading them out. He was eight years old when his mother died so, when I came along a year later, he'd often display a great deal of resentment that I was trying to take his mother's place. It took a lot of work on my part, but he gradually got to the point where he tolerated me. Some days, he even liked me.

As he was now entering his pre-teens, I hoped that, as his hormones took over, he wouldn't revert to resentment. Instead, to my relief, the exact opposite happened. We became closer and closer. He even came to me for advice on personal matters and problems.

His sister, Stella, was four years younger. We were close from nearly the very first day. Her memories of her mother were much less vivid than Albert's and she was more accepting of me. After Rosa was born, Stella eagerly took on a role of helpmate. As a working mother in a stressful career, her help was much appreciated. Now, they even share a bedroom.

As Jonas pulled the car in front of our house in the early evening, Albert burst through the side door followed closely by Stella. Will carried Rosa as he strode along behind the kids. As I had suspected, Rosa had one of those quick kid things and was now feeling fine. The doctor in the emergency room gave her a shot of antibiotics, and the fever quickly dissipated.

If having the kids stream out to greet me wasn't enough, the smile on my husband's face could get me through anything. Will's face took on a questioning look when he noticed that we drove up in Jonas's car, not mine. That look changed to horror and dismay when I told him what had happened. We decided we would discuss it in greater detail later when the kids were in bed.

Jonas ate dinner with us and then stayed with us overnight rather than driving the rest of the way to Brooklyn. After dinner, the kids settled down to do their respective things while we updated Will on the results of our trip.

"I usually can read people but I couldn't get a fix on the local cop, Sykes. There's something about him that didn't seem right. When he issued that ultimatum to me, I was tempted to have you go up there and get Federal all over his ass. Then, when he knew exactly where I was when I was shot at, I knew he was in on something. Foster saw it, too. I figured I'd come back home like John said to get my bearings and work with the resources I have at my disposal here."

"I for one am glad you're back."

I scooted over on the couch and nestled in Will's arms where I felt nice and safe.

"Thanks, hon. And thanks for letting me go on like this. My heart's still racing and we're no closer to finding Eunice than we were before. I should have stayed up there. I should have followed my instincts that Rosa would be fine. Emma had everything under control, and you were coming home. I shouldn't have skedaddled like I did."

Jonas responded. "You didn't skedaddle, Frannie. You were being a mother. Somebody shot at you. You were wise to leave. I'm the one who should have stayed, but when I saw you with blood on your face and glass in your hair, I couldn't let you go on alone."

I reached over and took Jonas's hand.

"Stop beating yourselves up, both of you. You both did right. There was little more you could do."

"Thanks, hon."

"From the way you described the shot and the damage to the car, my guess is that it was buckshot that shattered the window since it didn't get through to you or the window on the opposite side. If it was a high-powered rifle, you might be dead now."

"Thanks so much for that clinical analysis."

"Trying to keep it real. Just sayin' that sometimes it's best to retreat and regroup."

"That sounds much nicer than skedaddling, doesn't it?"

"Yeah, it does. I think it may be time for the FBI look into what's happening up there. So, what's next for you?"

"Well, I want to see if there's anything I can learn about Officer Sykes and *Beyond Revelation*. They're connected somehow. I know it. We've gone on and on here but haven't once asked about you. You working on anything interesting?"

"We've got an ongoing intergovernmental task force with NYPD to smoke out some of the worst drug kingpins. I looked up Jane Kelly. I hoped that, with Kent down in DC, the NYPD would have come to its senses and reinstated her to her old job. But it wasn't to be. She was still walking a beat as a street cop. She was miserable and about ready to quit. So, I made a few phone calls and, before I knew it, she's now working for me. She's got to put in a few weeks at Quantico but, with her experience, they short circuited a lot of her training."

"What?" The vehemence with which I said this surprised even all of us.

"What's the matter? Jane impressed both of us when she worked with us. She'll be an asset to the Bureau. I thought you'd see this as great news."

It was great news. I really liked Jane Kelly and was happy that her demotion had been short-lived. However, I could not help but feel that twinge of jealously I previously felt when she and Will were working together. She was beautiful and funny. As a law enforcement professional, she had much more in common with Will than I. She was also closer in age to him than I. I never suspected that Will had ever cheated on me, nor did I believe he would, but still.

I was jealous enough when she was an associate working for an entirely different agency. Now she would be working directly under Will—let me rephrase that, directly with Will—on a day-to-day basis. I felt very insignificant in comparison.

"I am happy for her. She'll be a tremendous addition to your team."

The next morning, my first task was to sit down with Heather to see how her father was doing and see if she had mended relations with her family. Then, I needed her to perform some of her research investigation magic on *Beyond Revelation* and on Officer Andy Sykes. I needed her to dig deep and find out as much as the Internet offered on these subjects.

Once I got her going on these tasks, I had to sit down with Frank to see if we still had a functioning business venture here. I had full confidence in Frank, but we were so thin that if any one of us were out for several days, the impact could be devastating. I walked down to see him.

"Hi Frank, how you doing? How are we doing?"

"We've been better. I've had to fill airtime with some puff pieces. I've interviewed a couple new on-air candidates I want to run by you before I make them offers."

"Frank, I trust you completely. You know that."

"I know that, but I don't feel comfortable spending your money without your input or sign-off."

"Frank, I just don't have the time. We're no closer to locating Eunice than I was two days ago. Jonas is understandably a wreck. He said he'd come in to work today, but late. Poor guy needs the sleep. In the meantime, I've got to keep working on this. Hire whoever you think will help us."

"Okay."

"If it's any consolation, I think Eunice's disappearance is connected to a bigger story. I've only scratched the surface, but I'm getting the sense it could be a huge story. Think you can keep things going without me for now?"

"Yes, I can keep things going. Do what you have to do."

I returned to my office and then it occurred to me that I should go back to my old source, Reverend Malcolm McKenzie. I called him.

"Hi Reverend, I need help from somebody versed in the world of religion and your name was at the top of the list that popped into my mind."

"Well, you have me intrigued. What religious question are you about to pose?"

"*Beyond Revelation.* It's a religious retreat or community of some sort. Have you ever heard of it?"

"Which one?"

"Which one what?"

"There are I would guess ten *Beyond Revelations* now. It started in Montana about fifteen years ago. It was such a success that five years later one sprouted up in Colorado. Then, a couple years ago, they established small retreats in states throughout the country."

"It's the one in Massachusetts I'm concerned about."

"Well, that's one of the more recent communities. Like I said, the Montana one's been around for about fifteen years. It's the nerve center. Colorado is big, but it's still a satellite. In any case, they're both so remote that it takes days to reach civilization, if anyone ever has the inclination to leave."

"No one leaves?"

"Not that I know of. These are insular communities indoctrinated in the belief that the Rapture, the Second Coming, is imminent. They believe they are in the right place to ascend to heaven when it happens. From what I understand, people enter the community with this belief and then the indoctrination continues every minute of every day after that. They also believe that modern conveniences—cars, televisions, iPhones—are all the work of the devil. This makes it a lot easier to keep people on the property."

"Isn't it then a little odd that they established the Massachusetts community in such a populated area? I was there. A town center is only an hour walk away. I can't imagine that every single person who joins these communities remains forever enchanted with this life. I'd think there would have been at least one defection over the years, especially when the temptation of modern life is so close and so tempting."

"Those were my thoughts exactly when I heard the satellites were starting up. The Massachusetts community and many of the others seemed a definite risk, but rumor has it is that they have a way of addressing any defections. They monitor people continuously and, if they detect any dissatisfaction or diminution of spirit, they either re-indoctrinate them or, if that doesn't work, they ship them out to the remote locations. It's also rumored that they use drugs to make the person more compliant. They have a couple private jets at their disposal to move people around so discontent does not have a chance to spread."

"It seems you can find anything on the Internet but whenever I look for anything on *Beyond Revelation* all I get are dead ends. You know me well enough to know that I wouldn't have come to you without doing some research on my own first. But there was next-to-nothing."

"The members may not have access to modern media but that doesn't mean the leadership doesn't. They hire people whose job is to monitor the web and then scrub it clean."

"Is there a leader?"

"There are two. For lack of better terms, there is a secular leader and a religious leader. The secular leader, the one who paid for it all, is billionaire Robert Benson."

"I read about him in a local newspaper article when the Massachusetts compound started up."

"Benson is a New York guy. I've met him a couple times. He was a big-time contributor to my campaign and would attend fundraisers in the area."

"Think you could introduce me so we can meet?"

"I don't see why not. He's always out there, hungry for publicity and adoration. The religious leader, by contrast, is a recluse. He lives exclusively on his compounds, at least I think he does. I hear that nobody interacts with him directly. He'll reach out to his flock periodically by video, but not in person. His name is Caleb Smith, but I doubt that's his real name. Very mysterious, but one thing is obvious. He's rich, both in his own right but also from the millions he's bilked from various flocks over the years. He's not as wealthy as Benson, but still quite a nest egg. I met him once at a conference twenty years ago. He was one of those men whose eyes could penetrate right through you; kind of like they used to say about John Brown. Very freaky, which is saying a lot in this line of work where all of us are freaks."

One thing I always liked about Reverend McKenzie was that in one breath he would be full of conceited bluster, but in the next he'd be self-aware and self-deprecating.

"If *Beyond Revelation* is so secretive and insular, how do they recruit new members?"

"They insulate the members but they have a cadre of highly paid recruiters. They go to churches and scout out vulnerable members. They're like jackals who look for the young or injured members of the herd and then they pounce. Their tactics are to entrap and then brainwash. These people are very high tech."

"How do you know all this?"

"One of the recruiters came to me when I was still just a country preacher. He wanted to bare his soul, but he also wanted to remain alive. I had just made my national name with my speech and he looked me up. He was not enamored by the cult anymore and needed to tell someone about their practices."

"Did you pass anything on to the authorities?"

"Pass what along? While everything I described may not be the most ethical, it's all perfectly legal."

I was about to leave when he asked me a question.

"Why do you have an interest in *Beyond Revelation*?"

"A friend of mine went missing in the same town as the compound and I've gotten some information that leads me to believe *Beyond Revelation* may somehow be involved."

"Interesting."

"And I think they may have a local cop on the payroll. When I started getting close, he showed up to harass me and keep me away."

"Well, just be careful. They are a cult and there's no predicting how they may act when they feel threatened."

"Careful is my middle name."

7

I returned to the office and found Heather there, waiting for me.

"How's your father doing?"

"Much, much better, thanks. The thing's he's most pissed about is that he has to make some lifestyle changes. That'll be the tough part. He's a stubborn coot."

"I'm so glad you're back together again."

"Me, too."

I was about to tell her I learned there were many *Beyond Revelation* when she advised me of the same thing.

"Francine, did you know there are at least eight of these communities? The biggest is in Montana."

How she could so often be a step ahead of me, especially when it came to gleaning information from the web, was truly impressive.

"Yes, I just found that out myself."

"Well, I couldn't find out much about any of these compounds or even on the order itself but I discovered one interesting fact about the towns near them."

"And that is?"

"There were a number of residents that went missing in each town over the past years."

"People go missing in towns all over the country. What's so unusual about these people?"

"They're all people of color."

"Start from the beginning."

"Once I discovered there are numerous *Beyond Revelations* around the country, I looked for commonalities. I focused on three of them, Montana, Colorado and Massachusetts. I examined the demographics of the areas around these compounds and the closest town had a predominantly white population. I examined the past three censuses and noticed a gradual sprinkling of minorities over time, but no great shifts.

"I then dug deeper into who the minorities were and if anything happened to them. In Montana, I found police reports for four African-Americans—Vernon Boyd, Sharon Cauthen, Harvey Goolsby and Monica Lacey—and in Colorado, police reports on three Blacks—Carl Smith, William Dixon and Laura Friday—all of whom disappeared without a trace over the course of a decade. You know what happened in Massachusetts. In each instance, the person had only recently moved into the town and then disappeared before he or she could get settled. Are they related? I don't know."

I examined Heather's work before speaking.

"Heather, this is incredible investigative journalism. I don't know whether I would have ever thought to look for this. These could be coincidences, isolated unrelated events but, as Will is fond of saying, always proceed as if everything is interrelated until proven otherwise. The coincidences will drop out eventually, but if you start off assuming things aren't related, you'll miss things as you glide right over the connections without ever noticing them."

Heather pulled out her pad and pen and jotted this latest nugget down. I continued.

"See if you can dig up information on any of these missing people. Families, friends, people who may have reported them missing, I'd like to speak to them first."

"What about the local police or sheriff's department?"

"We'll probably have to talk with them at some point but, given my suspicions about Officer Sykes in Fairbrook, I don't want to play our hand too early and tip off somebody about what we're looking for."

"I looked into Sykes' finances but I haven't noticed anything yet."

"Keep looking. He's involved somehow; I know he is. In the meantime, I'll fill in Will."

I dialed my husband and told him what Heather had told me. I hoped that, after our conversation, he was going to tell me that the FBI would get involved.

"Fava," he patiently told me, "I'm running into a lot of roadblocks here. You yourself mentioned the possibility of coincidences and we have no hard evidence that *Beyond Revelation* is in any way involved with these disappearances. I've made some phone calls, but I'm being emphatically advised that these are still local and state cases. This involves religious institutions. The FBI would get crucified if we rushed in based on the flimsy evidence we have right now. We still have protocols put in place after the Branch Davidian fiasco in 1993 to keep such an incident from happening again. I'm sorry. I really am."

"I know you are. We'll keep plugging away."

"Be careful. You've had one window blown out."

"We will. Love you."

We were on our own. I hoped Heather would get some names for me to talk to. I needed to do something. My phone rang, it was John.

"Hi John, how you doing?"

"I've been better."

"Why? What happened?"

"I wanted to let you know that Karen Gagnon is dead."

"She's dead? How?"

"Word has it she wandered out of her house in the middle of the night for one of her drunken walks but, instead of wandering through the woods like she normally would, she walked along the tracks. A train hit her."

"You don't sound overly convinced that this was how she died."

"Karen had a sad life, but she was a good person. She didn't deserve to die like that."

"Nobody does. But you didn't answer my question."

I heard nothing on the line.

"John?"

"I'm still here. No, I'm not convinced. I think someone killed her and then put her in front of a train. I'm not sure of anything anymore. I've tried to reach Harry, but he's still not back. I'll do everything I can, but this isn't the town I love anymore."

"I know you will. Let me make some calls."

I hung up with Foster and dialed Will once again.

"Will, I know we just talked about the lack of evidence to warrant FBI involvement, but things have changed. I just got a call from John. Karen Gagnon is dead. The official line is that she was drunk and walked in front of a train, but that seems fishy. People are dropping like flies in this town, Will. I'm worried about John's safety now. Something might happen to him.

If the local cops know the FBI is watching, maybe they'll be on their best behavior. Please, Will."

"I'll call the police department right now and make it clear we're interested in what they're doing. It's Fairbrook, right? We have a field office in Springfield. I'll call them too and come up with an excuse why they need to be involved."

"Thanks, hon."

"I'll let you know what happens."

8

After her initial success, Heather was having trouble getting additional information off the Net. She theorized that whoever was in charge was very proficient at covering their tracks, making it difficult to dig into *Beyond Revelation*. One thing I admired about Heather was that her frustration did not deter her. Instead, it made her more determined. I knew it was only a matter of time before she found something.

She called the newspapers in both Montana and Colorado that had reported the missing persons but they threw up one bureaucratic roadblock after another and she was getting nowhere. Likewise, she left message after message at town offices, but with no return calls.

I didn't have a clue what to do next when my phone rang. It was a Manhattan number. Normally, if I didn't recognize a number, I would let it go to the machine but there was too much happening to pass on answering this time. I answered.

"Hello."

"Hello, is this Francine Vega?"

"Yes, it is."

"This is Robert Benson. I understand from Reverend McKenzie that you would like to speak with me."

"Yes, very much so. Thank you for calling."

"Can I ask the nature of what you'd like to talk with me about?"

"It's about *Beyond Revelation*."

"I see. I'm probably not the best person to talk about that. Caleb Smith has the most knowledge."

"But you've provided the financing. You must have some influence or working knowledge. In addition, Caleb Smith does not appear to be reachable. He's downright elusive, as a matter of fact."

"I'm not sure what influence or knowledge I have, but perhaps we should get together. Everything would have to be on background."

"Agreed. When do you think we could meet?"

"I'm free for the next couple of hours. Could you meet me at the Brews Brothers Coffee Shop on the corner of 76th and 2nd in say a half hour?"

"That would be perfect."

I did not know what to expect from this meeting. His attitude about *Beyond Revelation* seemed rather detached to the point of being a third person participant despite having poured in millions of dollars into this venture. Perhaps it was a tax write-off or maybe just a toy for a rich man to play with. I headed out and hailed a cab.

I arrived at the coffee shop at the agreed upon time. It was one of those establishments with a raised stage area for guitarists, singers, poets, you name it.

There were six other people, each of whom was on a laptop or some electrical device, but none that resembled the Internet pictures I had of Mr. Benson. I ordered a cappuccino from the multi-pierced and tattooed barista and took a seat on a worn upholstered chair in the corner. An hour and a half and two cappuccinos later, I decided he was a no show and got up to leave. I was through the door when he waltzed in.

"I had to decide whether you were serious. I've been out in my car, watching you."

He pointed up at a surveillance camera on the wall.

"You're very pleasant to look at."

"So my husband tells me. Mr. Benson, I really don't have time for your, for lack of a better term, foolishness."

"Everybody ought to make time for a little foolishness each day. Don't you agree?"

"Not when somebody's life may be on the line."

"Now you have me intrigued, Ms. Vega. Let's sit down and talk for a bit. Oh, I instructed Hailey, our fine barista, to not charge you for the cappuccinos so you won't find them on your credit card bill. I own this fine establishment. If you show up at 7:30 on any Tuesday or Friday, you'll catch me playing my guitar and singing old ballads and folk tunes right here. I'm not half bad, if I say so myself."

I sat back down at the chair I had recently vacated and he across from me.

"Now, before we begin, I want to let you know that what I told you on the phone about *Beyond Revelation* is true. I really don't keep track of what happens at the compounds on a day-to-day basis."

"What can you tell me? Are these really the places to be when the end of days finally arrives?"

"Oh yeah, all that stuff. Do you want to know why I got involved in *Beyond Revelation*?"

I nodded.

"We have the highest incarceration rate of any country on earth. We don't need more people in our prisons, wasting their lives away. I envisioned *Beyond Revelation* as an alternative. People have to make a commitment to stay there perhaps for the rest of their lives, but it is their choice, not someone else's. These folks are searching for something, anything that will give meaning to their lives. Some people believe the way is through drugs or through a love of money. I'm offering them an alternative, one in which they can live for others."

"You don't especially believe the end is near, that the second coming will be soon upon us and that everything described in the Book of Revelation is about to come true?"

"I don't have a clue. My partner, Caleb, seems to believe it, and he passes that belief on to our initiates. They believe it, and that's all that matters to me. So, tell me, Ms. Vega, why do you have an interest in *Beyond Revelation* and whose life may be on the line?"

I trusted this eccentric. If *Beyond Revelation* was up to something nefarious, I didn't think he was a party to it. Conmen and charlatans have fooled me before, but I didn't think that was the case with Mr. Benson.

I was at a dead end. I was no closer to locating Eunice than I was when I started. Jonas was at the end of his rope. Several people were dead. Even Heather was hitting dead ends. I had to do something, and confiding in Robert Benson might be beneficial. I laid out everything I knew.

When I finished, Benson did not say a thing but sat there chewing on his coffee stirrer. Finally, he spoke up.

"I've known Caleb Smith for over twenty years. I bet you're expecting me to say that I could never think of him being involved in what you're implying. Well, ten years ago or even five, that definitely would have been the case. However, five years ago he got strange. Let me amend that. He was always strange, but a decade ago, he went over the edge. I haven't seen him in person over that time. I don't even talk to him. I get emails and texts from him. In each case, it's from a different email address or number, like I was tracking him down."

"Do you have his picture or can you describe what he looks like? We got nothing."

"I've only met him in person a couple times. The last time I saw him he had shoulder length hair and a long beard. He had thick glasses and wore a baseball cap."

"No offense but why would you even talk to someone like that let alone give him millions of dollars?"

"He came up to me and told me something about my past, something personal that no one else would know. I was intrigued."

I couldn't fathom this type obsession with any person or idea.

"Of late, the tone of his messages indicates he's still got the religious fervor but it's now tinged with something more sinister. In short, he's a zealot and I've never found zealotry of any stripe to be a good thing."

"Is there anything you can do to look into this for me?"

"I said I didn't involve myself in the day-to-day, but I'm not totally divorced from its operations. As the chief benefactor, I get statements on all large transactions and expenditures. Let me go through those statements and see if anything jumps out."

"Do you trust that people aren't lying to you on the statements?"

"They tried lying to me once, and I immediately shut off the money spigot. They learned their lesson."

"They may not lie, but they may play games and hide things in other ways."

"Ms. Vega, I did not become a billionaire by letting people get things over on me. If anything is there, I'll know. I'm sorry about your friend's disappearance and all the other things that have happened. I hope things straighten out for you soon."

"Thank you."

By the time I left the coffee shop, it was after five. It was hardly worth heading back to the office so I jumped on the subway for home. I could do nothing more today. I would start fresh tomorrow.

When I arrived at the office the next morning, I looked in Heather's office and found her slumped over her computer keyboard. She was wearing the same clothes she was wearing yesterday.

"Heather," I called out. Nothing. I shouted louder. She stirred.

"Huh?"

"Have you been here all night?"

"I, um, yeah. I finally got somewhere a couple of hours ago. By then it wasn't worth going home, so I crashed here."

"If this is gonna be a habit, we'll either have to get you a couch or you use the one in my office."

I noticed that I did nothing to dissuade her from working late.

"So, what you find?"

"Remember that I was having problems getting any information on the people who disappeared? I hacked into the newspaper's database. Hacking in wasn't too difficult. It was searching through hundreds of folders and files that took so long. Finally, I found some contact information for Vernon Boyd, a person who disappeared in Montana. He was originally from Detroit. His father, Franklin Boyd, was the one who reported him missing. Here's his address and telephone number."

"That's great work, Heather. Thanks. You okay on the hacking stuff?"

"Yeah, I cover my tracks well."

I was going back and forth whether I should call Mr. Boyd or jump on a plane to speak with him in person. The advantage of the former included the saving of both time and money. I could just pick up a phone and call. I could get a feel whether there was a relationship between what was going on in Massachusetts and in Montana. However, I long ago discovered that people are much more willing to talk face-to-face than they are to talk over the phone to the disembodied voice of a person they've never met before. Karen Gagnon was a case in point. She never would have confided in me if I weren't sitting with her, looking into her eyes, letting her know I was sincere in my inquiries. I wondered whether my talking to her ultimately resulted in her death but I couldn't let thoughts like that keep me from doing what I needed to do. I am a journalist and my job—my life—involves asking questions.

Believe it or not, I had some non-*Beyond Revelation* work to do so I settled down to work on some other projects, but my mind wasn't in it. I picked up my phone.

"Hey, J., tomorrow morning, we're flying to Detroit."

9

First thing the next morning, Jonas and I were on a plane out of LaGuardia to Detroit.

"Explain to me again why we're going to Detroit when Eunice is in Massachusetts."

"There are just too many coincidences. There has to be some connections between the *Beyond Revelation* compounds. We aren't getting anywhere in Massachusetts so maybe if we can answer some questions in Montana, it might lead to answers in Massachusetts. The one person connected with Montana that we know about is Vernon Boyd. He originally came from Detroit and I'm hoping we can talk with his father to get some info on his son."

We got off the plane and went to the taxi stand. When I gave the cabbie the address, he put on his 'off duty' sign and refused to take us there. Having grown up in Spanish Harlem, I understood what it was like to be from a neighborhood that, while it had its problems, the fear generated from its image far exceeded the true danger.

Rather than go through another rejection, we went to the car rental desks and rented a car for the day. We'd drive there. I'm sure I would have been fine on my own, but I was happy to have Jonas along.

I decided not to call Mr. Boyd before we left New York. I know we were risking he might not be home or that he even might not live at that address anymore, but I didn't want to scare him off. I preferred to call him once we got to Detroit; it would give him less of a chance to blow us off.

I called, and he was at home, which was lucky considering it was a workday. I explained why we were in Detroit. He said he would be happy to meet with us, but he didn't want us to come to his home. We agreed to meet at a coffee shop not too far from where he lived.

We plugged the address into the GPS and headed out. It was about a forty-minute drive from the airport. The word to best describe the view out the window as I drove would be depressing. Long vacated storefronts and boarded-up buildings punctuated the landscape. There were a fair number of people on the street, far too many of them young men, primarily men of color. A few of them cast looks our way as we drove by, but most didn't bother looking up.

We arrived at the coffee shop, Joe's Eats, and walked in. It was a standard eatery with reddish worn upholstered booths and stools. The place was clean and well-maintained, far better than the neighborhood surrounding it. Since it was between breakfast and lunch, there was only a handful of people, none of whom I thought could be Mr. Boyd.

A pleasant, middle-aged waitress named June ambled over to take our orders. We each ordered a cup of coffee but told her we may order more when our other party arrived.

About ten minutes later an average-sized man with gray hair and very dark skin entered. He walked with a cane like he had hurt his back rather severely at least once in his life. The waitress called out to him.

"Well, how are you this morning, Mr. Franklin?"

"I'm doing very well, Miss June. Lovely day, isn't it?"

"Yes, it is. What can I get you today?"

"Just a coffee for now." He surveyed the diner and surmised, probably from the fact that my face was probably the whitest in at least a ten-block radius, that we were the people he was to meet. "I'll be joining these fine people seated over yonder."

Franklin Boyd limped over to our booth. Jonas and I got up, introduced ourselves and invited him to join us. He said he hadn't had breakfast that day and asked if we would mind if he ordered something to eat. I said neither had we, and we would join him. June came back over, and we all ordered.

"So, do you have information on my boy?"

"No sir, I have no information on Vernon. It's just that your son's disappearance is very similar to disappearances of other people in Massachusetts and Colorado. We're just collecting information that will help us put a puzzle together. Hopefully, as we put this puzzle together, we can get a better picture of what happened to your son."

"Massachusetts? Colorado? What the hell do they have to do with my son?"

"Have you ever heard of a religious organization called *Beyond Revelation*?"

"No, they have something to do with Vernon?"

"We don't know yet. Why don't you tell us about Vernon and how he ended up in Montana."

"Vernon was rather wild in high school. He got into some trouble, nothing big, but it seemed like he was getting into a pattern that could lead to nothing good. Thing is, he recognized this in himself. He knew if he didn't change, he'd be dead at a young age. Then when he dabbled in using heroin, we both knew we had to do something, and fast. He just wasn't strong enough to resist anything here so he had the idea of moving to some place that had fewer daily temptations. He was open on where to go to. Montana seemed like a good spot for him to start over.

"He found himself a nice little place out in the middle of nowhere. The population of the town was almost all white, but he said he felt accepted. He'd call me every other day. I'd send him some money once a week. It was from my disability. Then, after about a month, nothing. I kept calling and calling. No answer. After a week, I called the local cops. They were worse than useless. A couple weeks later, I drove there myself. There was another family living in my boy's place. I went to the cops and they accused me of lying, of making the whole thing up. They also suggested that, if he had been around, maybe he fell into the wrong crowd and was off doing drugs again.

"I asked around town and one shopkeeper said he thought he recognized the picture but couldn't be sure. My boy kept to himself, so I don't believe he'd have made any new friends. I tried calling the person who owned the house he was living in, but the number was disconnected.

"Now, Vernon wasn't an angel. He's lied to me in the past, especially when he was on drugs. But he wasn't lying here. He was making a new start and was so happy. I just want to know my boy's okay."

"That's what we want, too. Do you know whom you spoke with in Montana?"

"I kept notes of everybody I spoke with and what they told me. You're welcome to them."

"Yes, that will be helpful."

He handed over a sheaf of papers. I looked through them.

"You'd make a good reporter, Mr. Boyd."

"In another lifetime, maybe."

10

"Did we accomplish anything here? I don't feel we're any closer to finding Eunice than we were yesterday."

"You ask a good question, Jonas."

It really was a good question. What were we doing? We were running all over the country on a whim, on a gut instinct. But what if my gut was way off? That's one more day that we would not have an answer about Eunice. Still, as Will has long said, build your case brick by brick. Sometimes a brick is misshapen and won't fit, so you have to chip at it and mold it to make it fit. Sometimes a brick is not good, but you won't know that until you examine and test it. I tell myself this but it doesn't help, knowing that a friend's life is in the balance.

I'd just gotten back home when my phone rang. It was John Foster.

"Francine, we've had an interesting development. *Beyond Revelation* is opening its doors, holding an open house, of sorts. They sent an invitation out through the churches saying that they've been closed off from the public for too long and want to reestablish themselves with us. They want us to come in and meet the congregants. They presented this as a periodic reintegration into the community."

"When is it?"

"Tomorrow, from 10 to 11."

"Not much lead time, is it? The timing of this open house wouldn't have anything to do with our suspicions about them, would it?"

"Hmmm, let me think on that one."

"Let me check with Will and our babysitter but I'll get a night's sleep and be to your place by 9 or so. Work for you?"

"Perfect. I'll see you then."

I hung up and noticed Will standing there.

"Back up to Massachusetts?"

"*Beyond Revelation* is opening its doors for one hour tomorrow morning. I have to see this place. My gut is still telling me that Eunice's disappearance is tied to that place."

"What time you need to be there?"

"I told John I'd be at his place by nine."

"Hold on."

Will pulled out his phone and walked into the other room. A few minutes later, he returned.

"I got you some company for the trip. Jane Kelly, or rather Agent Kelly, will go with you. I can't get away from this RICO case we're on now, but I don't want you going there alone Someone shot at you. Jane can be your chaperone, but she can also look for a reason for the FBI to be involved in this case. She'll be here at four tomorrow morning and then the two of you can be on your way."

I was about to protest that I can take care of myself, but he shot me a look that ended the discussion. Frankly, I was happy to have someone along who could watch my back, someone with a gun.

As expected, Jane arrived at our house precisely at four. It was nice seeing her. I really had not spoken with her since the maelstrom of the Zyklon Killer and the Presidential election over eight months earlier. On the trip up to Massachusetts, I filled her in on *Beyond Revelation*, but that didn't take too long since Will had already fully briefed her. We chatted about more personal things.

"I hear your daughter is growing by leaps and bounds."

"Yes, and now that she's walking, we can't slow her down."

"My kids are teenagers now."

The revelation surprised me. I was also somewhat ashamed of myself. We had gotten close to Jane, but it was entirely on a professional level. I focused on my job and I only saw her in her role as a New York City Detective who could help me do my job. I knew next to nothing about her as a person. What made me even more ashamed of myself was that my only opinion of her personally was as potential competition for my husband's affections. The only basis for these feelings was my insecurity. Jane is beautiful. She's closer to Will's age than I am. She works in the same field as Will and therefore would have shared experiences that I never could offer. There wasn't anything between Will and Jane, but that didn't stop my brain from running amok.

These irrational feelings therefore never allowed me to see beyond Jane as competition, as a woman who could easily replace me. It shouldn't have shocked me she had two teenaged kids, but it came as a complete surprise.

"You have two kids?"

"Yes, Sean, who's sixteen, and Amanda, who's fourteen. They're great kids, but they're teenagers. You can imagine how challenging it can be, especially for a single mother."

"Widowed or divorced?"

"Divorce. It turned out that Steve wasn't quite the gem I thought he was."

"Similar to my ex. I didn't learn about Eddie's alcoholism until after our marriage. Once I learned about his problem, I stuck it out a few years, but I was never having a kid with him. He was too irresponsible. I knew our relationship was heading south, and I didn't want to subject any kids to the ravages of a breakup. We parted on good terms, but you know what I mean."

"I do."

"Your ex, is he involved in the kids' lives at all?"

"No, I have no idea where he is, but that's okay. I'm not sure how good an influence he'd be, so it's just as well. Will tells me you're a great mother to his kids and your daughter."

"I try, but it's constantly a feeling along process. Albert is a work in progress. Stella warmed up to me immediately. They should put out how-to manuals on being a proper step-parent."

"I'm sure there are scores of them but none ever seem to apply to your particular situation."

We worked our way up into New England and within three hours we were riding on the road beside *Beyond Revelation*.

"See that razor wire? That's where we'll be in a few hours, in the compound beyond that wire."

"They are serious about maintaining their privacy, aren't they?"

We made our way into town and were soon driving alongside the town common.

"This is a lovely town, just look at those brilliant colors," Jane remarked.

"It is, but I find myself totally out of my element here. Give me a New York City street corner any day."

"I'm in between. I grew up in suburbia. Bergen County. Jersey. So, who again are we going to see?"

"John Foster. He's a lawyer who does mostly civil stuff: real estate, wills, things like that. He handled the original sale to Eunice's cousin. He's been very helpful. He's been almost too good to be true, but in his case it is true. I Googled him and if the guy was never a Boy Scout, he is one now. He's a Vietnam Veteran who won a Purple Heart. There's really not much on the guy to dig up except an incident where he and his father shot a guy Foster had witnessed in Vietnam committing an atrocity. Authorities cleared both of them calling it self-defense. Other than that, he is Everyman, married to his boyhood sweetheart, raised kids and now is helping raise his grandkids. He's even living in the same house he grew up in. He's close friends with nearly everyone in town, many of whom grew up with him."

"It's funny. In both of our businesses, we see so much of the bad in people on a daily or even hourly basis that we are skeptical of anyone who is good. We constantly expect the real person to emerge, the person who's in it for themselves, who's playing an angle."

"It's often safer to be the way we are. I find it better to be pleasantly surprised than repeatedly getting kicked in the head."

"Perhaps you're right, but what is the price we pay?"

We turned left at the traffic light in the center of town and were at Foster's house in under a minute. As expected, John Foster was waiting for us and had coffee and pastries ready.

"Francine, it's great to see you again."

"John, this is my friend Jane Kelly."

"Nice to meet you, Jane. I was expecting to see Heather again."

"No, I gave her a break this time. And, after getting shot at the last time I was in your fair town, my husband thought I perhaps needed some protection. He's working on a big case and he asked Jane to tag along. She's an FBI Agent."

"Technically, I'm still a probationary agent but that gets a little long-winded so agent will do just fine."

"It's a pleasure to have you here, whatever your status is. For the purpose of our visit today, however, let's say you're a member of our church. I have a feeling they're going to be on their guard with Ms. Vega in attendance. I don't think they were counting on your tenacity, Francine. That's why they sent out the notice just yesterday announcing that the open house would be this morning. They thought they could ram this through and then say to everybody that everything's okay. You may surprise them, Francine, but they'll be ready for the contingency of you attending. We'll just keep the fact that Jane's an FBI agent between us. If they know there's also an FBI Agent roaming the grounds, they'll close ranks and fold their tents."

"That works for me," Jane responded.

Foster looked at his watch.

"We'd better get a move on. Finish your coffee and we'll head on over."

We did as we were told and John drove us to the area designated in the flyer. Along the way, Jane appeared to be texting on her phone.

"Sending a message to your kids?" I asked.

"No, I expect they'll confiscate our phones. I'm entering a code that will digitally fry everything if someone enters the incorrect password."

We got there about fifteen minutes early and there were thirteen town residents there, four from John's church, six from the Sacred Heart Catholic Church and a couple people he did not know. Before too long, six SUVs arrived on the scene. The drivers and passengers poured out of the vehicles. A pleasant-looking man with long gray hair pulled back in a ponytail addressed us.

"Thank you all for coming today. My name is Pastor Mark Fredericks, I'm one of the spiritual guides here at *Beyond Revelation*. We have been remiss in not inviting you to visit us much earlier, but we all know how time can get away from us. We promise to do much better. We hope to be good neighbors, not just those people who live on the 'other side of the wire'. We will begin your tour shortly, but I'd like to make a few remarks before you head out.

"As you all know, our mission here is to prepare our congregants for the end of days, for the rapture. You will, therefore, find this to be a place of joy. How can you have nothing but joy and contentment when you're certain you're going to heaven? To attain this elevated state, our members have all agreed to put aside all the temptations of the modern world, to separate them from the sins of Gomorrah.

"Many people—make that most people—find that they cannot do this. The draw of that smart phone or television set is too strong. We wish these people well and pray for their souls, but they cannot be one of us. That does not mean they could not someday see the light and join us. We just pray it's not too late.

"The people you'll run into here who have chosen this path of enlightenment may seem unfriendly, but they are not. Our congregants did not universally accept the idea to hold this open house today. There are some who do not welcome the intrusion of the outside world. They perhaps are the wise ones, for they know that the devil is crafty and resourceful and will do whatever he can to offer temptations and that not everyone is the tower of strength they think they are.

"While I and the other leaders of *Beyond Revelation* believe it valuable to test our resolve periodically, we have to be cognizant of the fears of our congregants. For this reason, we ask you to respect the wishes of those congregants who wish to be left alone. Please do not approach them. We also ask that you all leave all your phones and other devices here. We will keep them safe and will return them to you at the end of the tour."

On cue, a half-dozen people, all dressed like they were from the cast of *The Book of Mormon*, moved forward. Each was carrying small plastic sandwich bags and a Sharpie. One member also had a small burlap sack. They each went up to groups of two or three of us and asked us our names, which they wrote on the plastic bags. They then put the phones in those bags and then put them into the burlap sack.

Only one person had objections to having their phones taken away. A middle-aged woman said her father was sick in the hospital and could not be without her phone. Pastor Fredericks apologized but said there could be no exceptions and the woman left.

"I hope you all have a nice tour. Your guides will now show you around."

With that, Pastor Fredericks turned on his heels and walked away. I had hoped to ask him a few questions, but the pace of his exit showed that he was not interested in any more conversation.

The person who took our phones would be the tour guide for Jane, me and John Foster. Her name was Greta. Even before she collected our cellphones, Fredericks pulled Greta aside and said something to her privately. I noticed them both look in our direction, so I surmised that they were talking about John and me. I had never met Fredericks before, but he seemed to know about me and my trip up to Fairbrook a few days ago. I was wondering if he was specially instructing her on how to handle me. What I was hoping was that Greta would focus on the two of us giving Jane freer rein to observe things that we may miss.

Each guide had his or her own golf cart parked off to the side to drive to each building in the compound. Jane climbed in the front with Greta while John and I sat on the back seat, looking to the rear.

Our first stop was the chapel. It was rather mundane, but at the altar there was an impressive stained glass window depicting the Last Supper. There were about twenty rows of pews with an aisle down the center. Bibles and hymnals were on the back of each pew. When I went to grab a book to take a look at it, Greta brusquely dissuaded me from doing so.

"Those are for congregants only. Thank you."

Not wanting to make a scene, I retracted my hand.

We each had several questions about the services. Greta handled each question with alacrity. We moved on to our next stop, the residence halls.

The residence halls were rather attractive, for what they were. I expected drab college-style dormitories, but they were hardly drab. In fact, the word I would use to describe the living quarters is festive. There were a few of the congregants milling about, but none paid us any attention. In fact, they acted as if we didn't exist.

After a few more nondescript buildings, our next stop was the kitchen/food hall. This was your standard food dispensing facility with long tables and rows of chairs. The kitchen seemed well-stocked, modern and clean, with stainless steel tables and shelves. Greta said there was one full-time chef who oversaw the meal preparation and managed the kitchen, but congregants handled all other functions on a rotating basis.

From there our last stop was the recreation center. They had a pool table, a ping-pong table and a pinball machine. One congregant was playing pinball and did not acknowledge our existence. Greta informed me that this was to be the final stop on our tour.

"Greta, I'm curious about your infirmary. Where do people go when they're sick?"

Greta glanced at her watch.

"I don't know if there's enough time to show you that facility."

"There's a time limit on the tour?"

"Oh yes, we've only allotted an hour."

"We'll be quick."

"I don't know."

John spoke up.

"I was a medic in Vietnam. I didn't become a doctor, but I'm fascinated by medicine and medical care."

"Okay, but let's hurry."

Greta ushered us through the infirmary. There were five beds, two of which were occupied. Both occupants appeared to be asleep. We hurried through the building and were back at the common room at the appointed hour. Greta was greatly relieved that we did not run over the time. Because we were so rushed through the infirmary, we hadn't asked any questions about the health facilities, so we asked them now.

"The hospital seems rather small. Is it equipped to handle everything? What if someone needs emergency surgery? Can you handle that?"

"We take care of our own."

"You have doctors on staff?"

"We take care of our own."

I had hardly noticed Jane slipping away from us as we were having this discussion. At one point I glanced over and saw she was sitting on an ottoman bench against the wall. She was slowly moving the ottoman away from the wall. She was on to something and it became my job to distract Greta. John sensed it as well, so he joined in the conversation.

"Greta," he asked, "we ran across maybe fifteen people during this tour. I'm sure there are many more. Where are they?"

"Some remained in their rooms during the tours. The others are out in our fields. It's harvest time."

"I noticed all the people we encountered were Caucasian. Are there any people of color in your congregation?"

"Not at the present time. We are open to people of all races and ethnicities. We do not exclude anyone who comes to us."

"I hear that nobody has ever left *Beyond Revelation* once they enter. Is that true?"

"We screen our people very well to determine their commitment. They don't leave because they are fully aware of the dangers their souls are in. This is the best place on earth for them when the Rapture begins. They know that to leave could be the difference between heaven and hell. In addition, we care very well for our people; they have no reason to want to leave."

I glanced over and Jane nodded. She had gotten what she was looking for. She got up and rejoined us.

"Well, Greta, this has been an informative tour. You sure can be proud of what you've accomplished here. *Beyond Revelation* is a model community."

"Thank you very much. Thank you for joining us today. We'll just get back to the cart so you can be on your way."

We returned to the parking area and, after retrieving our phones, we climbed back into John's car and headed into town. I knew Jane had found something, but she didn't want to divulge it immediately. Patience is not one of my virtues, but I didn't push her; I figured she had her reasons.

John put on a pot of coffee while Jane examined her phone. Then she asked us to enter our passwords so she could examine ours. She put each phone through a series of tests and then she powered them off. After she did this, she handed them back.

"I wanted to make sure they didn't do anything to our phones before we talked. It doesn't appear they tampered with them, but to be sure let's keep them powered off. I don't want them to hear what we have to say."

"So, what did you find? I figured you were on to something when you went and sat down."

"If you noticed it, they probably did, too. Did you notice there were cameras all over? I bet there isn't one square inch of that compound that they don't record 24/7. It doesn't appear they monitor the feeds in real time because I would have been outed."

"Will you tell us already what you found?"

"This."

She bent over and pulled up her pant leg, revealing a Glock pistol as well as a second smart phone, one that didn't get confiscated.

"I told you I anticipated they would confiscate our phones so I grabbed a backup before we left New York. I'm just glad they didn't have a metal detector. I would have set that thing off for sure."

She activated the phone and went to her photos. She tapped on one to enlarge it.

"They didn't see this when they were sanitizing the place for company."

She turned the phone for us to see. It was a picture she took of the wall directly behind the ottoman on which she was sitting. Written in red, which appeared to be blood, was one word.

SLAVE

11

"Are you saying that they kept someone in slavery on this compound? Do you think that's what happened to Eunice and her cousins?"

"That's about as good a theory as any."

"What can we do?"

"Let me talk with Will and others at the agency to see if this is enough to get a warrant to search the place. He may say that a judge may not issue one because I didn't identify myself as an FBI Agent before entering. Their lawyers would argue that I conducted an illegal search of a religious establishment."

"But they wouldn't have let you in if you told them who you were."

"Yeah, it's a bit of a double-edged sword here. I think I acted appropriately, but I may have compromised any evidence I may have collected. Then, any future evidence even tangentially related to this could be deemed 'fruit of the poisonous tree' because I obtained it as a result of this illegal search. I'm sorry, Francine."

"Oh, no, that's okay. As you said before, there are cameras all over the place. They must have looked at the film of you pulling your hidden phone out and taking the shot. They would have discovered the word by now. They would have scrubbed it clean. I'd bet anything that if we went there now, there would be a strong smell of bleach. I guess that means we're back to square one."

John spoke up.

"Not in the least. We've at least confirmed our initial feelings about *Beyond Revelation*. We can now throw out other theories and focus our efforts instead of guessing. Granted, we didn't inspect every building, but I can't believe Eunice is still there. They would never have invited the town if there was any chance we'd stumble in on her. The whole thing was a show to convince us she was never there, that they're what they say they are, a bunch of religious fanatical nuts.

"Now, unless they were hiding her very well, I see two possibilities regarding Eunice. They could have shipped her out to Montana or one of the other sites, probably in the dead of night."

Then he stopped. Without thinking, I responded.

"You said two possibilities."

John just looked at me and I immediately understood the other possibility, one that none of us wanted to acknowledge.

"There's got to be some way of determining if they moved her to another location. They have access to private planes, right?"

"I'll try pressing Robert Benson again. I don't entirely trust him, but maybe he was sincere about helping us. He said he still had to sign off on every big-ticket item. Private plane excursions would undoubtedly fall under that list."

Jane then asked, "Does anybody else have trouble with the absolute wall of silence this place falls under? Any organization, especially one like this where a person's whole being is sublimated to the whole, has to have a disaffected member or two. There's got to be somebody out there who would spill the beans on *Beyond Revelation*. We have to figure out how to find them."

"The infirmary," I blurted out.

"What about it?" John asked.

"As up-to-date as the infirmary may be, it was tiny. It must have faced medical issues it couldn't handle. They would have to use area hospitals and medical facilities for cases like these. Somewhere out there is someone who became sick, went to a hospital and could not go back. Let's find that person to see what we can extract."

I pulled out my phone and dialed.

"Heather, it's Francine. Do you think you can search hospital records for the hospitals near the *Beyond Revelation* compounds? You can? Great. What I want you to look for admitted patients who may have been congregants of *Beyond Revelation*. Then, I'd like you to follow up on the status of these people to see if there are any who didn't return to the compound. Think you can do that? That's the girl. Oh, John Foster sends his regards. I'll talk to you later. Thanks."

Jane and I were about to say our goodbyes to John Foster when he turned to Jane.

"Agent Kelly, I meant to ask before but does you being here mean the FBI is taking an active interest in this case."

"No, I'm afraid it doesn't. I'll discuss my findings with my superiors when I get back and recommend that we take it on, but I can't make any commitments."

"I see. If you do take it on, could you include investigating what's happened to Harry Dumont, our police chief? He's gone missing. Officer Sykes claims he left for a fishing trip with his grandkids, but when I called his daughter, she said he wasn't there. She hadn't heard from him in days. I'm worried about him."

"I'll add that to the list of reasons for us to get involved."

"Thanks."

After that, we were on our way back to New York.

"This keeps getting deeper and deeper, doesn't it?" I asked. "Do you think with what you saw that there is enough for the FBI to get involved?"

"I think so, but I don't know. I'm still getting my feet wet with the Bureau. It would be enough for the NYPD, but the FBI is a different beast. Many more protocols and regulations exist regarding what they get involved in. I guess they need to do that because they're national and need consistency across the country in how they apply the law and allocate resources. Also, if something goes wrong, it makes national headlines that can set the Bureau back immeasurably. The new Director is especially image-conscious and does not want to take any undue risks."

"You miss the NYPD?"

"Not yet. Everything is so new and exciting now that I don't have time to think about my old life. Plus, I still have a bad taste in my mouth over how they treated me at the end. That'll pass though, I'm sure. Anyway, when we get back, I'll sit down with Will and his bosses to get us involved."

"I'll work on my husband. He's a wonderful man, but he can sometimes be a bit of a bureaucrat."

"That's one of the secrets to longevity in this field, I'm afraid. You take too many risks and eventually one of them will trip you up."

I thought about my precipitous fall from grace at Allied Broadcasting due to a risk I took. "I hear ya," I replied.

12

The next morning, I was back at my desk, trying to work on a story, any story, that would take my mind off of Eunice and *Beyond Revelation*. It was rather futile, but I plowed ahead. At around 10:30, my intercom buzzed. The receptionist said there was a man in the reception area to see me. He said it was something personal and urgent.

I really didn't have the time or inclination to add anything more to my plate, but I had many feelers out there for leads on *Beyond Revelation* and on other stories. I could not afford to blow anyone off. I asked the receptionist to show the gentleman back.

The man, a rather dapper slender man in his fifties with a graying beard and full head of wavy hair, walked into my office.

"Mrs. Vega, my name is Francisco Rodriguez. I am an attorney with the firm of Ashman & Williams. I am here on behalf of a client of mine, Eduardo Vega."

My blank face told him the name meant nothing to me. He continued.

"Eduardo Vega is your father."

"I have no father. There was a person—a male—who abandoned my mother and me on the streets of New York when I was a baby."

"But he is still your father."

"I have neither the time nor the interest to hear anything more. I suggest that, if you have any desire to pursue this further, you take it up with my mother."

"But your mother is deceased."

"Yes, I believe you're correct. I guess you're out of luck, aren't you? Good day, sir."

Mr. Rodriguez turned to leave, but before he reached the door he turned around.

"Mrs. Vega, I wanted to let you know that your father is dying. He has only a month, maybe only a couple weeks, to live."

"Well, that would only complete the process. In my eyes, he died over thirty years ago. Thank you for the news. Goodbye."

Rodriguez was about to say something else but then thought better of it.

"I'll leave my card on the table here if you change your mind. He'd like to meet with you to apologize before he dies. Good day."

He left. I sat there stewing. I stared at the card. Why I didn't rip it in half and throw it in the trash, I don't know.

Most of what I said to Rodriguez was true. My father was dead to me and I had no qualms about him dying, but I wasn't entirely truthful about the point at which I considered him dead. I went through my childhood hoping against hope that he would walk back into my life. Many of my friends in school had fathers they could look up to and brag about. Some of the kids had parents who had divorced, but I can't remember any of them saying disparaging things about his or her father, even if he was not still on the scene. Whenever the talk of fathers came up, I would make myself scarce.

I wanted to talk to somebody about this visit. I tried Will but his phone went to voicemail, so I walked down to Frank's office.

"Hey Frank, got a minute?"

"Sure, what's up?"

"I just got a visit from a lawyer representing my father."

"Your father? Really?"

"Yeah, the guy said my father was dying. The lawyer said he'll be dead in a matter of months if not weeks. He wants to see me before he dies. He is feeling guilty, I guess."

"Interesting."

"I kicked the guy out of my office, telling him I had no father. Now, I'm wondering what to do."

"You want me to tell you what to do?"

"No… yes… maybe. As far as my father is concerned, he was dead to me a long time ago. This changes nothing, and yet, it changes everything."

"My two cents is to see him. The man he is or was shouldn't alter the type of person you are. I can't think of any situation in which you wouldn't be the better person, Francine. This is just another one of those cases. So what if you give him something he doesn't deserve? It's not like he'll be able to lord it over you. He's dying."

"I still don't know."

"Where is your father?"

"I don't know. I didn't give the lawyer a chance to tell me. He did leave me his card."

I handed it over to Frank.

"Ashman & Williams? They're a high-powered firm. They don't come cheap. You have no idea what your father did?"

"None."

"Curious. You have quite a dilemma on your hands. Let me ask you one last question. What do you believe your mother would want you to do?"

"I don't know."

"Growing up, did your mother badmouth your father?"

"No, we just never talked about him."

"Did she ever divorce him?"

"I don't know if she did or didn't."

"That should tell you something right there. A woman with a new baby who gets dumped by her husband in a new country never disparages him? Sounds to me like you're answering the question what your mother would do."

"I guess I am."

I returned to my office, closed the door and dialed the number on the card.

"Mr. Rodriguez, this is Francine Vega. I changed my mind. I'd like to see my father."

"I am happy to hear that, Ms. Vega. The travel arrangements are all set."

"Where is he?"

"In Havana."

"Havana? As in Cuba?"

"Yes, Cuba."

"And you can get me there with no problem?"

"Everything is all arranged."

"I'll get back to you."

I went back to Frank.

"He's in Cuba, of all places. He must be pretty important down there. The travel arrangements have been all lined up."

"When are you going?"

"I can't leave while I still have work to do trying to find Eunice. I'm willing to see him but I can't jettison my top priority for it. If he dies first, so be it."

I thought I had the perfect out. I'd look magnanimous by appearing willing to see my father, but I'd never have to go through with it until my I finished my job helping to locate Eunice. Then Will called.

He was returning my call, but he had news of his own. I filled him in on my father. His reaction was like Frank's, using words like interesting and curious. Then he advised me he'd gotten authorization to pursue a preliminary investigation into *Beyond Revelation* and into Eunice's disappearance.

"I have to say that Jane taking a picture of SLAVE convinced my higher-ups. Everything else we could tell was just hearsay and speculation but a picture always resonates."

He and Jane were to head out to Montana and then Colorado. They'd leave within the next two days. His contact in Springfield, Massachusetts would start pressing the Fairbrook cops to get answers of what was happening in that small town. It was the first positive feeling I'd had since Jonas came in to see me.

I went over to tell Jonas the news.

"Hey J., I just got a call from Will. The FBI is officially involved in Eunice's disappearance."

"That's good, I guess."

His lack of enthusiasm was not what I expected. "I thought that would be good news."

"It is, but Frannie I've seen too many stories just like this that don't end up good. When you or another reporter announces that the cops had just found a body in an alley or an abandoned building, I'm usually too focused on the camera shooting you to get involved in what you're saying. This is different."

"I know it is. We'll find her. You've got the best working on it."

"I appreciate everything you and Will are doing. I really do."

"Oh, on a different note, you'll never guess who contacted me. My father."

"Your father? Did he hear you have money now?"

"That's what I thought but it turns out he's dying. I didn't actually talk to him. He sent a lawyer. He wants to make amends with me. He wants me to go to Cuba to see him. I initially said no way. He hasn't been there for me. I won't drop everything to run to him. The more I thought about it, I decided I wanted to see him. My mother would want me to. But I won't go see him until we find Eunice. That's my priority."

"I appreciate that, Frannie, but didn't you say the FBI was working on this now?"

"Yeah, but what does that have to do with it?"

"Well, you said yourself it's in pretty good hands now. You can be spared a day or two to go see your dad. He doesn't have much time left, does he?"

"No, a couple weeks, a month tops."

"You owe it to yourself. Maybe you'll learn something about why he skipped out. I know it's eaten you up over the years. Worse comes to worse, you'll find out he's a total asshole and you'll feel vindicated about despising him."

"I don't know. I got the station to worry about."

"Frank's good at this stuff. You know, I had a wonderful father. I'd give my right arm to spend another couple minutes with him. You got an opportunity for a couple minutes without losing a limb. Take it."

"You're wise, you know that?"

"I knew you didn't keep me around just for my good looks."

I called Rodriguez that afternoon. I got a hint about my father's importance when I was told there was a Cuban consulate plane ready to go out of Teterboro. After making sure that Emma could take care of the kids, I told him that I'd be able to leave first thing in the morning.

The following day I got up and first thing our nanny/housekeeper Emma showed up. I don't know what we would have done over the years without Emma. She'd been with Will for nearly ten years now and the kids adore her. If she weren't so valuable and allowed both Will and me to do our jobs, I'd be jealous of her. Instead, I was appreciative.

It brought home the value of having someone like Emma when Will got a call from Jane just before we were both to leave for the airport. Jane said that Amanda, her daughter, came down with the flu overnight. She didn't have anyone like Emma she could call at a moment's notice. She'd have to get her daughter to the doctor and take care of her until she could arrange for someone to look in on Amanda. Jane hoped she could join Will on the Colorado leg of the trip. Will said he understood completely. He emphasized that her daughter's health was the priority. He'd go solo in Montana and would be fine. I got a little nervous when I heard him say that, given the history with *Beyond Revelation* to date.

"Do you really think it wise to go there with no backup?"

"I'll be fine. I'll hook up with an agent from the regional office that covers Montana. I'm just going to observe and ask a few questions. I'm always careful. You know that."

I still wasn't comfortable, but I trusted my husband's judgment on such matters.

At around ten in the morning, our respective car services arrived. Will was flying out of JFK, I out of Teterboro. Neither of us had direct flights, but for drastically different reasons. In Will's case, he had to get to Garfield County in the eastern part of Montana. There appeared to be no direct flights from the New York area to anywhere in Montana so he had to fly to O'Hare Airport in Chicago where he would switch to a plane to Helena, the State capital. From there he would charter a plane to Jordan, Montana, the Jackson County seat. From there it was a two-hour drive to the *Beyond Revelation* compound.

For me, I would fly from Teterboro to Barbados and then from Barbados to Havana, Cuba. The reason for the need for a connecting flight was political. To fly directly from the United States to Cuba would have required clearances and paperwork, which could take weeks or even months. Flying from a small airport like Teterboro to an intermediate location of Barbados would make it possible to get to Havana with a minimum of red tape. All I would need was a passport. One thing would be certain: my accommodations on a consulate plan were far preferable than Will's coach class flights and transfers.

We arrived in Havana late in the afternoon. Rodriguez offered to put me up in the finest hotel in Havana, but I refused. I wanted to see my father, spend the requisite time with him, and then get back on a plane home. Rodriguez said he understood. A car was waiting for us at the airport and we went directly to the hospital. I would have liked to see the city, and the country itself, but I focused on making an in and out.

The hospital was more modern than I imagined it would be. My guess was that this was the hospital for Cuba's rich, famous and powerful. We took the elevator to the third floor. Rodriguez walked me down the hall to the room at the end. He let me walk in alone.

On the bed was a white-haired sallow-skinned man who weighed at most ninety pounds. His eyes were closed but I could see his chest almost imperceptibly rising and falling so I knew he was still alive. A tube supplied oxygen to his nostrils, but there appeared to be no other tubes or monitors connected to him. Rodriguez had told me that the doctors had taken him off life support and were now just managing his pain. Rodriguez did not volunteer what illness afflicted my father, nor did I ask.

I stood there at the foot of his bed and watched him for a minute. Here was the man who gave me life but was never there for me. He was never there for all of my life moments. He was never there when I needed him most, like when my mother suffered through the pain of cancer and died. He was never there, and never would be, for his granddaughter. How could I feel anything for this man? And yet I did.

Was I the type of person Frank said I was or was I an overly sentimental schmuck playing the eternal Pollyanna, hoping against hope that there's some good in everyone?

It did not appear he would awaken, so I turned to leave. I'd come back later. Perhaps he'd be awake then. I was almost to the door when I heard a raspy whisper.

"Usted vino."

"Si," I responded. I turned around and headed back to the bed. It occurred to me that a normal daughter would reach and take her father's hand in a situation like this but there was nothing normal about this situation, so I just stood there with my hands at my side. Neither did he reach for me.

"Your mother," he continued in English, "wanted that you...speak English so...we will use...that language, okay?"

I nodded. He could only speak a few words with each breath, so I knew I had to be patient if I were to hear him out. I appreciated that he conversed in the language he thought I would be most comfortable. It was a good start.

"What should I call you?" I asked.

He smiled a sad smile, most likely the only kind he had left.

"Eduardo would be...fine."

An uncomfortable silence ensued. He was struggling to find words, both physically and emotionally. Finally, he spoke.

"You...have done...well. I see...you...on television."

"You've kept up with me and my life?"

"Yes...in that drawer...open."

He weakly pointed over to a side table. I opened the drawer. In there was a gold locket on a necklace. I pulled it out.

"Open."

I did as I was directed and opened the locket. On one side was a picture of my mother. On the other was my picture, as a baby.

"For you...or...for Rosa...when...she is...older."

He looked at me one more time, smiled, and then closed his eyes. They never opened again.

I walked out to hallway where Rodriguez was standing.

"I'd like to go home now."

We walked back down the hallway. Rodriguez spoke briefly to a nurse, who gravely nodded her head and walked into my father's room.

We got back in the car. We proceeded to the airport. Neither of us spoke a word the entire trip. I hadn't put the locket in my purse, but instead I clutched it in my hand close to my chest as I stared out the window. I saw nothing as my vision was turned inward, examining my thoughts.

I had no greater insight about my father now than when I landed in Cuba. As evidenced by the locket, he had feelings for my mother and me. He kept track of me throughout my life, even down to knowing I have a daughter named Rosa. Why did he leave us? Why did he never try to contact me in the past? Did he contact my mother over the years and if so, why didn't she ever tell me? The answers to these questions and more went to the grave with him. I did at least leave with a feeling that my father cared about me. That was something I never knew before.

We arrived at the airport and worked our way over to the consulate plane. When we arrived, the pilot was having a heated discussion with an official-looking man in a suit. Before long, I realized that their discussion centered on me. After a few more minutes, the man in the suit turned and walked away. It was obvious from the body language of the pilot that the situation had not been resolved. The pilot headed over to us.

"That man was from our State Department. He advised me you cannot fly to the United States, Ms. Vega."

"What?"

"You are on a no-fly list and are not allowed to fly into the United States. Our plane could bring you as far as Barbados, but then you would be held there."

"I don't understand. I can't be on any such list. Perhaps my name is the same as some terrorist."

"He showed me the paperwork. It had your passport number on it. I will be happy to assist you in straightening this out, but I've been involved in similar situations before. It could take a week or more before U.S. officials concede their mistake. In dealing with Cuba, U.S. officials sometimes are over-zealous in their approach, even when there's been an obvious error."

Then the obvious occurred to me.

"No, this is no mistake, no error. This was purposeful. It came straight from the top."

"What do you mean?"

"President Kent and I have a history and this is one of his petty revenges."

"The Nazi concentration camp affair?"

"Yes, that one."

"They can't bar you from reentering the country, can they? You're a U.S. citizen, right?"

"Born and bred in New York City, but I don't think that matters much these days."

"I will have my driver take you to a hotel. You can stay as long as you want, courtesy of the Cuban government."

"Thank you. Let me make a phone call first."

"Of course."

I stepped off to the side and called Will. He had a special government phone. It wasn't as prone to signal failure, but he was in Montana where I'm sure signal strength is weak or non-existent, and I was unsure if I could reach him. If I remembered correctly, he was staying over in Helena overnight and was taking a plane to Jordan first thing in the morning. I supposed that Helena, as the state capital, would be in the one area of the state where signal was the strongest. I dialed. He picked up on the second ring.

"Hi hon, did you see your father?"

"Yes, and I'll fill you in later but right now I have a more immediate concern. The American government won't let me fly back."

"What?" he screamed.

"My reaction exactly. I'm on a no-fly list. Rodriguez, the attorney who facilitated the meeting, thought it might be a mistake even though they had my passport number. He offered to work on my behalf to straighten out the situation but he's said it could take over a week to resolve something things like this."

"How do you think this happened?"

"You know as well as I do."

"Kent?"

"That's the only explanation I can think of. His treatment of Allied Broadcasting showed how vindictive he can get. He expected that, as a journalist, I'd travel out of the country so he put an attachment as a terrorist threat to my name for that eventuality. Whatever the cause, I'm stuck here now. I can't afford to be away that long. My gut told me not to make this trip in the first place; I guess my instincts were correct."

"Tell Rodriguez to work his end of things. Maybe it was a computer glitch or some such SNAFU that can be easily corrected, but I think you're correct. This sounds like one of Kent's petty revenges. Let me make a few phone calls to see what I can do from here. You're at the airport now?"

"Yeah, but Rodriguez says he'll put me up in a hotel, at government expense, no less. His driver will drive me there."

"Why don't you stay at the airport until you hear from me? You might have a better signal there than at a Cuban hotel. If I'm able to pull off what I'm thinking, it may be easier to extract you from there than from the middle of Havana."

"Extract me? It sounds like something out of a *Bourne* movie."

"Hopefully we can minimize the chase scenes. I'll call you back within a half-hour. Love you."

"Love you, too."

I told Rodriguez I wanted to wait at the airport, at least until I heard back from Will. I didn't mention about 'extraction.' I wasn't sure of the strict legality—or illegality—of what Will was planning, so I thought the less said, the better. Rodriguez said that would be fine if I remained here. He had some business to attend to—including making some calls on my behalf—so he would take a taxi into town. The driver would be at my disposal whenever I was ready.

Will called back twenty-five minutes later.

"Okay, I've run into roadblock after roadblock. Kent really has it in for you and he's using every means he has at his disposal. He's making it as hard as possible for you to get back into the country. The only helpful response I've gotten is that you should go to court."

"I'm stuck here indefinitely?"

"No. With every roadblock I encountered, the more pissed I got, so I had to think outside the bureaucracy. I made a few other calls. You should be home tonight. Since I'm stuck out here in Montana, Jane will coordinate things for me from New York."

"I'm not entirely sure I like the sound of this."

"It'll work out fine. We've done this plenty of times before."

His voice sounded confident, but there was something that betrayed a nervousness.

"What you need to do," he continued, "is get to the pier at the end of Avenue de la Ponce, right near the Miramar Hotel once it gets dark. That should be in say, two hours. Can you get there then?"

"Yes. I can."

"A man named Alejandro will meet you there. He'll guide you and will be in contact with Jane. Let me give you a number to contact Jane in case anything happens or Alejandro doesn't show. She'll be using a burner phone for this operation. You ready? It's 212-555-8976. Got it?"

"Yes. What do I tell Rodriguez?"

"Nothing at this point. I don't want him trying to stop you. You can call him once you're back home. Okay?"

"Okay, I guess."

"You'll be fine. Trust me."

"I do, but that doesn't mean I'm not nervous. You be careful up there."

"I will be. I'll let you go now. Love you."

"Love you, too."

I hung up. The first thing I did was to get the lay of the land. I went to the front gate of the airport, but I didn't step out. I didn't want Rodriguez's driver to see me. For a second, I toyed with the idea of him driving me to the pier since Rodriguez said the driver was at my disposal but I didn't want the driver reporting in before I had left the country.

The taxi stand was directly in front of the terminal. There were plenty of cabbies idling about waiting for fares. That shouldn't be a problem. The trick would be to get by Rodriguez's driver. He sat in his car beside the taxi stand.

While I was standing there contemplating what to do, the driver got out of his car and headed for the front door to the airport, right where I was standing. I made a dash for the nearest bench and grabbed a newspaper that was laying there. I held the paper up to my face at an angle that shielded me but still allowed me to track his movements. I wanted to see if he was coming in to look for me or whether he had to go to the bathroom.

I lucked out as I saw him head into the men's room. I decided this would be the best time to make my break. I walked out into the stifling heat and headed over to the first cabbie.

I had neglected to exchange any American money for Cuban pesos so I asked him, in Spanish, if he accepted US dollars. He shook his head no. I asked the second, who also said no. By this time, I was nervous that the driver would reemerge but the third said yes, he would take them but he'd charge me a significant commission. I said that would be fine. I climbed in. As we were leaving, I could see the driver come back out and climb into his car. I felt a little sorry for the guy, cooling his heels like this, but I couldn't take the risk.

I told the driver where I wanted to go. It turned out to be only a couple miles away and I knew I was being ripped off when the driver asked for $50.00. I was about to pay it, but then I reconsidered. I handed him two twenty-dollar bills, which still significantly overpaid for the ride. He didn't bat an eye as he said gracias and went on his way.

I walked into a little park near the entrance to the pier and sat on a bench. Nobody else was around. The neighborhood appeared to be relatively upscale, but that did nothing to allay my anxiety as I periodically looked around. I still had a good hour before darkness descended and I was nervous that someone would notice me and how out of place I seemed to be.

Forty-five minutes later a casually dressed tall thin man with graying hair entered the park. He looked directly at me. Then he reached inside his jacket. I froze, not knowing what to do or if I should do anything at all. He pulled his hand came out. In it was a pack of cigarettes. My heartbeat returned to normal. He extracted a cigarette and walked up to me.

"Do you have a light?" he asked in Spanish.

"Si," I responded as I reached into my purse for a box of matches.

He thanked me and went to hand the box back to me, but I said to keep them. He smiled and departed.

I don't know why I was so nervous. I felt like I was doing something clandestine. Any minute the cops would haul me away in irons to some roach-infested jail. All I was trying to do was get home. Could anyone blame me for that?

The sun was setting. I thought I would head to the pier to meet the mysterious Alejandro. I left the park to walk toward the pier. I made a left onto the street, but before I did, I glanced around to make sure I wasn't being followed. I was. To the right, leaning on a lamppost a block and a half away, was the man I'd just given the matches. He was looking directly at me.

I hurried my pace and glanced around. He had left the post and was following me. I quickened my step and so did he. By the time I reached the pier, I was nearly at a full trot, but he was gaining on me. I contemplated not turning onto the pier since he would trap me once I entered, but I didn't have much choice. I was unfamiliar with the streets and could easily get lost. The man would undoubtedly know his way around and most likely was a stronger runner. Also, I still had to hope that Will was his usually reliable self and had made the arrangements for Alejandro to meet me.

I was about halfway down the pier when the man called out to me. I could not understand what he was saying, but he was now very close. I needed to stand my ground. I turned around while I reached into my bag for the pepper spray I always have there. When the man got close to me, I let loose the spray. It was a direct hit in his eyes. He screamed out as he put his hands up to his face.

I was now close enough that I knew I could give him a swift knee to the groin when a second voice spoke to me.

"That wasn't a very nice thing to do to my friend."

I turned and standing there was another man who had just emerged from the shadows. He was short, balding and very overweight.

"You're Alejandro?" I asked.

"In the flesh, of which I'm sorry to report there is a lot."

I turned back to the man I'd just squirted. He was still in considerable pain from the pepper spray. I pulled a water bottle out of my bag.

"I'm so sorry. Here, lean your head back and I'll flush your eyes with some water. Why didn't you say anything in the park?"

Alejandro repeated what I'd just said, but in Spanish. The man, Francisco, did as we requested. The water seemed to help.

"Francisco only speaks Spanish. It was my fault he didn't identify himself earlier. I asked him to locate you and then monitor your movements, nothing more, and Francisco is very good at following orders."

"So, what do we do now?"

"We wait. I have a cozy little cottage over here. I brought in some pernil with rice and beans and plantains if you're hungry. I have a shortwave radio there. As the pilot gets close, he'll call me and we can take my boat out to meet it. Please come with me. Francisco, will you be alright?"

Francisco, looking at us through little slits, motioned he would manage, so we walked on.

"Please tell him again how sorry I am. I've had my share of close calls and attacks over the past few years so I react first and talk afterwards."

"It's understandable. Francisco will be fine. He has a lovely wife who will nurse him back to health. Will has told me all about you, so I know of your run-ins."

"You know Will well?"

"We've been friends for over twenty years. I got into a bit of a scrape in the States some years ago—I won't go into details—and Will caught me. He could have thrown the book at me, but he recognized I was young and foolish. He came up with a much lesser charge. I did two months in prison, but it could have easily been five to ten years. He's got a good feel for people.

"He came to see me in prison to make sure I was okay. Then he saw me after I came out to make sure I would not be stupid again. I told him I would return to Cuba. He thought that was a good idea. A few years later he called me out of the blue. He wondered if I could help him out from time to time. He said I'd get paid for my services. He made it clear that the choice was up to me. I said I'd try it. Fifteen years later, we're still working together."

"You do anything considered dangerous?"

"Sometimes, but only if I get caught, and I'm very careful not to get caught."

"Is what we're doing now considered dangerous?"

"Again, only if we get caught. Cuba is no different than any other country. The Cuban government doesn't like people from other countries messing around in Cuba. They want to know what's going in and out. But when Will told me you were in trouble, I knew what I had to do. Shall we go in?"

We entered the building he euphemistically called a "cottage" but was more of a shack. The interior was comfortable, however, and moderately well appointed. On the table were a couple bags from which Alejandro pulled some Styrofoam boxes.

"Here, let me pull out two plates so we can eat. The food still feels somewhat warm but I could heat it up for you if you'd like."

"No, that would be fine."

"I hope you like pork. As my waistline shows, I eat perhaps eat too much of it but, every time I eat pernil, it transports me back to my mother's cooking."

"For me, it's arroz con pollo. I remember coming home from school and as soon as I walked into the apartment the delicious smells of the dish cooking would fill my nostrils. I make a good arroz con pollo myself, but it still takes a backseat to my mother's."

"I make absolutely no claim to any culinary skills so I have to rely on a dependable local restaurant."

We dug in. The roast pork pernil with the accompanying rice and black beans and plantains were all delicious.

"So, how did you and Will meet?" he asked.

"He interrogated me because of my association with a well-known Muslim leader the FBI suspected may be a terrorist. He wasn't, but things sometimes get crazy in our country when it comes to Muslims."

"And with people from my country, too."

"So true. It turned out there was a terrorist plot that Will and I got embroiled in, but it was a plot against Muslims, not by them."

"The scheme to blow up Mecca from a few years back?"

"The same. The two of us were in that crucible together and along the way we fell in love. Unfortunately, the crucible has had a way of following us ever since."

"Will has a way of bonding with people during stressful times, doesn't he?"

"I guess you could put it that way."

"You are in Cuba to see your father?"

"Did you know him?"

"Only by reputation, but it is a very good reputation. Did you get to see him?"

"Yes, I was with him when he died."

"Oh, I hadn't heard. I'm very sorry."

"Thank you. But it was the first time I'd ever met him, other than when I was a baby. I don't really know how I feel. I don't even know what he did throughout his life."

"The Castros had many people on the government payroll without having an official position. Your father was one of those people. The difference was that most of these people lived off the public dole without doing anything. Your father made a difference. He advocated for the downtrodden and people who were being crushed by the system. Other people who tried doing what your father did found themselves in jail, but he could work with officials without threatening them, so they allowed him to live and prosper. Even through the regime change of the past decade, they tolerated him. He had rare gifts."

"He just wasn't much of a father."

"Well, at least you found out something about the man."

The radio crackled a bit and then they could hear a man's voice.

"Big Al, come in. This is Heavenly Wings."

Alejandro threw a switch on the unit and picked up the microphone. He obviously was not in the mood to do the ham radio banter as he responded.

"Hi Herbie."

"Is the package ready for pickup?"

"All ready. Where are you?".

"About twenty minutes out."

"Okay, we'll meet you at the pickup spot."

"Roger. Be sure to have a light on so I don't run you over in the dark."

"Will do. See you soon."

"Roger. Out."

Alejandro switched the radio off.

"Herbie likes to play the spy game and talk in code. He thinks someone is listening in. Maybe they are, but I find it rather tiresome. Just talk in a normal conversation."

"That radio seems like such an antique. What is it? World War II vintage?"

"Close. That's why we use it. In case Herbie is correct and someone is trying to listen in, they would probably do it on a somewhat more modern piece of equipment. They probably wouldn't be able to home in on the frequencies of this antique."

"Rather clever of you."

"Shall we head out?"

We walked out on the pier and climbed into a thirty-foot fishing boat with two outboard engines. We untied and pushed off as Alejandro started the engines.

"Herbie was correct about one thing. Once he was picking someone up and there was a bright moon. When I went out, I forgot to turn a light on. Herbie came in and clipped the top of the boat. A foot or two lower and it would have been catastrophic for both of us. He reminds me every time but believe me, I don't need reminding."

We powered our way out of the marina and were soon out on the open sea. Alejandro looked around to make sure there wasn't anybody following. He also had turned on his radar/sonar unit, which was far more up-to-date and sophisticated than his radio to make sure there were no patrols about. If the coastal patrol intercepted his boat, he would spin a yarn of fishing at night, the only time his wife would let him out. There were no patrols evident in the immediate area, so he didn't have to resort to this ruse.

We went to a spot about a mile and a half from shore. It was far enough away not to be too noticeable from the shore, but not too far for this boat. Alejandro turned off the engine, and we waited. Ten minutes later we heard a low drone coming in from the west. He turned the beacon on as the plane approached. A short while later, the boat's two giant pontoons skidded on the ocean in front of us and came to a stop about twenty feet away.

Alejandro re-started the motor to work his way over. The door on the plane opened and a slender man with a Vietnam Veteran hat and a gray beard and hair that was pulled back in a ponytail leaned out.

"Big Al!" he called out.

Alejandro grimaced at the name but grinned and bore it.

"Hey Herbie, this is Francine Vega."

"So, you're Will's lovely bride? Pleasure. Hop on board."

I gave Alejandro a hug.

"Thanks for everything."

"Give Will my regards."

I climbed out of the boat into the plane. The water was choppy so it was a challenge making the transfer, but with the help of my newfound friends, I made it. I waved to Alejandro, strapped myself into the copilot's chair and we were off.

"How the hell did Will land a doll like you?" Herbie asked.

"Maybe I landed him?"

"Will? He's okay if you like those official, by-the-book types. But you, wow, you're by far my foxiest extraction."

I laughed.

"That's something to add to my resume. You know Will long?"

"Hell, yeah. We go way back. We met in a Key West bar about twenty years ago. I got a bit of a drinking problem, which I'm proud to say has been under control for fifteen years now, and I got myself into a bit of a scuffle with a biker gang. Will was hanging out at the other end of the bar and saw what was happening. I had no idea why, but he took a liking to me—he later said it was my Nam hat—and walked over to intervene. The bikers were more than glad to give him a thumping, too, until he pulled this huge gun from his belt and aimed it at the main guy's head. That gun was pure Dirty Harry. I expected him to say, "Go ahead, make my day, punk." But he didn't. The bikers just turned and ran.

"Will walked back to his seat and resumed his drink. I walked over and sat down beside him. He asked me what I did, and I told him I was an outta work pilot. He told me if I cleaned myself up, he could help me get a plane and he'd have some periodic work for me. Well, the man was true to his word."

"He always is."

"I cleaned myself up and he got me back on my feet. I do flying gigs all over Florida, but whenever Will calls for something like this, I drop whatever I'm doing."

"You said you met Will twenty years ago and cleaned yourself up but you said your drinking problem has been under control for fifteen. Why the difference?"

"I went on a bender. My daughter had committed suicide and I couldn't handle it. Will tried calling me for a job. When he couldn't reach me, he came down and tracked me down. He found me back in the bar where we first met. Well, he took me home, poured a gallon of coffee in me and nursed me back to health. Been clean ever since."

Like John Foster in his hometown who seemed to have gone to school with everyone we met, I wondered if there was anybody in the clandestine world that Will had not helped.

"You make many, what do you call them, extractions from Cuba?"

"More than you'd think. People think we're enemies with the Cubans but we're not. They're good people who want the same things we want."

"What did you do in Vietnam?"

"I was a chopper pilot. I helped to evacuate the wounded."

"A noble job."

"It was a job, no more, no less. I was no more noble than the poor guys on the ground getting shot at. I was luckier, that's all."

"Where are we headed?"

"Lake Okeechobee. There'll be a car there to pick you up. We'll be there in a couple hours. Sorry, but that's about as fast as this heap will go."

"That's okay. It's a very relaxing flight."

It was so relaxing that the next thing I knew, we skidded along the waters of Lake Okeechobee, jolting me awake. I opened my eyes to a lovely moon shimmering on the lake water as we taxied our way to Herbie's dock. He expertly guided the plane into its spot and cut the engine. He jumped out of his seat and attached lines to secure the plane to the dock. He then helped me out.

"I'd love to host you in my humble abode, pretty lady, but yon chariot awaits you as we speak."

Parked beside his house was a black SUV. I could see two people sitting in the front seat, but I couldn't make out their faces.

"Thank you, Herbie. You're my knight in shining armor. I've learned a lot about my husband on this trip but you've confirmed one thing about him I already know. He has a way of seeing good in people where others may not."

"Give him my regards."

"Will do. Stay away from bikers."

"Good advice. Bye now."

I walked up the path to the house and then to the car. As I got close, the two people got out of the car.

"Agent Broderick, Agent Kelly, you don't know how much of a pleasure it is to see you two."

"I can't say I've ever had a woman say that to me before, Ms. Vega," was Agent Broderick's monotone response.

I've known Agent Broderick for over three years and I still could not tell when he was joking. I wasn't even sure of his first name. Will called him Rick, but he never elaborated whether that was his first name or just a shortened version of Broderick. Almost everybody else knew him as either Broderick or Agent. Whenever we met, I was always Ms. Vega. He was always Agent Broderick. He was the quintessential dour law enforcement official, but what he lacked in humor he made up in loyalty and competence. Will had been after him to advance up the chain at the bureau, but his response was always that he was happy where he was and that he had progressed to the level of his competence. I for one was very glad he was competent at his job since he once saved Will's and my lives when we were captured in Israel.

I was very glad to see Jane with him.

"Hi, Jane. Is your daughter feeling better?"

"Hi, Francine. Yes, very much, thanks. I'm glad to see you made it back okay."

"It sure is nice to be back in the U.S.A. You and Will won't get into trouble for pulling off this stunt, will you?"

"What's Kent going to say? 'I made up some stuff to keep an American citizen from re-entering the country?' I don't think that would play very well. Will knew that and pulled all this together. He's called on a lot of friends and people who owe him."

"Over the past day I found out a lot about my husband's past and the people he's impacted over the years."

"Oh, how was the meeting with your father?"

"He passed away while I was there."

"I'm so sorry."

"I'm still trying to figure out how I feel. I spent thirty-plus years hating this man, thinking he just up and left us. Turns out the truth is more gray than black and white, but I still don't have any answers on what he was all about. Then, when I finally get to meet him and ask him some questions, he up and dies on me. Oh, well."

"Shall we head out? Broderick will drive you back to New York. First, he's going to drop me off at the Orlando airport. I got a text from Will telling me to meet him in Colorado. He said he had a lot to tell me about *Beyond Revelation*, but he didn't feel comfortable doing it electronically. He'd rather tell me in person."

It occurred to me I had powered down my phone. I wasn't getting any service, so I figured I'd save my battery. I powered it back on. As soon as it came back on, I had a ton of notifications, some from messages, some from Twitter and other social media outlets. I ignored those and went straight to messages. I saw two from Will. I opened the first.

"Will's telling me the same thing he told you. He's got a lot to update me on *Beyond Revelation*."

It would have really upset if he had sent a message to Jane but not me on this subject. It did my heart good to see that text. Then I opened the second.

"Oh no," I exclaimed.

"What's wrong?" Jane asked.

"Jane, when did he send you the text?"

She pulled her phone back out.

"Fifty minutes ago."

"That's about when he sent me mine, but then he sent another one about five minutes ago. He's in trouble."

"What did he say?"

"The text reads: FRANCINE. Trap Alan 11199a."

13

"I don't understand. He sent you a text with your name and you think he's in trouble?"

"That's not my name."

"Huh? Come again."

"Not to Will. He never calls me Francine. To him, my name is Fava. He would only use Francine as a code. He would type this if he thought he might not have time to type anything else. Something happened. He's in trouble."

"What does 'Trap Alan 11199a' mean?"

"I don't know, but it means something. Alan refers to Alan Westbrook, our friend who was killed last year by the Zyklon Killer."

"I remember his story, although I never got to meet him. Wait, Westbrook as in Westbrook Broadcasting?"

"Yes, he left us money in his will. We used it to start up the station."

"That's some friend."

"It turned out we were the only friends and family he had. He was brilliant, but he was also a very sad and lonely person. Anyway, I don't understand what 'Trap Alan 11199a' means, but it'll come to me. Will would not send a message with a meaning I couldn't figure out."

"Are you sure you're not over-reacting?" Jane asked.

"Hopefully, I'm wrong about him being in trouble. I'll try calling him."

I dialed. The call immediately went to voicemail. I left a message.

"No answer. Something is wrong. I need to go to Montana to find him."

"Maybe his phone crapped out. Maybe he's in the air now and is unreachable."

I looked at my watch. According to his schedule, he was to be in the air, going from Helena to Denver, right now. From there he would take another plane to Grand Junction, which was way out in the western part of Colorado. Grand Junction was at least a real city compared to the places he visited in Montana, but it was still in the middle of nowhere.

"I guess you're right. I'm tired and everything is such a jumble."

"Let's stick to the original plan. You go back to New York, and I'll go to Colorado to meet him. The worse thing we can do is to run all over the Montana wilderness to find him."

Broderick dropped her off at the Orlando airport and then we were on our way back to New York. Broderick was never much of a conversationalist. Although I slept on the plane, I was exhausted, so I settled down in the back seat and went to sleep. I didn't even wake up when he stopped for gas in North Carolina.

I finally woke up when he stopped again in Maryland and he came back to the car with a couple boxes of fried chicken.

"I thought you might be hungry."

"I am. Thank you. You know, I've known you for over three years and I don't know your first name. Will calls you 'Rick' but I don't know if that's your actual name or if 'Rick' is just a shortened version of Broderick."

His deadpan response was: "It's Agent, ma'am."

I burst out laughing. I even detected a hint of a smile on his lips. Undeterred, I plodded forward.

"I also don't know if you're married or if you have kids."

"I'm married to the job, ma'am."

He delivered this line in the same deadpan manner, but in this case I couldn't tell if he was trying to be funny or whether he didn't want to tell me. After a few seconds of staring off into space, he spoke again.

"I was married. Her name's Wendy. We'd known each other since elementary school. Then I was working on a mob racketeering case and one witness was this high-rolling billionaire named Lawrence Lanier. Perhaps you heard of him. They assigned me to protect him before the trial. One day he and Wendy met. The rest, as they say, is history. As soon as the trial was over, he and Wendy jetted off to some Caribbean Island. I suppose they're still there. I contemplated going after her, using my FBI resources to track her down, but then I reconsidered. Even if I got her back, who knows when the next guy would come by to turn her head? I want someone who's devoted to me. I'm sure she's out there. I just have to be patient."

"I'm sure that woman is out there."

We ate the rest of our chicken in silence. Broderick threw our boxes away and we were back on the road again.

"Thanks again for coming to retrieve me, Agent Broderick. I'm sure being a chauffeur does not fall into your job description."

"My job description is to do whatever Will asks me to do."

"You're that devoted to my husband?"

"Yes, I am. I know that he would do the same for me. In fact, he has."

"Rick," I said using Will's name for him rather than my usual Agent, "you know Will even better than I do. Did you agree with Jane that I was over-reacting or misreading Will's text?"

Agent Broderick said nothing for a minute as he stared ahead on the road. Then he spoke deliberately.

"I don't think you're over-reacting at all. The one thing I know about Will is that everything he does has a purpose. If he used a name he never calls you, he has a reason. I agree with you he may be in trouble. Jane is very good, but she's still learning the ropes. Hopefully, he'll meet her in Colorado but we need to proceed from here as if he won't."

"What are you going to do?"

"First, as soon as we get back, I'm going to place a track on his phone to see if we can determine where it is. He's got a specially configured phone. Even if it's turned off, it still releases a signal. It can be tracked. It would have to be virtually destroyed to stop sending a signal. It's also a satellite-based phone and it's not dependent on the availability of cell towers in the area. Even out in the wilderness of Montana, we can track it."

"You're getting me worried."

"We should be." He paused for a second. "I'm sorry to be so blunt, but that's the situation. Jane is worried, too. She's more diplomatic than I am."

"I appreciate your candor. Is there anything I can do?"

"You spoke with the money guy for *Beyond Revelation*, didn't you?"

"Yes."

"See if you can talk with him again. From what Will told me about your meeting with this person, he might be alarmed by what's happening. That means he has some idea of what is happening. You could press him to give you some ideas on the workings of this group. It could be useful."

"Okay, I'll call him first thing in the morning."

"Oh, even though Jane and I may have different thoughts on the level of danger Will is in, I totally agree you should not be heading out to

Montana. You'd get lost and we'd end up having to track you as well as him."

"I appreciate that vote of confidence."

"No offense intended."

"None taken."

Before too long, we pulled into my driveway. It was late, so I didn't get the reception of the kids streaming out to greet me. The front door opened and Jonas surprised me by stepping out.

"J., what are you doing here? I'm sorry, it's great to see you. I should have said that first."

"Emma called me. She had some emergency. She asked if I could come over. It's nice to know I'm at the top of your emergency call list. The kids are all in bed."

"Thanks, J., for coming out here."

"How you doing?"

Before I responded, I ran over and gave him a huge hug. Tears were welling in my eyes.

"J., I'm so worried about Will. He headed out to Montana to visit the *Beyond Revelation* compound out there and see if he could get any information on Eunice's disappearance. I got a text that led me to believe he may be in trouble. I feel so helpless."

"There, there, Frannie. It'll all work out fine."

Jonas held me as we silently stood there in the driveway. Broderick was standing off to the side, reading something on his smart phone. Then he typed in a few things, after which he walked over to us.

"Ms. Vega," he was back to his formal FBI Agent persona, "I have a change in plans. I have to get to LaGuardia to fly to Colorado and then to Montana. I have to get there for a flight in forty-five minutes."

He walked towards his car but Jonas stopped him.

"You're beat. You'll never make it if you have to park your car. Let me drive you and I'll drop you off."

Broderick thought it over for a few seconds.

"Okay. We'll take my car. I've got lights and sirens if we need to get through traffic. You're technically not authorized to drive my vehicle, but screw it. Ms. Vega, I'll call you along the way to fill you in what I just learned."

Jonas called back to me.

"Okay if I come back here to sleep after I drop him off? I don't feel like making the drive back home."

"Of course. I'm really beat, so I'll probably be asleep when you get back. I'll leave the door unlocked. Drive carefully."

He waved in response as they piled into the car and sped off. My nerves were so on edge that my mind went immediately to one of the last times Jonas left our house. He only made it as far as the FDR Drive. His car stalled and when he got out to check on it, it blew up from a bomb meant to scare me. He was lucky it didn't kill him. I quickly erased that memory. I had more than enough on my mind to worry me about present problems; I didn't need to dredge up the past.

14

I made my way into the house. I checked on the kids. They were all sound asleep, blissfully unaware of the danger their father might be in. I stood by each of their beds and watched them sleep. I was envious of the peace they were enjoying. I hoped some of that feeling would permeate my being. It didn't work. While as I was standing there, my phone buzzed. It was Broderick. I took one last gaze at my daughters and left the room so I wouldn't wake them.

"Hi, Agent Broderick."

"Jane texted me. She's at the Denver airport, waiting for me to join her. She beat me to the punch and had our office track Will's phone. It's still in Montana. When I get to Colorado, we'll go on to Montana together and look for him."

"What do you think happened to him?"

All the worst possibilities raced through my mind. My one consolation was the resourcefulness of my husband. Broderick responded as if he could read my thoughts.

"I don't know, Francine, but the one thing I know is that if anyone can get himself out of a situation and take care of himself, it's Will. I'll be in touch to let you know what that situation is."

"Thanks."

I went to my room. I went through the motions of getting ready for bed. With Will's and my schedule, there are many nights that we don't share our bed, but tonight would be especially tough. I doubted that I would get much in the way of restful sleep, but the sleep I'd had over the past few nights had been spotty and not exactly in the most comfortable positions, so I had to try. It would be nice to lie in my own bed.

I laid down and my mind raced all over. What on earth could Will's message mean? Trap Alan 11199a? Trap Alan 11199a? What are you telling me, my love?

Eventually I settled into a sleep. I'd only been asleep for a short while when I heard a bang. My initial thought was Jonas had returned. I was a little put out he made such a loud noise. He's a careful and considerate type of guy who would know the kids were sleeping and wouldn't want to wake them. Then again, he didn't know the layout of the house so he wouldn't know where things were in the dark. I went back to sleep, assuming he'd find his way.

Then I heard a second bang. This one sounded as if somebody had knocked something over. I wrapped my robe around me and walked into the hallway. There was enough light filtering in from the street so I didn't turn on the light.

I was about to call out to Jonas, but then I reconsidered. Instead, I ducked into my room, grabbed my purse, which had my phone and pepper spray, and then I hurried towards Albert's room. I entered. I reached down and shook him in his bed.

"Albert," I whispered loudly, "wake up."

On the second shake, he opened his eyes, but just barely.

"Wha?" he asked.

"Come with me."

He dutifully got out of bed. I took his hand as we walked to his door. I stuck my head out and looked both ways. Whoever was there had not yet made it up to the second floor. We hurried out and rushed into Stella and Rosa's room. I closed the door behind us. I looked around to see if there was anything I could use to barricade the door. I found nothing suitable, so I improvised.

I went to the lamp in the corner. I unplugged it, put my foot on the base of the lamp and gave it a hard yank. Luckily, the lamp was a super cheap one we had found at Target and the wire came out of the lamp easily. I tied one end to the door handle and the other I tied to a nearby bedpost. It wasn't very secure, but maybe it would slow down the intruder enough for me to get some pepper spray in his eyes and perhaps hit him over the head with something. What that something would be wasn't clear, but I'd work on it. I was kicking myself for not going into the safe to pull out Will's spare Glock.

Stella woke up.

"Hi Fava!" she exclaimed.

I leaned over to her and gently put my hand over her mouth. With my other hand I told her "Shh".

It was then I could hear footsteps on the stairs. I dialed 911.

"911, what is your emergency?"

"There's an intruder in my home. I'm with my three children in a bedroom on the second floor. I just heard footsteps on the stairs so he is coming up here. The address is 850 Astoria Avenue in Queens. My name is Francine Vega."

"Mrs. Vega, I'm dispatching a patrol car. It should be there shortly."

I grabbed Rosa and held her in my lap while Albert and Stella huddled close to me. The footsteps were getting closer and closer to us when I heard the front door open and close.

"J.," I shouted out at the top of my lungs, "there's someone in the house. Get out. Cops are on the way."

The footsteps I had heard approaching were now running away down the hall and then down the steps. I heard the report of a gun and then a crash and a door slamming. I had to go see what was happening.

"Albert, you're the man of the family right now. You stay here and protect your sisters, okay?"

"Okay."

I sprinted down the stairs, flipped on the lights, and I saw Jonas lying on the floor.

"Oh my God!"

I kneeled down beside him and searched for a wound. Thankfully, I found none. I surmised that he hit his head when he dove out of the way before the shot. He was coming to when an NYPD officer burst through the door with his pistol drawn.

"Move away from the suspect, ma'am. We'll take it from here."

I stayed right where I was, beside Jonas's side.

"You're crazy. He's the victim. He's my friend."

"Move away. Now."

"You idiot. The person who broke into my place ran right by you."

The cop refused to budge and kept his weapon trained on us. At that moment, Albert, after hearing the commotion, appeared at the top of the stairs. The officer, startled, turned and fired his pistol in Albert's direction.

"No!" I screamed as I bolted up the stairs to Albert. I noticed the bullet had splintered the railing, leading me to believe the shot was errant and did not hit my son. I breathed a sigh of relief when I found him, cowering against the wall, but unharmed. I ran over and hugged him tightly.

"Everything's all right, my brave boy. Everything's all right."

I held him for a few seconds, feeling him calm down somewhat. For the briefest of seconds, I contemplated lecturing him about not doing what I told him to stay with his sisters, but I just as quickly reconsidered. Now was not the time. I was sure that, in his mind, he was protecting his sisters and me. He had too much of his father in him to not run toward danger when someone threatened the people he loved.

"I have to go down to deal with this policeman. Will you be okay?"

Albert tentatively nodded his head.

"Yes, Fava, I'm okay."

I smiled. It was very rare that he called me Fava. Will had long called me by that name and Stella immediately adopted my nickname, but Albert had been more resistant. I gave him one more hug.

"You are a brave boy. Thank you for coming to my defense. You should go back to your sisters. They might be frightened. Okay?"

He smiled in return, although it was a meek smile, and got up to head to their room. I headed towards the stairs but before I got two steps, Albert ran back to me to give me one last hug. He often seems so grown up I forget he's only eleven years old. I hugged him back and we both went our ways.

I stormed back downstairs. The cop, realizing what he had almost done, was standing there in shock, staring at his gun. I walked over and slapped him hard across the face. Just as I did, his partner entered and, seeing me slap the officer, trained his gun on me.

"You're under arrest for assaulting a police officer."

The original cop spoke up.

"No, Freddie, I deserved it. I panicked and shot at her son. Is he okay?"

I softened somewhat at seeing the officer's reaction.

"It's a good thing you're a terrible shot; that's all I have to say."

"Yes, it's a good thing."

By this point, Jonas was still on the floor but sitting up. He still looked a bit dazed.

"Who's that?" the second cop asked as he eyed Jonas suspiciously.

"He's my friend, Jonas Clarke. He's staying with us for the night. He was injured when the person who broke in got spooked and ran. Somewhere in the wall you'll find a slug from the shot he took at Jonas. Luckily, he also was not a very good shot. Will you please put those guns away and help me get him up on the couch?"

The officers complied with my order and we lifted Jonas onto the couch. I went to the freezer and pulled out some ice, which I wrapped in a towel. I gave it to him to put on his head.

"Can you tell me what happened?"

"I had just fallen asleep when I heard a bang. I thought it was Jonas. He was returning from dropping someone off at LaGuardia. Then, when there was a second bang, I got out of bed. I still thought it was Jonas who was stumbling around in the dark because he didn't want to wake us by turning on the light. I quickly surmised it was an intruder. I gathered the kids and we all hid in the bedroom. I could hear the intruder coming up the stairs and approaching when Jonas came back. The intruder was startled and ran back out, firing at Jonas along the way. That's all I can tell you."

"Did either of you get a good look at the suspect?"

"No, he never got to the room we were in."

Jonas shook his head no.

"Who else is in the house?"

"My three kids, one son and two daughters. That's all."

"No husband?"

"My husband's away on a case. He's a special agent with the FBI."

Upon hearing that he almost shot the kid of an FBI agent, the face on the officer who fired the shot turned ashen. He was probably imagining his entire career going down the toilet.

The other cop continued his questioning.

"Have you noticed anything missing?"

"I really haven't looked around, so I don't know."

"Take an inventory and let us know."

"Will do."

"Is there anything you'd like to add?"

"Just that the NYPD needs to do a better job of training you guys. You come in and automatically assume that the Black man is the suspect, not a victim. Your partner here almost murders my son because he is so jumpy."

I turned to the young officer.

"How old are you?"

"Twenty-three, ma'am."

"How long have you been on the force?"

"Eight months."

"Only eight months and your partner sends you into a situation by yourself? I understand now. Listen, I don't know what discipline the NYPD will impose on you, but I won't be pursuing anything. Use this as a lesson. Don't prejudge people and think before you discharge your firearm. You seem like a good guy. You immediately realized your mistake and it's tearing you apart."

"Thank you, ma'am."

I wasn't entirely sure that I would let the matter drop, but I saw no need in tormenting the rookie officer further at this point. I figured I'd discuss the incident with Will when he got home. And I still firmly believed he would come home to me, although every time I thought about the current situation, it petrified me.

The other cop, annoyed that I pinned some, if not most, of the blame for nearly killing Albert on him, curtly announced.

"If there will be nothing else, we'll be on our way."

"Aren't you going to do any investigation of the crime scene? There won't be any forensic staff here to at least dust for prints?"

"I called and there have been two multiple murders in this precinct tonight. All the crime scene investigators are tied up there. I can have someone come, but it won't be here until tomorrow, at the earliest."

I told them they probably should come if for no other reason than to retrieve the slug intended for Jonas. They asked if we needed them to drive Jonas to the hospital. I raised this with Jonas and he said no. He did seem a lot better than before. The officers departed.

The more I thought about the evening, the more convinced I became that this was not a simple break-in or robbery attempt. The intruder did not look for valuables on the first floor. Instead, this person was making his or her way up the stairs without hesitating.

I couldn't help but think *Beyond Revelation* was behind this break-in. We were getting close to something; we'd hit a nerve of some sort, and they were reacting. If this was true then I felt even more nervous about Will's fate.

My priority was to make sure the kids were safe and sound. Jonas had settled down on the couch and had fallen asleep, so I didn't have to worry about him at the moment. I headed upstairs. I walked in. The kids were all on the floor. Albert was sitting up with his back against the wall with one girl on each side, both sound asleep. I stood there for a few seconds to absorb the beautiful scene. Then I picked up Rosa and tucked her in her bed. I repeated this with Stella. I turned back to Albert and held out my hand. He got up and took it as we walked out of the room.

"Albert, you probably should go back to sleep but I'd like you to help me with something. Do you think you can help me?"

His eyes lit up. Albert is the type of kid who loves being useful. He adored his father and the times they worked on projects together. He should have gone back to sleep. The following day was a school day. But he had just gone through an ordeal; someone shot at him. Sleep wouldn't come too easily, so he should be useful.

"I want you to pretend you're your father and help me collect evidence. Think you'd like to do that?"

"Wow! Can I? What are we going to do?"

"Let's go get your father's kit out of his office."

This was actually Will's backup kit. He had his full one with him at all times when he was working. His kits contained a whole assortment of forensic investigation tools, many of which I did not understand what they did. One tool in the box that I knew something about were the materials to lift, preserve and save fingerprints.

One evening I asked Will to show me how to look for and lift fingerprints. I asked partly because I thought it something I should know in my line of work as a journalist. I'm always reporting on criminal investigations and it's good to have firsthand experience on anything I report. Who better to get trained on this than by an FBI Special Agent? But, to be perfectly honest, I asked Will to show me how to lift fingerprints because there was nothing good on TV that evening. Whatever the reason, Will walked me through the process step-by-step. Is there something wrong with me I found working with him this way rather arousing? Who knew that lifting fingerprints could serve as foreplay? Through it all, I gained a working knowledge of how to collect fingerprints.

I digress. I intended to use this newfound expertise this very evening. Besides possibly gathering some useful evidence, it was a golden opportunity to bond with my son. That's an opportunity I would never pass up.

I fully realized that by collecting evidence myself I was potentially compromising the crime scene for when and if the crime scene investigators showed up. I didn't care for several reasons. First, after the half-hearted performance by the NYPD, I doubted that they would seriously pursue the intruder. Second, if they investigated this break-in, they would look at it from a break-in/attempted robbery standpoint. They wouldn't have any reason to look for other motives—including ties to *Beyond Revelation*—for entering our home. This would hamper the investigation.

I was still shaking in fury at the officer for shooting at Albert. I was also livid at both officers for automatically assuming that Jonas was the suspect because he was African-American. Taken together, I would not just sit around waiting for the NYPD to get me answers.

The first thing I did was to get two pairs of latex gloves, which Albert and I both put on. The ones we had were way too large for both of us, but Albert's hands swam in them. He didn't care; he was too excited.

It occurred to me that the whole exercise could be a waste in time if the intruder wore gloves, but we had to proceed. Will had always said not to make any assumptions; that might cause you to miss a key clue.

I grabbed an erasable marker and a roll of masking tape. We would use the markers to mark surfaces such as the front door and any walls he may have touched. The tape would designate any possible areas that a marker may ruin or we couldn't designate with a marker.

We did our best guess in retracing the steps of our intruder. It was my stupidity and tiredness that allowed him to waltz in through the front door. Knowing that Jonas would be coming back soon, I left it unlocked. When our uninvited guest arrived, all he had to do was turn the doorknob. That was the first place we marked. I had Albert draw a circle around the knob and the part of the door where he may have pushed his way in. He also marked around the doorjamb where he may have put a hand as he entered.

In the entryway, he might have fumbled around in the dark and put his hand on the wall as he walked along. I didn't want to mark up the wallpaper with the marker. Wait, let me correct that. I wanted to deface the hideous wallpaper that was here when I moved in, but I didn't feel that I had the right to do this. Will's first wife, who died a few years before we met, had most likely chosen the wallpaper and it would therefore have sentimental value to Will. So, I asked Albert to place a big piece of masking tape on the wall to signify that we should test here.

We had a bit of a setback. Albert tried to tear off a piece of tape, but he didn't remove his latex gloves first. The tape stuck to the gloves and shredded. He was getting increasingly frustrated but calmed down when I advised him it was okay for him to take his gloves off for this phase of the project. He'd put a fresh pair on after completing the taping.

We moved our way up the stairs and down the hallway to the girls' room, marking as we went along. Finally, we completed the marking. Now we moved on to the next phase.

I opened Will's kit and took out the fingerprint powder and brush. We went back down to the front door.

"Okay, Albert, what we'll do is dip the brush into the powder and then we brush over the areas we marked off. You don't need too much powder, but you don't want too little either."

I wanted to show him how it worked so we walked over to a section of the living room wall.

"Press the wall with your finger right here. Press the wood so we'll get a better print."

Albert complied with my request. I dipped the brush into the powder and then brushed the wall where he touched. I aimed the flashlight at the powdered area.

"Look!" I exclaimed. "There's your fingerprint! Now what we do is to take this special tape and press it down on the print. Then we carefully pull it away. You don't want to lift it too fast."

I did as I described. Once I lifted the tape, I showed it to Albert.

"There you are, preserved for posterity. You better behave yourself; now that we have your prints, we'll be able to track you down."

Albert's face beamed at the fact that he had fingerprints. He laughed when I told him he better watch his step.

"Now, let's see if we can find other fingerprints."

We began dusting and documenting, working side-by-side. Albert would get so excited when he found one. His enthusiasm was infectious, but I had to caution him that fingerprints would be everywhere, especially on the front door. Some would be mine, some would be his father's, some would be Emma's, some would be deliverymen or visitors to our home. I hoped that among all of these innocent prints would be one that would lead us in the direction of finding out not only the person who had invaded our home but who ordered it. Each print that we found we put into a folder, being careful to write on the bag where it was captured.

We worked our way into and up through the house. After the front door and entryway, the number of prints dwindled significantly. Albert was getting a bit downhearted that he wasn't finding more.

"Albert, a lot of police work is boring. Reporting is the same way. Sometimes you have to do a lot of mindless work and tedious digging into records to find the answers to questions you may have. Sometimes, you look in the wrong places and totally waste your time, but that's part of the job. You just have to tell yourself that the work was not a waste of time. Instead, what you did was to eliminate a possibility. Understand?"

I think he grasped as much as his eleven-year-old brain could process, but he was still bored. When I asked him if he wanted to stop and go to bed, however, he said no. He wanted to complete the job with me.

"Every day I look at you and see how much like your father you are becoming. You're turning into a rather fine young man."

His face beamed. Comparing him with his father gave him renewed energy and determination to plow ahead. We'd gotten to the top of the stairs and I was working on the railing while he was examining the wall. If I'd thought it through more carefully, we probably should have reversed areas we were testing. He was average height for his age but, since his age was only eleven, he couldn't easily reach areas where a full-grown man might put his hand. There was one such area at the top of the steps. Undeterred, he got himself a footstool to stand on. I hovered near him since he was standing on the stool at the top of the staircase. I could easily see him losing his balance and toppling down the steps, but he was fine.

He dusted and then called out to me.

"Fava! Look!"

I walked over and he directed the light toward his new find. It was an entire palm print of his right hand and nearly perfect full prints for his first and second fingers and a partial of his thumb and pinky. We pulled out the tape, captured the print and entered it in the folder.

I thought through the possibilities for this handprint. The most logical was that it was the intruder who Jonas spooked when he arrived home. He ran down the hallway and then he had to change direction and it would only be natural to hold out a hand and push off the wall before careening down the stairs.

The only other possibility was Will. Maybe he lost his balance and put his hand on the wall to steady himself, but that did not seem like him.

"This might be the print we've been looking for, Albert. But let's not get too far ahead of ourselves. There are alternative possibilities, but I'm optimistic. Let's finish the rest of the hallway and then try to get some sleep."

We dusted the rest of the hallway, finding a few more prints but nothing of note. When we were through, we had forty-five fingerprints that we had to analyze.

"Albert, thank you so much for helping me on this. I couldn't have done it without you. I think we both could use some sleep now. It's three o'clock. If you think you need to stay home from school, I'll understand."

"No, that's okay, I'll go to school. Fava?"

"Yes?"

"Is Dad okay?"

"I hope so. We'll have more information by the end of the day. Agent Broderick and Agent Kelly are both out looking for him. They're the best. They'll find him; you shouldn't worry."

I did my best to sound convincing. I silently repeated what I just told him to convince myself as well.

"Let's get some sleep."

He looked somewhat mollified as he headed toward his room. I walked toward my room at the other end of the hall. I was just about ready to turn the knob and enter my room when I heard someone running behind me. Startled, I turned around only to find Albert jumping into my arms. He'd given me hugs before, but normally it was after Will reminded him to give me one. This one was entirely spontaneous and initiated by him.

I hugged him tightly as I told him how proud of him I was. Finally, he loosened his grip. As he went back to his room, he called out.

"Good night, Fava."

"Good night, Albert. Sleep tight."

15

All things considered, I got a rather solid three hours of uninterrupted sleep. When the alarm went off at six thirty, I was blissfully unaware of everything. I wasn't worrying about Will. I wasn't thinking about *Beyond Revelation*. I wasn't thinking about my father and all the questions I still had about him. I wasn't thinking about the President of the United States and the petty grievance he still had against me. I was blissfully lying in my own warm bed. Reality soon made itself known when I heard a bang from downstairs.

I grabbed what has become my ever-present weapon of choice, my pepper spray, as I tore out of my room toward the stairs. I was about halfway down the stairs when Jonas called out to me.

"Sorry, I dropped one of your mixing bowls."

I burst out laughing. It was the uncontrollable, irrational laugh of relief. Jonas looked at me like I was crazy. I finally controlled myself.

"Sorry, J. It's just that after everything that's happened over the past week, the sound of a clanging mixing bowl is like music to my ears. What are you doing, anyway?"

"I thought I'd make you and the kids some pancakes. There's coffee in the urn."

"Thanks. How's your head?"

"It still hurts some. I was thinking of going to the doctor this morning if it's all right. I just want to get it checked out. Ever since the explosion, I've tried to be careful."

"You do whatever you feel you have to."

"Frannie, what exactly happened last night? I'm still blurry."

"We had an intruder, but you arrived home just at the right time and scared the guy off. The cops came, and they were useless. One of them—a rookie—shot at Albert. They wanted to arrest you, I guess because you were a Black man."

"Is Albert okay?"

"He's okay. He was a little shaken, but then we dusted the whole place for prints. It was a fun bonding exercise."

"You did that while I was out cold on the couch here? You shoulda woke me up to help."

"You were out like a light. Plus, you did your part just in scaring off the intruder."

"Was he looking to rob you?"

"I don't think so. I really believe he was connected to *Beyond Revelation*. I think we've hit a nerve. We'll see if the prints give us any leads."

Around seven, I called Will's office. Normally, I would call Will and if he's not there I'd call Jane or Broderick but they were out of pocket. Will had one more assistant who would go to the ends of the earth to help his boss: Agent Bernard Willoughby.

Agent Willoughby was almost as buttoned up as Broderick, but I at least knew his first name. The explosion when Jonas' car blew up had also severely injured Willoughby. After a month in the hospital, he was released but he was confined to a wheelchair and could no longer perform field duties. He retired from the Bureau but called Will after only three days, begging to come back. Technically, Will should have told him no, that he should just enjoy a well-deserved rest in his retirement. However, Will heard the anguish in his voice and persuaded his superiors that Agent Willoughby still had a lot to offer even if he couldn't be in the field and the FBI took him back.

Will confided to me he wasn't entirely sure there was enough office work to warrant putting Agent Willoughby back on the payroll, but he couldn't cut him loose. He was convinced that, if Willoughby stayed retired, one day he'd put a gun in his mouth and pull the trigger.

Even though it was only seven in the morning, I knew that Willoughby would be at his desk. I dialed. He answered on the first ring.

"Agent Willoughby, it's Francine Vega."

"Have you heard anything from Will yet?"

"No, I was going to ask you the same thing but obviously you haven't heard anything either. I was wondering if you could help me with something."

"Shoot."

"Someone broke into my house last night. The NYPD were next to useless. They probably won't be dusting for prints until today, that is if they get around to it at all. So last night I dusted the place for fingerprints."

"You lifted prints?"

"I'm a woman of many talents, Agent Willoughby. One evening, Will gave me a lesson on how to do it."

"I've heard of agents getting into it with their wives and girlfriends using their handcuffs but lifting prints is a new one."

"Let's not go down that road. Anyway, I have a collection of prints I'd like to see if they're in the system. There's one especially that I'm curious about. We took it from an area on a wall where there shouldn't be any."

"Well, I don't know."

"Bernie, don't get bureaucratic on me. I believe this may somehow be related to Will's disappearance."

"Can you get the prints to me this morning? I'll run them through the system and see what I can come up with."

"Thanks, Bernie. I have them all in a folder. I'll drop them off to you on the way to the office. Do you think I could send you a picture of the one I'm especially concerned about?"

"Let's try. It might not be clear enough, but let's give it a shot."

"Should I send it to Will's email address?"

"That'll be fine."

"Thanks."

I dug out the folder and took several photos of the print from the top of the stairs. I experimented with different lighting angles until I had one that I thought was as clear as I thought it could be. I sent the image on its way.

By this time Jonas was in full gear making breakfast. The smells of bacon and pancakes permeated the air. I went upstairs to wake up the kids, but they were already on their way down. I looked at Albert and he seemed refreshed considering the lack of sleep he had. I made the offer one more time for him to stay home from school, but he was resolute. He would go to school no matter what.

About that moment, Emma showed up to babysit for Rosa. She usually helped with getting Albert and Stella ready, so it surprised her that they were almost ready. Now that she was here, Jonas and I left for the subway to get to work. Jonas took the train into Brooklyn so he could go to the doctor. I took the train to lower Manhattan to go to the FBI office.

When I walked in, Willoughby was there with news for me.

"Francine, great job lifting that print. It was crystal clear, and I got a hit. I didn't get anything initially, but I was only checking domestic databases. On a hunch, I went international and Interpol provided a match. The prints belong to a Russian named Alexi Slatzky."

"A Russian?"

"Yup. I don't have any other information on him except that he was arrested in France a few years ago. That's why his prints are on file with Interpol. There's no information on the status of those charges. He's also on various watch and no-fly lists. Hm, he was on a no-fly list, but still he got into the country. Where have I heard that before?"

"Ha, ha, very funny. Anything else?"

"Nope. There are some notes that information has been redacted from the official file. Your best bet would probably be to check with the State Department to see if they can give you hints as to what was deleted or to give you anything they have on this guy in their files."

Willoughby shifted in his wheelchair and winced.

"You okay, Bernie?"

"Yeah, I'm used to the pain. I think we already have what you're looking for but why don't you give me the rest of those prints for me to go through."

I handed him the folder.

"You take care of yourself."

"You, too. Let me know if you hear from Will."

"Will do. And thanks for your help."

16

It seemed like ages since I'd been at my desk or in front of a camera or doing anything remotely work-related. It felt good to be back on my home turf. I looked in on Jonas and then Heather, and then I went to see Frank.

"I'm so sorry to hear about your father."

I felt ashamed that I hadn't really kept Frank at all current about what had been happening with my life. I was ready to call him right after my father died, but then the whole visa/no-fly mess happened. I then meant to call him after I got back on U.S. soil, but then I got word that Will may be missing. I meant to call him along the road, but I was too exhausted. I meant to call him once I arrived home, but then we had the break-in.

"Thank you, Frank. I'm still processing what that means to me. I assume Jonas gave you some basics on my last 72 hours."

"Not much. He'd gotten word that your father had died and that you were stuck in Cuba. That's about it. I figured you'd fill me in sooner or later."

"I hope you have some time. We'll need a little time for me to bring you up-to-date."

I told him everything that had happened to me over the last 72 hours. He offered sympathy, gasped and offered advice all at their appropriate times. When I finished, he looked thunderstruck.

"I'd tell you how things were going here but it would all seem somewhat anticlimactic. What are you going to do next?"

"I have to find out more about Alexi Slatzky and why he broke into my house. What would a Russian who's not even allowed in this country want with me? Or was he after Will? Maybe Will killed his brother, and he arrived, looking for revenge."

"Was that the second or third Die Hard movie? I have trouble keeping them straight."

"Frank, this is serious."

"I know it is, Francine. My point is that you can't get too ahead yourself. You start speculating and then you're going down roads that don't lead you anywhere. Don't forget all the things that have made you a great reporter. Follow your leads, collect your clues, build your story. You speculate as part of the process, but make sure that speculation is done in an orderly manner that can be tested and either accepted or thrown out."

"I'm just so overwhelmed by everything. I'm a reporter, not a scientist."

"They're not mutually exclusive. You're under a lot of pressure with Will and your father and everything, but that can't impact your judgment. There's nobody better to figure this all out than you but we need the best that you can be."

I was about to give him a sarcastic retort, but then I stopped. Instead, I sighed and gave him a warm look.

"Do you think I'll ever get to the point where I'm not working for you?"

"Sure. I have to retire someday, don't I?"

"Oh, how are things around here?"

"Don't ask. Let's just say that I secured a new contract for a 2:00 AM infomercial for Fligli non-stick cookware. They really are amazing. Things just slide right off."

"I'm sure they are amazing. Do we need to hire somebody to help you out since I'm not much help these days?"

"Not yet. I have a few storyline ideas that should increase our viewership. Give me a couple days for them to mature in my mind and then we can sit down and talk."

"Deal."

I went back to my office, nervous about our network's future but confident that, if anybody can make us a success, it was Frank. In the meantime, I needed to get back to the task at hand. I called Heather in.

"Hi, Francine, any word on Will?"

"No, I'm hoping to hear an update from Jane or Broderick this morning."

"I'm sorry about your father."

"Thanks. It is what it is. I'd like you to do some research for me."

"Shoot," she responded as she pulled a reporter's pad out of her pocket.

I had to smile. One of the first pieces of advice I gave her was to have a pad or some way to take notes on her at all times. You never know when a story may present itself. You don't want to tell someone 'hold that thought' while you run to get yourself a pen and some paper. Given her high-tech proclivities, I would have thought she'd take notes on an electrical device, but I guess she thought she'd be a more authentic journalist by using an old-fashioned pen and pad.

"I'd like you to find out whatever information you can dig up on Alexi Slatzky. He's Russian, and he's on Homeland Security's No-Fly List. That's all I know about him."

"How do you know him?"

"He broke into my home last night. We were able to get his fingerprint."

"Wow, who's we?"

"Albert and me. You should have seen that boy. He was just like his father, plowing ahead to help me dust the place and find clues at three o'clock this morning."

"Nobody was hurt during this break-in, were they?"

"No, thankfully. But the guy showed up with a gun, which he fired at Jonas. Luckily, he missed. It was also lucky the cop missed Albert when he shot."

"It sounds like quite an evening."

"It was, and I'm glad it's over and done with."

"I'll see what I can find out."

Heather got up and headed back to her office to start her assignment.

I debated who to call next. I wanted to call Edward McKenzie. He's Reverend Malcolm McKenzie's brother who worked at the State Department. At least I assumed he still did. The last time I'd spoken with him was in the previous administration. He was a career guy, but if President Kent ever got word that he was friendly with me, Kent would undoubtedly figure out some way to punish him. Kent was that vindictive and would gladly slap around anybody who ever came in contact with me.

I also thought I would wait until Heather had finished her research on Slatzky. Edward McKenzie was nice and would help me, but he could also a be evasive if it suited him. I've read enough spy novels where someone like Slatzky was playing both sides and no one would want to jeopardize his status and usefulness. Having information and background about Slatzky would make it more difficult for McKenzie to smoke me.

The other person I wanted to call was Robert Benson, the money man behind *Beyond Revelation*. The old movie, *All the President's Men*, presented the truism 'follow the money' and boy was that true in this case.

I may be jaded, but I had trouble believing so many people were willing to give up everything to go live in a place where you totally forsook the rest of the world as they patiently awaited the rapture and the second coming. There had to be something more, some other incentives. The money man would be the place to start because money was such a strong motivator in most peoples' lives.

I called him and, after going through the gatekeepers appropriate to a CEO billionaire, I spoke with him. However, once I told him what I wanted to talk with him about, he abruptly said he had nothing to say on the subject and he hung up. That was an unexpected dead end. Ten minutes later my phone rang. I didn't recognize the number but I answered anyway. I was greeted by a loud car horn honking and a lot of street noise. I was about to hang up when the caller identified himself.

"Francine, it's Robert Benson."

"Mr. Benson? I can barely hear you, it's so loud," I shouted into the phone.

"They're doing some construction here. Let me walk away."

A minute later, the extraneous noise greatly lessened and I could hear him.

"Better?" he asked.

"Much."

"Sorry I couldn't talk to you earlier. Can you meet me at the public area in the Citicorp Building in say fifteen minutes?'

"Sure, I'll see you there."

Fifteen minutes later I was at the agreed to meeting spot. He sat at one of the white metal chairs at a table. He had two Starbuck Coffees in front of him.

"I didn't know if you took anything in your coffee so I got it black. It's their bold blend. Given your Hispanic heritage, I figured you'd prefer a strong coffee."

"Black is fine and the stronger the better."

"I'm sorry about this cloak and dagger stuff. I'm afraid there are ears in my building."

"You're being bugged?"

"I think so. I'm having a firm come in to sweep the place but I'm not even sure who to trust in my own firm so I have to be careful. That's why I called you back from the street using a store-bought cellphone."

"Who's bugging you?"

"Who do you think?"

"*Beyond Revelation*."

"Bingo."

"You're their sugar daddy, no offense meant. Why would they bug you? Couldn't you just turn off the spigot?"

"It turns out I'm only a minor investor now. Let me back up and explain what's happened over the past week. After you told me about the disappearance of your friend, I made a few inquiries. I tried calling the Massachusetts compound and got absolutely nowhere, so I called Montana. They at least told me they'd investigate and get back to me. About a half hour later I got a call back. It was Caleb Smith. I hadn't spoken to Caleb in over a year and was pleased to talk with him.

"We exchanged a few pleasantries and then the conversation turned nasty. He advised me they'd found another party who was willing to provide much more money than the amount I'd invested in *Beyond Revelation*. I found that inconceivable given the money I poured in over the years. Before you try doing any calculations in your head, let's just say it's in the nine digit area.

"I was about to protest when he instructed me to look at my text messages. I opened up the messages he had just sent me and there were pictures of my kids and one picture of me that would, well let's just say, if released, it would ruin my marriage and my career.

"I got back on the phone and he told me to drop the inquiries I'd made earlier. Like I said to you, I'd known Caleb for over twenty years. I believed in him and his cause. One thing I may not have been entirely truthful about earlier was that I do in fact passionately believe in the stated mission of *Beyond Revelation*. I believe we need to prepare for the rapture, for the second coming. I thought I was doing good works in financing this venture. I hoped that my contributions would not be overlooked when the End of Days came about. I hoped I'd secured a place in heaven for me and my family.

"I started to ask questions when *Beyond Revelation* expanded so substantially a few years back. Caleb gave me assurances that it only had to do with a hunger for a true religion that was not being satisfied by the established churches. I naively bought this explanation. Now that I was asking pointed questions about what they were doing, however, I was turning into a liability. I don't know if Caleb and the mission of *Beyond Revelation* got corrupted or whether Caleb had played me all along. I'm thinking the latter. He needed a meal ticket until he could find a new one. Boy, do I feel like the world's biggest fool."

I let that hang in the air for a moment before speaking up.

"You were doing what you thought was right. Now we have to continue doing right. Do you have any idea what *Beyond Revelation* is up to these days?"

"I really don't."

"You said the group's rapid expansion raised questions in your mind. Why?"

"I'm a businessman. I've seen too many examples through the years of businesses that have met with success, but then expanded too quickly. They couldn't handle the volume or they couldn't maintain quality. Eventually, these businesses went under. I thought this venture, even though it's not a business, would meet a similar fate and I was concerned. My concerns were dismissed and I accepted their dismissal. It turns out I should have remained concerned. The expansion was being done for a distinct reason that had nothing to do with saving souls. I just don't know what that reason is."

"Do you know where they're getting their alternative funding from?"

"No, I tried looking into their books the other day but they've been closed to me."

"Do you know a man named Alexi Slatzky?"

"No, the name doesn't ring a bell. Who is he?"

"He's a Russian who broke into my home the other day. I have no direct evidence but, for some reason, I associate him with *Beyond Revelation*. I probably have no justification, but the possibility has stuck in my mind."

"Russian? Wait a second. It must be a year ago now when the electronic notifications I received about *Beyond Revelation* financial transactions changed. I used to get monthly statements of balances and transactions. I'd also get a notice whenever any transaction exceeding $25,000 took place. I trusted Caleb so I'd just give them a cursory glance and then I'd file them. Well, about three months ago I got a notification of a huge deposit to the *Beyond Revelation'* account. I'm talking over $1 million. What really caught my eye was that the bank noted that it had to convert the amount from Russian rubles to dollars before finalizing the deposit. I called Caleb. He told me that a Russian businessman, someone similar to myself, had contributed to the cause. He joked that I was still his number one man. Again, I trusted him and thought nothing of it.

"Now that I think about it, that was the last of those types of notifications I received. I still got statements, but they showed a stable balance that neither increased nor decreased substantially from month to month. Looking back, I think I wasn't supposed to see that Russian deposit. Some clerk hadn't gotten the memo and sent me the notification, just like he or she always had. Well, they immediately corrected their system. Caleb probably opened a second account into which he could deposit Russian funds, eliminating fear that I could see the record of deposit. Again, I was the world's greatest fool."

"I believe my break-in is related to these deposits. If that's the case, they'll probably be after you as well. You probably should augment your security and the security for your family."

"I did that right after my conversation with Caleb. I hired a private security firm."

Benson fixed his gaze to an area behind me to my right. I turned around and saw leaning against the wall about fifty feet away a man in a stocking cap, jeans and bomber jacket.

"That's Ron. He follows me wherever I go."

I waved at him. He waved back.

"Mr. Benson, is there anything else you can tell me?"

"No, I don't think so."

"One thing I didn't mention is that not only is my friend, Eunice, missing but now my husband has disappeared. He went to Montana after which he fell off the face of the earth. The only thing that keeps me going is my faith in my husband's ability to take care of himself. I have to believe he's still alive, but the more I learn about *Beyond Revelation*, the more afraid I get."

"I'm so sorry. And I'm sorry I ever played a role in making them viable. If I can be of any help to you, let me know. Here's a number you can call that's not traceable."

17

When I got back to my office, Heather was waiting for me.

"Been waiting long?"

"Just a few minutes. I got some background on Mr. Slatzky. The guy has quite a record throughout Europe. He has arrest records in France, Belgium, Austria, Italy, Greece and The Czech Republic. A lot of extortion and money laundering. No violent crimes. The problem is he's never been convicted. I find it hard to believe that there's been this much smoke but never any fire. He must have a highly-placed friend or guardian angel who gets him out of jams."

"Have you thought to cross-check his activities with anything that was happening in the country or region at the time?"

"Yup. In each case there was a labor or some such demonstration taking place in the same city as the crime. There was some speculation in one of the police reports that Slatzky's efforts, if they didn't outright support the labor unions, they at least egged them on, or at least the more violent aspects of these actions."

"It would seem he's an advance man when something is brewing. Anything else?"

"I wanted to see if I could figure out how a guy like this could sneak into the country. I noticed in one of the police reports that, when they caught him, he was carrying an American passport. The name on it was Stanley Smith."

"Smith? Not very imaginative of him, was it? Did they confiscate the passport?"

"It doesn't say, but, given the way they allowed him to walk, I'd imagine they gave it back."

"Me, too. Do you have a way of figuring out if Slatzky entered the U.S. as Stanley Smith?"

"I tried but Homeland Security has improved its cyber security. It'll take me some time to figure out a way in without getting caught."

Heather was especially upset with herself at not being able to answer one of my questions. Often in the past when I'd ask her about some information that she could only have obtained through legally dubious methods, she'd respond: 'Don't ask.' If she felt she disappointed me, I could imagine her pressing on until she got it, perhaps exposing herself to arrest.

"Don't worry about it. I'll call my contact in the State Department. I'll check with him. Please, do nothing more on it. The info you got me is great and very helpful."

She seemed relieved. I knew she'd find a way to hack into Homeland Security because it was a challenge, and she's not the type who would ever back away from a challenge. But if she were to do it, I wanted her to do it at her leisure where she could give it full attention, not in a hurry where she might forget something and leave herself exposed.

"There is one thing more. Do you think you could access the financials of *Beyond Revelation*?"

"I think so."

"Good. I'd like you to check and see if there have been any large-scale deposits or expenditures over the past year."

"How large?"

"Anything out of the ordinary; anything that doesn't fit the pattern of the rest of the transactions. Especially look for anything that smacks of Russia."

"Russia. You got it."

I was nervous. I hadn't yet heard from Jane or Broderick about Will. I had to tell myself they were still on their way to Montana, but still I tried their numbers. Both went to machines.

I went into my contacts list. It was time to contact Edward McKenzie to gather what he could tell me about Alexi Slatzky. I dialed his number at the State Department office in New York. A woman answered.

"I'm afraid Mr. McKenzie doesn't work here anymore."

"Really? I would have bet any money that he was a State Department lifer."

"He was let go after the change in administrations."

"It doesn't sound like you supported his being let go."

"No, we lost a lot of experience and knowledge. They treated him pretty shabbily. I'm convinced he was fired because he's the brother of the man who ran against the President. It was such a sick display of partisanship. He's a good man who provided a valuable service to his country."

"Do you have a number where I can reach Mr. McKenzie?"

"I'm afraid I'm not at liberty to give you that. I'm sorry."

"I understand. I can get his number elsewhere. Thanks for your time."

I would call The Reverend to ask him if he could give me his brother's contact info. Even though Edward McKenzie no longer worked for the State Department, I was certain he'd still be able to dig up some information on Alexi Slatzky. Or, if he didn't have access to such information, he'd still have plenty of contacts who I could call. I could start cold-calling myself, but it would take me way too long to learn what I needed to know. I needed contacts that I'd already cultivated.

I was about to dial when my phone buzzed. It was Jane.

"Jane, what can you tell me? Have you located Will?"

"Hi Francine. We arrived in Jordan and tracked down his phone."

"He isn't with his phone?"

"No, I'm sorry. His phone was smashed. They threw it behind a tree in the woods. Like I told you before, our phones are specially designed to send out a signal even if it's disabled."

"You have to find him, Jane. You just have to."

I was nearly in tears at this point.

"We'll do our best, Francine."

I thought about his original message: 'Trap Alan 11199a'. What could it mean? Then it dawned on me.

"Is there a diner in town?"

"Yes, the Kingfisher Diner. It's about the only viable business in this whole place."

"Today's the 18th of November, right?"

"Right."

"Then he'll be at that diner at 9:00 tomorrow morning."

"How'd did you get that?"

"We trapped Alan Westbrook at a diner. He's sending me a message that that's where he will be. The numbers are the date and time. He'll be there tomorrow at nine."

"I don't know. That all seems like a stretch to me."

"Here's my theory of what happened. I think they took him hostage a few days ago. Anticipating his capture, he typed a hurried message, one that only I would understand. Then his captors tried to destroy his phone, thinking they'd rendered it untraceable. He must have evaluated the bad guys and figured he could easily escape. He chose a date and time where he could rendezvous with you."

"I never would have figured that out. I still don't entirely buy it, but it wouldn't hurt to be at the diner at nine. There's a little motel on the outskirts of town. We'll stay there tonight and then go to the diner. I hope you're right."

"Me, too. Be careful. These people are playing for keeps and I don't see any reason they wouldn't run you over if they had to."

"Thanks Francine, we will. Take care of yourself, too."

We hung up. I meant to tell her about our break-in, but it slipped my mind because I was so excited at cracking Will's code. I contemplated calling her back, but what could she do from the wilds of Montana?

I was proud of myself for figuring out what Will was telling me. I have never been so in tune with anyone in my entire life. Still, the theory I was spewing was entirely conjecture. The only fact that was indisputable was that my husband, the man I loved more that anyone or anything on earth, was away from me. I had no idea if he was still alive. And, if he was alive, he was out in the absolute middle of nowhere, cold and alone. When I get him back, I was going to read him the riot act for proceeding alone, without backup or a partner. But until then, I was totally frazzled.

I couldn't stand it much longer. I held it together for the kids and because I had a job to do but I was at the end of my rope. Will and I had gone through too much together for me to remain sitting idly by, waiting for the FBI to do its job. I needed to do something. I needed to act.

The first thing I did was to call Emma. I asked her if she'd be able to stay with the kids for the night. She said she'd be able to stay over. I had to admit how lucky I was. There are several people in my life who are worth their weight in gold. Jonas and Frank most definitely fit the bill. Emma is another one. I've lost track of the number of times I've called her at the last minute to ask her if she could help us out and her answer was a cheerful "Yes."

A few months ago, Will had to remind me I was a filthy rich woman and I could use my money to pull myself out of the hole in which I found myself. Because I did nothing to earn the money, but had it given to me, I rarely thought about it or accessed it. When Will suggested that I use the money to start a new network, I initially resisted. But when he said it would be something Alan would want me to do, I decided to dip into the funds. Now I would dip into the account again to retrieve my husband. Alan would also approve of this expenditure.

I went online to look up charter air services. I needed to get from the New York metropolitan area to Jordan, Montana in just under fifteen hours. I started calling. The first three had answering machines. An actual person answered the next two, but they had no planes available. And then a couple more answering machines. Finally, on the eighth company I got someone who would entertain the possibility.

"Hello, this is Barnswell Aviation. How can I help you?"

"I'm looking to charter a flight from the New York area to Jordan, Montana."

"Where the hell is Jordan, Montana?"

"Um, it's in Montana."

"Never heard of it but if it has an airstrip, I can get you there. When do you need the flight?"

"Now. As soon as I can get to you."

"Now as in today?"

"Yes."

"I don't know."

"Whatever the amount you would charge for such a trip, I'll double it."

"What did you say?"

"I said I'd double whatever you would normally charge."

"Well, it's an eight-hour round trip. I only have one plane that I would even attempt a trip like this in. My plane's a Falcon 50, top of the line. Just got it a few months ago."

He seemed very proud of this jet and expected me to be impressed. When I didn't react one way or the other, he continued.

It'll fly for four to five hours without refueling, so we'll have to gas up in the Chicago area. I have a facility there so that won't be a problem. I hope they have fuel in, where did you say we're flying to again?"

"Jordan. Montana."

"Right. I'll try giving them a call to see about fuel. It's $4,000 per hour plus fuel charges so the total bill for an eight-hour round trip would come out to about $35,000. I'd have to charge you additional if there's any significant lay-over time."

I could tell by the way he said this amount he was expecting me to either faint away or hang up. I did neither.

"So that would make the total amount I owe you $70,000. It's a deal."

"Wait a minute. You're serious?"

"Dead serious. Can you do it or not?"

"For that much money, damn straight I'd do anything. How soon can you get here to Teterboro Airport? I'm in Hanger 7."

"I'll stop at the bank and get you a certified check and then I'll come straight to you. It'll probably take me an hour, hour and a quarter."

"I'll file my flight plan and contact the airport in Jordan. These little strips have a tendency to close down after a certain hour if they don't have any planes scheduled to come in. I once landed my plane on a strip that was deserted, but they didn't bother telling me. They at least had the decency to leave the strip lights going."

"You're still around to talk about it so I guess you're a decent pilot."

"Not bad, if I do say so myself. See you in an hour or so."

I grabbed the bag I'd told Heather to have on hand for cases like this. Then I explained to Frank what I was doing, ordered a car service, and I was out of there. The bank, never ready to give up money, took a little longer than I planned but there was only very light traffic heading out of Manhattan through the Lincoln Tunnel and I was at the airport within the promised hour and a quarter.

It was eleven in the morning when I left the bank to head towards the airport. There was one more call I had to make before I was in the air. I dialed.

"P.S. 53. Sharon Middleton here. How can I help you?"

"This is Francine Vega, Albert Allen's mother. I need to speak with him. Would you be able to pull him out of class for a few minutes? It's very important."

"I'll go get him right away."

A few minutes later, Albert came to the phone.

"Hi Fava."

"Hi Albert. Have you been able to stay awake?"

"Yeah," he laughed.

"I have to head out of town and probably won't be back until tomorrow. Emma will stay with you."

"Where are you going?"

"I'm heading out to Montana. I'm going to bring back your father."

"Really?"

"Absolutely. In the meantime, I need you to watch out for your sisters. I need you to do everything Emma asks of you, okay?"

"Okay."

"That's my boy. I'll call you as soon as I can. I love you, Albert. I love you very much."

"I love you too, Fava."

We located Hanger 7, and I walked in through the huge open bay. The plane I was taking (or at least the one I assumed I'd be taking since I wouldn't know a Falcon 50 if I tripped over it) was sitting there. Two men were standing beside it. They turned to me as I walked towards them.

"Ms. Vega, I presume," the older gent called out as he reached out his hand. He was, let's be kind here, rotund. He was in his fifties, stood five foot four and, in my estimation, pushed the scales at close to three hundred pounds. The man with him was the exact opposite. He was tall and thin and had a shock of gray hair atop his head.

"I'm Eddie, Eddie Howes. We spoke on the phone. I'll be your pilot today. This is Willie Wilson. He'll be the copilot."

I shook both their hands. I then pulled the check from my bag and handed it to Eddie.

"I believe this is the amount we agreed upon."

He took the check and stuffed it in his pocket without looking at it.

"Whenever you're ready, we can get going."

We climbed in the plane and buckled in. Howes and Wilson went through their preflight checklist as they flicked one switch after another. We rolled out of the hangar and onto the tarmac. We taxied out to the strip and soon were in the air. Within a few minutes we were at our cruising altitude. I was reading a magazine when Eddie came back to sit with me.

"What is so all-fired important to pay an arm and a leg to head out to the middle of nowhere? I probably should have asked this before I accepted the job, but you're not involving me in something illegal here, are you?"

"No, not in the least. I'm heading out to save my husband."

"Save him from what?"

"He's been missing for three days. He's an FBI agent who was investigating a case and then something happened."

"Shouldn't the FBI be the ones who are looking for one of their own?"

"They are, but the last thing he did was to send me a message that let me know he's in trouble and how to get him back. Will and I are a team. I have to go."

"That's good enough for me. I just had to make sure. Like I said, I should have checked this out ahead of time but all that money dangling in front of me clouded my judgment for a few moments. I'm glad to know I'm not doing anything I'll get in trouble for. Can I get you anything to drink or a snack? Nothing fancy, but it'll stave off any hunger."

"I'd like some sparkling water, if you have it."

"Can do."

It took some doing, but he got out of his chair and then went to the refrigerator to get me my water. After that he returned to the cockpit, leaving me to my thoughts. The next thing I knew we were bouncing to a landing. Eddie stuck his head in.

"Refueling. We should be airborne in a half hour or so."

I took a sip of my water and looked out the window. It was a tiny airport, probably similar to our final destination. Within minutes, a tanker truck was working its way out to us and attaching hoses. The efficiency of the operation impressed me.

As Eddie promised, we were back in the air within a half hour. We had another two-and-a-half hours to go. I was getting hungry, and Eddie produced a rather nice assortment of cheeses and crackers and grapes. He offered me a glass of red wine to go with it, which I declined. I needed to keep my head as sharp as I could.

We touched down around five in the evening. I have to correct what I stated earlier. The airstrip where we refueled was a major hub compared to this strip. We landed just before the airstrip's sole employee left for the day. If we had been any later, he probably would have left the lights on just as Eddie had described.

I looked around as we deplaned. Ours definitely was the largest, and not to mention the most sophisticated, aircraft anywhere in the airport. Most were two-seater, single engine prop planes. Eddie confided to me he had been a little nervous about the length of the runway as we approached. He said he could see a row of trees getting larger and larger as he applied the brakes. I asked him if taking off would be a problem. He said no, takeoffs were a breeze for him.

Eddie and Willie volunteered to stick around for a day or so to bring us back, but I told him he could head back to Teterboro whenever they wanted. While a private jet is nice, I figured I'd head back with my FBI folks and they'd feel ill at ease riding in such luxury. To their credit, Eddie and Willie were gentlemen and they would not leave until they were sure I was settled.

We all walked over to the main terminal building. In fact, it was the only building on the premises. It was a not very imposing structure, but it at least looked solid and capable of keeping out the cold. The sole occupant, Hans Feyerbach, got up to greet us.

"Impressive piece of machinery you got there. Don't see many like it around these parts."

"Thanks," Eddie replied, "it is a sweet bird, my pride and joy. I tried calling earlier to check if you have fuel, but I didn't get an answer. I'm relieved to see that tank of jet fuel over there. I need to buy some off you to get us back to Chicago, if I could."

"That can be arranged with no problem. What brings you to Garfield County?"

"I need to get into Jordan. Is there a taxi I can call?"

"No taxis here. Jordan's the county seat and we got 350 people. Not much call for a taxi service. Most people who use this strip are crop-dusters, fire fighters and livery services from outpost to outpost. Most folks drive here, fly off, do their business, fly back and drive home. There is a guy in town, Alistair, who I sometimes talk into shuttling people here and there, but he's home sick with the flu."

"There's no way to get into town?"

He thought over the question for a couple seconds and then replied.

"I'm about done for the day and I'd be happy to drive you into town."

"Would you? That would be so kind."

"My missus would string me up if she caught wind of me stranding anybody, especially a female, here over night. You strike me as an urban type and I doubt you'd take too kindly to the sounds you hear throughout the night."

"Can I buy you dinner or anything?"

"Nah, I got a hot meal waiting for me back home. And you two, you need a lift, too?"

"Nope, now that we know Ms. Vega is safe, we can be on our way back home. We should be able to get in before midnight."

"Your airport lets you land that late?"

"Yup, planes come in and out at all hours. And we're a small airport compared to the rest in the New York area."

"Personally, I'll stick with our little strip here."

"It does seem nice. Well, we'll just fuel up, and then we can head out. Thanks for the business, Ms. Vega. Let me know if I can ever be of service."

With that, Eddie and Willie headed back to their jet while Hans ran the fuel line over to the Falcon. A half hour later, the jet was fueled up. Eddie and Willie took off and then Hans could close up.

Soon we were in his Chevy pickup truck heading east toward the town. Along the way, Hans regaled me with stories about his six-year-old son and fourteen-year-old golden retriever. Just as the son was getting to the age where he could go hunting and fishing with Hans, the dog had lost a step or two and could not keep up on these outings.

Before long, we were in town. I'd asked him if he thought I'd be able to find a room in town. He said that Hasting's Inn would probably have a room available. If I had arrived a couple weeks later when hunting season started, there wouldn't be a free room, but now the inn would be practically empty.

I offered to pay him at least gas money for rescuing me, but he wouldn't hear of it. Although his house was in the opposite direction, he wouldn't take a cent.

I walked into the inn. A sprightly young blond-haired woman greeted me. She said she had a lovely room that would be just perfect for me. I said fine. I then asked her if Jane and Broderick had checked in. At first, she was reluctant to tell me, especially since she was aware they were FBI agents. But then she looked me over and decided I didn't pose too much of a threat. She told me Jane was in Room 1 and Broderick was in Room 5. I was to be in Room 3.

I put my bag in the room and then I walked next door and knocked on the door of Jane's room. I should have had a camera to capture her expression when she opened the door.

"Francine, what the hell are you doing here? How'd you get here?"

It surprised me when she leaned over and gave me a big hug. It really wasn't her style, so I knew the show of affection was heartfelt. She invited me in. I explained my irresistible urge to come here and the machinations I needed to employ to make it happen.

"I can't even imagine how much it must have cost for you to get here."

"Don't ask, but it's worth every cent. Providing I'm right."

Jane said that she and Broderick were just about ready to go have some dinner. I was starving, so I said I'd join them. It would be at the only diner in town.

We knocked on Broderick's door. His look of surprise was as priceless as Jane's, but I did not get a hug. If that had happened, I would have wondered who had invaded his body and taken over.

Dinner was standard, non-glamorous diner fare, but it was fine. There was only one other couple dining there. Once hunting season started the following week and from then on through the holidays, hunters would pack the place.

Jane and Broderick filled me in on what they'd learned so far. They had canvassed the town with pictures of Will and some people remembered seeing him and talking to him. The two agents also asked around town about the *Beyond Revelation* compound. The reactions ranged from yawns to a feeling that something wasn't quite right about "those people".

They also asked if anybody knew anything about Vernon Boyd, one of the Blacks who lived in Jordan and disappeared a few years ago. A few people said they remembered Boyd but they thought he'd just moved on. They didn't realize his father had reported him as missing. They all said he seemed like a nice man. He was quiet and kept to himself, but was friendly when you ran into him on the street or in a store.

We finished our meals and headed back to the hotel. There wasn't anything else to do in this town, so we figured it would be an evening of watching TV and then going to bed early. I knew that I would not get much in the way of sleep that night. My mind would race between the dread of what I would do if Will didn't show up the following morning and the anticipation of seeing him again, safe and sound. I wasn't all that tired. Although I only got snatches of sleep on the plane, the sleep I did get was deep and restorative.

I settled in with the TV on a channel promoting home restoration projects. It's not as if I was planning any home restoration projects, but the selections were limited and this channel was the most inoffensive option. Even though I was not sleepy, I set the alarm for seven thirty to give me time to shower and get ready to be at the diner at nine.

I guess I was more tired than I thought since, the next thing I knew, the alarm was buzzing away. I was disoriented for a few seconds, but before long I was ready to go. I made some coffee in the room. Even though I doubled the packets in the machine, the coffee came out weak, but it was the best I could come up with. I got dressed and was ready to go. I was about to step out when there was a knock on the door. Jane and Broderick were both waiting for me.

We got a booth by the window, ordered coffees and stared out. At quarter after nine Broderick wondered aloud whether Will would show. I was wondering myself whether I had misread his message but then, just as I was thinking it, he came around a building across the street. He was dirty and disheveled and supporting a Black woman who was limping badly. It was Eunice.

I jumped out of the booth and ran to the front door. Will, who was about thirty feet away now, looked up. He saw me as he yelled "Fava" with a huge smile on his face.

I was about to run out onto the street to him when a black Ford pickup truck came racing down the town's main street. It stopped about twenty feet away when a burly bearded man who had been sitting in the back of the truck stood up. He was wielding a semi-automatic rifle that he aimed at Will and Eunice. Will saw what was happening and immediately shielded Eunice with his body. The gunman opened fire. Jane pushed me out of the way and started firing her pistol at the gunman and the driver. Broderick broke the window by the booth and started firing.

After his partner got off a few bursts, the driver gunned the engine and the truck sped away. I ran to Will with Jane close behind me. I knelt down by Will's side while Jane took a position over me in case there were any other gunmen. Broderick broke into a sprint after the truck, firing his pistol at the receding vehicle as he ran. When he ran out of bullets, he discharged his cartridge, which he quickly replaced to resume fire.

I held Will in my arms, his blood oozing between my fingers. I could feel it already. He was gone. Jane came over and reached down to feel for his pulse. Finding none, she gently moved him and me to the side so that Eunice could get up. She was unharmed, but in shock. Jane moved her away as I sat there, Will's body nestled in my arms. I gently rocked him back and forth, somehow hoping to comfort him.

Broderick had returned by this point. He ran to the car he had rented, gunned it and raced after the pickup.

I don't know how long I sat on the street with Will in my arms. I supposed I was crying, but I don't remember. At some point Jane helped me up. I didn't resist. She could have done anything with me at that point, I was so pliant.

18

Broderick arranged for a military transport plane to bring Jane, Eunice and me—and Will's body—back to New York. He would stay in Montana. His chase after the pickup truck had been for naught and now his job was to coordinate the manhunt for Will's murderers with State law enforcement officials and the regional FBI office.

Eunice needed medical attention, but she refused to be put in a hospital in Montana. She had such a tantrum we thought it best to have her accompany us back to New York. Jane wanted a chance to question Eunice about her abduction, transport from Massachusetts to Montana and Will's capture, rescue of her and their subsequent escape. It's always preferable to question a witness or victim while facts and event are still fresh in the memory.

After her initial tantrum, Eunice settled into a catatonic state. Despite Jane's gentle prodding and questioning, she was in such shock that she didn't speak a word all the way back to LaGuardia. Even when she was throwing her tantrum, she wasn't speaking in words; she just shouted and ranted incoherently. That didn't stop Jane from trying, however.

Personally, I was glad that Eunice preoccupied Jane. It gave me a chance to sit in my stupor and sorrow. I really couldn't take anybody trying to be nice to me right at that moment, no matter how well-meaning he or she may be.

In a perverse way, I was happy that Eunice was as catatonic as she was. I didn't want to hear her tell me how much of a hero Will was. I didn't blame Eunice for anything; she was the ultimate victim. But neither did I want her to remind me that I was responsible for my husband's death. I was the one who sent Will all over the country searching for her.

I was glad she was free. I would try to talk with her later, when she's able. However, I couldn't take it at that point. I had to be alone. I stared out the window the entire flight back. I could feel Jane's presence at one time during the trip back, but she understood my need for solitude and backed off.

When we landed, Jane asked me if I wanted to accompany Will's body to the FBI morgue. I didn't know if that was standard procedure or whether I was a special case because of Will's and my relationship. I declined. I didn't want to seem unsentimental, but I had to deal with the living. I had to go home to my children.

Jonas offered to be with me when I broke the news to the kids. I thanked him but told him no. It was something I had to do by myself. I am their mother; it was my responsibility.

I opened the front door and called out. Emma appeared first, holding Rosa's hand. Rosa broke free and ran to me. I held her close. Emma looked down on me with a tear emerging from the corner of her eye. Next, Stella appeared at the top of the stairs. She ran down to me. Albert appeared from the kitchen. He took one look at my face and turned around to head back into the kitchen without saying a word. I wanted to go to him, but I supposed he was like me; he needed to be alone.

I sat down with Stella on one side of me and Rosa on the other. Since Rosa was too small to understand, I directed my comments to Stella. I explained slowly and detailed how much of a hero her father was. The more I talked, the more I both upset myself over losing Will and thrilled myself at being with such a fine man for even the short time I did.

I hugged my girls closely. Stella and I began crying. Rosa didn't understand why we were crying, but she started as well. Either she did not want to be left out or perhaps I was squeezing her too tightly.

As we were hugging and crying, Albert hurried by us and climbed the stairs. I could hear the door to his room close rather loudly. I left him alone for the rest of the evening. There would be plenty of time to talk later on.

The next morning, I knocked on Albert's door to wake him up. In response, I received a terse and angry: 'Go away, leave me alone'. I debated knocking again, telling him we needed to talk, but I let him be. We all grieved in our own ways. We'd talk eventually.

Broderick called us later that day. They found the pickup truck. The shooter had died from wounds sustained during the shootout and his body was still in the truck bed. He had bled out as his accomplice drove away. Not that it mattered, but the FBI wanted to determine whose bullet killed him, Broderick's or Jane's. I did not care.

A few hours later, they captured the driver and were interrogating him, but Broderick said he had lawyered up. There was nothing connecting the murder with *Beyond Revelation*. In fact, Broderick said that he had driven out to the *Beyond Revelation* compound and it was deserted. Not a single person remained. There were some remaining personal items, indicating a very hasty evacuation. Since there was, to anyone's knowledge, no roster of people who lived at *Beyond Revelation*, it would be impossible to track them down.

Broderick said that, now that the killer had been apprehended and had clammed up, he would return to New York and be back in time for Will's funeral. I was pleased he would be able to attend. He meant a lot to Will.

Will's autopsy uncovered nothing new or unexpected. Three bullets had wounded him, but two were not life-threatening. The third pierced his back as he was shielding Eunice. It went between the fourth and fifth ribs straight into his heart, killing him instantly.

Once I got back home, I called Frank to let him know I was back. He told me he and Jonas had already begun handling the arrangements for the funeral and burial. Frank called the FBI district office to see if they had anything on file about funeral arrangements Will may have made if his death were to occur. The woman who answered initially told Frank she could not give out that information, but she relented after admitting being a friend of Will's. Frank apologized for overstepping, but I told him I appreciated his efforts.

Since neither Will nor I were much in the way of churchgoers, the funeral was to be held at the Franklin Funeral Home in Astoria, Queens. There would be no wake or calling hours. I didn't need person after person telling me how sorry they were and how great a man Will was. I knew all that.

When my mother died eight years earlier, I went through all the bells and whistles of a wake, funeral and celebration of her life. However, there were several substantial differences between the circumstances of her death and Will's. First, my mother died after a long bout of cancer. When she passed away, her suffering ended. It was almost a relief. Will was stolen from me suddenly, in the prime of his life, and mine as well. Rather than a feeling of relief, I had a profound feeling of bitterness.

Another big difference was that I knew practically every person my mother knew. In a way, we both grew up together in New York City. She was a newly arrived immigrant; I was a newly arrived baby. Then, as we both grew, we shared many experiences and acquaintances. At all the services and ceremonies surrounding her death, the people who came to pay their respects were all familiar faces. Not only were they familiar faces, but they arrived with familiar stories with which I was intimately familiar. I shared many of their stories.

Conversely, Will and I were married for just under three years after a miniscule engagement. He had a marriage and two kids. He had a law enforcement career that I was not part of. He had a world of acquaintances and experiences foreign to me. When his former wife's brother comes up to me, what can we possibly have to say to each other? I know Jane, Broderick and Willoughby but I never really got to know his other FBI colleagues. What could I talk about with them? I know I'm a reporter and am paid to ask questions and dig for information but now hardly seemed the occasion to put these skills to use. Instead, I wanted to crawl into a hole and die.

I therefore was perfectly happy to have had nothing more than a funeral (and maybe not even that), but Jonas told me we should have people over to the house. He said it would be important for the kids to have people around to get a sense of the man their father was. They needed to heal. Being shut away from the ritual of grieving would only inhibit the healing process. I thought it over and ultimately agreed that he was correct.

Albert would not speak to me. He took his meals up to his room so he wouldn't have to be in the same room as me. I felt that we had regressed all the way back to when Will and I were first married. He thought I was trying to replace his mother who had died a few years earlier. He never said as much, but he held me responsible for his father's death. In a way, I was.

The day of the funeral, I got the girls dressed. I went back and forth about whether they were too young to attend. I remembered a line from an old movie about a mother who was going through a similar dilemma and her attitude was that she should not shield children from death or they will be afraid of it when they get older. I knew many people would look askance at me bringing Rosa, who wasn't even three, but I wanted to celebrate Will's life, not just mourn his death. And what better way to celebrate that life than through his daughter, through our daughter.

Albert got himself dressed and was ready to go but would not ride with me. He rode with Frank and his family. I still planned to talk with him, but it could wait.

The funeral was a blur. Hundreds of people attended. They had to utilize multiple rooms with monitors so that all could view the service.

I was struck by the number of Will's FBI colleagues who came to pay their respects. This included the Bureau's Associate Deputy Director. Numerous other people Will had helped over the years came, people like Alejandro and Herbie, the two men who had gotten me out of Cuba. There were a couple people he had sent to prison but then helped out once they got out. Again, this spoke to Will's character.

A chaplain who knew Will from their time together in the Army presided over the service. He said all the right things about Will being taken from us too soon, about his beautiful children now without a father, about his service to his country cut too short. I was too lost in my own sorrow to pay much attention.

After the service, attendees were invited over to my house for some refreshments. I don't know who provided the refreshments or how they got there, but I can guarantee that Frank and Jonas both contributed to making it happen.

I made the rounds and accepted condolences from an endless supply of people. At one point, there was a lull in the line of people who wanted to give their sympathies, so I sat down on one of the folding chairs in the living room. I supposed I looked as dejected as I felt. I looked up. Jonas was making his way in my direction. I smiled. If there's one person who can always put a smile on my face, it's Jonas. I smiled at him and he smiled back but, instead of sitting down beside me to cheer me up with one of his folksy sayings, he walked right by me. He kept walking until he came upon Albert, who was sitting by himself in the kitchen. Jonas sat down on a stool beside him and talked to him. He went on for at least five minutes. Albert kept looking down but would occasionally nod in response to something Jonas said.

Jonas stopped talking, and Albert nodded. Then Albert cried and he ran into Jonas's arms. Jonas gave him a big hug and then said one more thing to Albert. Albert nodded one more time and got up from his stool. He came out to the living room and walked up to me. I stood up to greet him. He hesitated a second and then burst out in tears as he ran to me. I knelt down and gave him the most motherly hug I could muster. He hugged me tightly in return.

We stayed like that for several minutes. Then, when we pulled apart, he looked me in the eyes.

"Fava?"

"Yes, Albert."

"Why did Daddy die?"

"He died the way he lived, helping others. Your father died saving someone else's life. You know, throughout your life you'll hear about people who they call heroes. Sometimes they deserve it, sometimes not. You can be proud to tell anybody you meet that your father was a true hero. He was a hero every single minute of every single day. He lived a life to protect us. There was never a finer man than your father, but you want to know something?"

"What?"

"I think you're growing into a man as fine as your father. You have all the makings. I can tell. I hope you'll let me help you become that man."

"I will, Fava."

"That's good. Why don't you go see what your sisters are up to? You're the man of the family now and I'll need your help around here. Think you're up to it?"

He smiled his response through his tears and left. I looked up and saw Jonas smiling warmly at me. I walked over and gave him a bear hug, the kind I always demand of him. I'll never know what it was Jonas said to my son that turned him around, and I'll never ask. I'm just so indebted to this man. He restored my spirit and will to live.

I turned around and standing there was John Foster.

"John! Thank you so much for coming. I can't tell you how much it means to have you here."

"Heather called me and told me what happened. I'm so sorry."

I gave him a big hug. I was on a roll now, hug-wise.

"I thought you'd be in Singapore by now with the kids."

"I was practically out the door when Heather called. I contacted my son and told him the kids would have to stay with me for a while."

"Where are the kids now?"

"A close friend of mine is looking after them."

At that point, Jane walked up to us. She greeted John warmly.

"How are things in Fairbrook?" Jane asked.

"I'm very concerned about my town. Harry, Chief Dumont, is officially missing. His family is beside itself with worry."

"I'm sorry to hear that. He seems like a good man."

"He is. Oh, one more thing, *Beyond Revelation* is no more."

"Really?" I asked.

"Yeah, it all happened in one night. They packed up lock, stock and barrel and skipped town. We probably wouldn't have realized it except for some kids who were playing in the woods and noticed the gates wide open. Kids being kids, they went in to check it out. When they went home, they told their parents. A bunch of us went to investigate and found it a ghost town. Oh, and that same day Andy Sykes disappeared. No one's heard from him since."

"When did this happen?"

"Last Friday."

"That was a day after Will was killed. Agent Broderick said the Montana compound closed up shop, too."

"Heather told me you suspected your husband's murder was orchestrated by *Beyond Revelation*."

"Yes, but I can't prove it. The gunman is dead, but they captured the driver. He isn't talking. As of now, neither has any direct link to *Beyond Revelation*."

"Will always told me to be wary of coincidences. His being killed and days later they close up shop? I think Will found out something and they wanted him silenced, but the FBI can't go any further without evidence."

We both looked at Jane, expecting her to provide the answers. She had nothing to offer.

"Look," John said, "I didn't mean to bring all this up. Today should be a day for celebrating your husband's life. I'm sorry."

"No, that's okay. The best way to celebrate Will is to uncover the truth about how and why they killed him. And believe me, I won't rest until I do just that."

"I believe you."

We chatted for a while longer, mostly about my children and his grandchildren. It was good to talk about some mundane things not related to Will's or anybody else's death. We were standing in the living room near the door leading to the dining room. We could hear a small group of people talking just around the corner. Nothing they were talking about seemed consequential until I overheard one of the participants ask a question.

"Had you heard that Allen was about to be reprimanded for using Bureau resources to rescue his wife who was stranded in Cuba?"

"And he wouldn't have been out in Montana if it weren't for some fool's errand she sent him on."

"Yeah, I heard that, too."

I heard this, and my blood immediately went to full boil. I stormed through the door.

"Are you saying it's a good thing he died? Otherwise, he'd have this blemish on his record? Is that what you're saying."

"No, that's not what we meant," said one of the four.

My outburst caused everything to come to an absolute halt throughout the house. No one even dared breathe at that point.

"Get out!" I screamed. "Get out of my house right now. I don't know who you are, but I can guarantee that you are not even one-tenth the person Will Allen was. Even dead in the ground, he's better than you are. Get out! Now!"

The group complied and turned to leave. I faced the rest of the gathering and raised my voice even more.

"In fact, if I didn't know you before today, get out now. I will not have anybody standing around gossiping and besmirching my husband's character in his own home. Go. Now. Get the hell out of here!"

People put down the plates of food they were eating and headed for the exit. A number repeated their condolences, but most left quietly. Eventually, I stood alone with only my closest friends remaining somewhat at a distance. They looked on me with worry on their faces about my mental state.

I'd raised my voice so loudly that the kids had emerged from their rooms and were standing at the top of the stairs. Like the others, they were looking down on me with looks of concern. I looked up at them and, after I calmed down, I motioned for them to come down the stairs to me. Tentatively, they started down. I sat down with them on the bottom steps.

"I'm sorry you had to see me like that. These people were our guests, and I should have been nicer to them. But I will not let anyone say anything against your father. I loved him with all my heart, just as I love you."

Stella responded immediately.

"We love you, Fava."

I looked at their faces. They all told me the same thing. It was exactly what I needed right when I needed it. I gave each of them a big hug and sent them back up to their rooms.

Exactly as I had demanded, only the people, fifteen of them, I had known before today were there. They found the scene with my kids touching, but they still looked on me with more than a little worry about my sanity. I didn't entirely blame them.

"Thank you so much for coming today. And thank you so much for sticking around after my little meltdown. I meant what I said. You are the people I've wanted in my life for all this time and you're the people I want in my life. I miss Will so much but having those kids and all of you around me will help me through.

"Now, there is one big advantage of having cleared out the house. There's more food for all of us."

I'd officially broken any residual tension as we sat down to eat. Afternoon morphed into evening, the numbers dwindled down as people went home one by one. I gave each of them—including Reverend McKenzie, Agent Willoughby, Richard Leitz, Major Audra Fairchild and even Janet Kahn, the woman who fired me—a personalized sendoff and thanks.

Before Edward McKenzie left I asked him if he still had contacts in the State Department who could help me get more information on Alexi Slatzky/Stanley Smith. I made it clear I thought Slatzky was connected to Will's death. I didn't want to appear to be the overzealous journalist I often am, plying a source at my husband's funeral on an unrelated story because that source happens to be there. Edward said he still had lots of connections at State from whom he could still get information. He'd ask one contact to dig into the agency database to see what information they could come up with.

Soon we were down to what I consider my core group: Frank, Jonas, Heather, Jane and my latest addition, John. Broderick considered staying and would definitely have been welcome. However, he's not the most sociable person to begin with and he had just spent most of the day being sociable. I think he reached his limit.

We were all sitting around the living room chatting about Will and other things. We talked about Westbrook Broadcasting and what our future looked like, not that I'd been that much a part of its present lately. Inevitably, the conversation settled on the one thing on all of our minds: *Beyond Revelation*.

We knew two people who had had an inner glimpse of the workings of the cult. One, Will, was dead and the other, Eunice, was still hospitalized and unable to tell us what was happening. Physically, she had recovered after a few days in the hospital. She'd been severely dehydrated and had obviously been beaten and perhaps tortured, but there didn't appear to be any lasting effects. Mentally and emotionally, however, she was far from recovered.

The doctors theorized that the combination of her treatment in the two compounds, Massachusetts and Montana, her escape, being on the run for a couple days and witnessing her rescuer murdered, and then die lying on top of her, was too much for her to handle. She was catatonic. Even Jonas couldn't break through to her. They thought she'd recover fully, but it would take some time. The problem was I didn't know if we had time.

Beyond Revelation may have closed down, at least in Montana and Massachusetts, but I doubted that this was the last we'd heard of them. We didn't know the state of the other compounds. Broderick was heading out to Colorado to check that facility. He had a friend from the academy who worked in the Denver office who would accompany him. Will's example had taught him a lesson. He would not go into any of these places without backup.

Heather's research had uncovered five additional *Beyond Revelation* compounds that had sprouted up in or near metropolitan areas throughout the country. Then she told us she may have uncovered at least seven more. She was unsure because they went by names different from *Beyond Revelation*. However, they all appeared to have one commonality, a link to Caleb Smith. She had no way of knowing, but I bet that if one were to examine the financials for these facilities, Russian money would be apparent. Caleb Smith and *Beyond Revelation* was up to something, something big. But what?

Jane said that the FBI's interest in *Beyond Revelation* had definitely cooled. The official who had authorized Will to look into the religious organization was mysteriously transferred to a backwater office. The official line was that, since Will could not file a report on his investigation, the Bureau had nothing to warrant further inquiry. There was no evidence linking Will's killers to the cult. The way the bureau looked at it, a couple anti-government wackos saw a perfect opportunity to take out a federal agent. They had their man and he would fry. *Beyond Revelation* had closed down and its members had scattered to the four winds. Case closed.

Jane said she heard that the Deputy Director had been a rookie agent that was part of the assault on the Branch Davidians in Wako, Texas back in the 1990s. That experience—and the resulting backlash—left him wary about taking on any religious groups.

Jane had also heard the murmurs about the possibility of Will's reprimand for ordering my extraction from Cuba. Jane apologized for bringing it up again so soon after my meltdown. I told her it was okay; I wouldn't kick her out. Will's perceived fall from grace was enough for the FBI bosses not to pursue anything further on this case. The only thing that would reopen this was for Eunice to provide some information on what *Beyond Revelation* was into, but she was in no shape to do so. I reached over and took Jonas's hand when Jane said this.

"That doesn't mean I won't continue to dig," I stated. "We all know that *Beyond Revelation* is responsible for Will's death. I intend to prove it, with or without the FBI's help."

"You know that Rick, Bernie and I will help you. Screw official FBI policy."

"I appreciate that. I know I can count on you, but you have two kids who depend on you. You can't risk losing your job or even worse. I'm persona non grata and that comes from the very top. Hell, the President is such a vindictive bastard he was willing to let me rot away in Cuba. He'd have no qualms about ordering your arrest, or Rick's or Bernie's arrest, if he got wind that you're helping me. I may call on you if I get stuck or if I get this inquiry to a point where a crime is uncovered but for now, I've got to go this alone."

"Not alone," Frank stated. "I'd commit the full resources of the company to help you but I can't really do that since it's your company."

Everyone laughed.

"And you know I'm in," Heather offered.

"Me, too, Frannie," Jonas volunteered.

That left John, but not for long.

"You can count on me, Francine."

"Don't you have to go to Singapore to deliver your kids to their parents?"

"I called my son just before I drove here to tell him I wouldn't be coming for at least a month. I enrolled the kids in school in Fairbrook."

"You didn't have to do this."

"Yes, I did. Besides the pain *Beyond Revelation* has caused you, I'm convinced this cult is responsible for the death of Karen, somebody I've known my entire life. Another lifelong friend, Harry, is missing and I fear he's dead. Someone who's connected to my Vietnam War buddy is dead. Carl Rutledge is still missing and may be dead. *Beyond Revelation* has torn apart the town I love, the town my father grew up in, the town I grew up in and the town my kids grew up in. I owe it to my community. Plus, it wouldn't hurt my grandkids to be exposed to small town life either."

"How'd your son take the news?"

"Not great but I think he heard by the tone in my voice that my mind was set. Ultimately, he relented. Anyway, I had the kids here and the old saying about possession being nine-tenths of the law came into play."

"Well, thank you. Do you think you can learn much in Massachusetts since they've cleared out?"

"There's always more to learn."

"Okay, we're all set. I kind of feel like we've just formed our own Order of the Phoenix here."

Jonas had a better name. "No, we're Fava's Army."

19

My weekly show was approaching, and I contemplated cancelling this week. It would have been understandable given Will's death. In fact, I think most people would have expected me to be respectful of my husband and call it off. To be honest, I really didn't feel like doing it; I didn't feel like doing anything at all.

I'd been able to hold it together through the funeral. All the people, even if I didn't care for them or know them or they made me angry, were constant distractions. Now it was the kids and me, on our own. We were all feeling a lot of pain. I knew time would help heal us, but we needed some healing right now and I didn't know how to do it.

In 2011, I'd helped produce a series of shows on how the families of 9/11 victims were coping a decade later. I'd only just started at the station, so I did not play that big a role. I was the one doing initial contacts and off-camera interviews. I would talk with them to get a feel for whether they were good candidates for a recorded interview. Thinking back, it was a fair amount of responsibility—making determinations who was to be on-air and who wouldn't—for a rookie reporter. I felt important.

It wasn't until years later that it dawned on me that they handed me this assignment because nobody else wanted to do it. The tragedy of 9/11, even a decade later, was still fresh in people's hearts and minds. Most of the veteran journalists had reported on that day and had experienced the rawness of the emotions and anger everyone was feeling. To go through it a decade later would have been too much to bear. I was their filtering process. My screening helped eliminate the people who still could not bear the weight of 9/11. It also helped to prepare folks for their on-screen interviews in advance. We wanted people to show emotion in their interviews, but we wanted people who could hold it together.

The station also wanted a show that was ultimately uplifting and inspirational. To show family member after family member who had fallen apart, unable to cope, would have been a downer for the viewers. The ideal interview would be someone who still missed their loved one but who had pulled themselves together to be a positive force in the world. They wanted people who had used his or her personal tragedy not as a crutch but as a springboard for good.

Now, here I was wondering if I could use my personal tragedy as a springboard for good. I was talking a matter of only days, not years, but Will Allen would not die in vain. I would carry on and be a positive force, for him. If nothing else, the kids needed me to be that strong. They needed me as an example. I'd done more than a few stories of parents who had fallen into a bottle of booze, never to emerge, after a tragedy. It's always the kids who suffer.

Will would want me to be this way. There was one time when Will had said something that rubbed me the wrong way and I lit into him. I let him have it with everything I could. I insulted him. I mocked him. I used my full arsenal of sarcasm. I threw every jab I could at him, many of them unfair and uncalled for. Many men would have responded in kind, escalating the shouting match to a point of no return or repair. Other men would have stormed off, resulting in a standoff of not talking to each other for days or weeks.

Will did none of these. He was silent during my diatribe. Once I blew myself out, what did he do? He stood there smiling. It was infuriating, to tell you the truth, so I asked him what he was smiling at.

"This is why I love you so much and why I think you're the perfect mother for my children. Perhaps you could learn to modulate your insults a bit. Some of them went over the line. But that's a minor flaw you can work on. When you see a wrong, you speak out about it. You take steps to correct it. Damn, I love you so much."

What could I do after that but give him a big hug and kiss? If I remember correctly, I believe I found myself so aroused I dragged him straight to the bedroom.

Now, even though he was gone, I still tried to see myself through his eyes. I had to keep on plowing ahead. I would do my show. The trouble was that the show was in four days and I didn't have a topic to discuss, let alone any guests to discuss them. I had some quick thinking to do and calls to make.

"Hello Richard, it's Francine."

"Francine, how you holding up?"

"I'm okay. Thanks for asking and thanks for coming to the funeral. It meant a lot to see you there."

"Well, I got to know you very well over the past year, but I also got to know Will during the Zyklon affair. He was a fine man. It's such a tragedy."

"I'm calling to pick your brain for a bit. I think of you as a mentor of mine."

"I appreciate that. Pick away."

"I've got my show on Friday. I contemplated not doing it this week. I know people would understand, given the circumstances, but for a variety of reasons I'm considering doing it. What I'm asking you is, should I go ahead and do the show? I haven't given one thought about the subject we'd discuss. I haven't done any planning. I haven't arranged for guests. I just feel I need to do it, both for myself and for Will. Your thoughts?"

"Then do it. Francine, I've seen you in action. There are few people I've met who are as quick on their feet as you are."

"Except for you, of course."

"But of course. A show topic will come to you in no time. Make it something you're familiar with. You also said you owe it to Will to do the show. Well, pick a topic that would mean something to him as well. It's going to be an emotional show for you. You'll have a tough time holding it together, so you'll need people there you can count on, people who are close to you and care about you. If you're talking about an issue that you knew Will would fight for, you can channel his fight."

"That's good advice."

"And in terms of guests, you already have one."

"I do?"

"Me."

"But you don't even know what we'll be talking about."

"We already established how quick a study I am, didn't we?"

"Yes, but how can you appear on my show? Aren't you contractually bound to Allied? Will they let you do it?"

"This will be one of those cases in which it's easier to ask for forgiveness rather than permission. Janet and I haven't been seeing eye-to-eye on a lot of things lately. I thought she was gutless in buckling to the pressure in firing you."

"It surprised me to see her at the funeral."

"It's all about appearances with her. She would have appeared churlish not to come. Oh, and regarding my contract, the language is rather squishy about outside appearances. I'm choosing to do a very broad reading of it."

"I'd welcome you on my show anytime."

"And I'd welcome you back on except Janet has more say on that matter. I do have one piece of unsolicited advice. Don't hold it on Friday. I think Friday night is a lousy time slot anyway, but this Friday especially so."

"Why?"

"Two reasons. First, it's the day after Thanksgiving. Nobody will be in the mood to watch."

"I'd forgotten Thanksgiving is this Thursday. I guess I don't feel that thankful this year. What's the other reason?"

"If you keep it on Friday, that gives you four days, including one that's a family holiday, to talk yourself out of it. You've made the decision, so do it. Make it tomorrow night."

"You're absolutely correct. We'll do it tomorrow night. I'll let Frank know we're shuffling the schedule."

"So, I'm on. I'll show up at your studio an hour before airtime, unless you want to have a meeting ahead of time to block the show out."

"I'll let you know on that."

"Don't wait too long before letting me know what we're talking about. Quick study or not, I'd like a little time to prepare."

"Will do. Thanks, Richard, for everything."

I hung up. My conversation with Richard energized me, but now I had to figure out what the hell we'd talk about. It had to be a subject on which I was conversant. Richard, as usual, had solid advice in telling me to choose something meaningful to Will. But what?

As I was pondering, Heather walked in. Her digging and hacking had gleaned more information that she was eager to share.

"I looked at the financials for *Beyond Revelation* and all its offshoots, at least the ones I believe are offshoots. As I told you, some are also named *Beyond Revelation* but a number have different names such as *The Rapture*, *The Horsemen* and *End of Days*. I didn't realize the connection to *Beyond Revelation* until I examined the financials and found a money trail leading from *Beyond Revelation* account to their accounts. The transfers happened a day or so after an infusion of millions of dollars into the *Beyond Revelation* account."

"How are you able to access all this?"

"Their cybersecurity system is shitty. Anyway, I haven't been able to track who owns the account the original monies came from, but all roads lead back to a numbered offshore account."

"My bet is on Russia."

"I wouldn't doubt it."

"So, besides Montana and Colorado and Massachusetts, how many of these compounds have you found?"

"I've come up with eight so far."

"Where are they?"

"In California there are two, one outside Sacramento and one near LA. There's one near Atlanta; another near Houston; one near New York City; one near Baltimore; another near Chicago; and the last one is in North Carolina, near Charlotte."

"Any connections or commonalities among all these cities?"

"Nothing I could find."

"Anything else?"

"Not at the moment, but I'll keep digging."

"Thanks. Great work."

I was thinking all this through when my phone rang. It was Broderick.

"Hi, Agent Broderick. How's Colorado?"

"We aren't in Colorado, Ms. Vega. We're in Montana, at *Beyond Revelation*. I never got to do a thorough sweep of the place."

"Were you able to get a warrant?"

"Don't ask."

I stifled a laugh as he used one of Heather's favorite lines when she was doing some questionable digging into a source or database.

"It occurred to me that, if Will was here, he may have left more clues. He did, but I don't know what it means. You may, though."

"What is it?"

"FAVA TKY BAM 13."

"That's it?"

"That's it. But what's just as significant is where I found it. It was behind a piece of furniture near the floor. And it was written in blood."

"Just like the 'SLAVE' that Jane found in Fairbrook."

"Exactly. I think Will put it there not only because it wouldn't be noticeable, but he knew Jane or I would think to look here. Any idea what it means?"

"Not a clue."

"He probably made it obscure so that, if they did find it, it wouldn't mean anything to them and they wouldn't bother to wash it away."

"Well, it means nothing to me. He was perhaps a little too obscure. I'll think about it and let you know if I have any brilliant revelations, no pun intended. Where you off to now?"

"We're heading to Colorado as originally planned. I'll let you know if I find anything there."

"Thanks. Bye."

20

FAVA TKY BAM 13? What are you trying to tell me, Will? I know that we, like most married couples, have our own codes and private language but we'd only been married for three years. It's not as though we'd been together for decades and could finish each other's sentences with ease. This cult robbed us of that.

The very thought of no Will to come home to or to call when I was having a tough day or even just to say hi left me with profound despair. At first a single tear escaped from the corner of my right eye, but soon it had plenty of company as I began sobbing. I put my head down on my desk and cried for I don't know how long. It was the first good cry I'd been able to have since Will's death. It always seemed I was holding it together for someone else whether it was the kids, my guests, Will. I needed this for myself.

I eventually settled myself down. I sat back up and dried my eyes off. After a half-minute, I heard a knock on my door and Frank walked in. I sensed he had been hanging outside my door waiting for me to compose myself. He gave me my privacy, which I appreciated.

"Hi Frank."

"Hi, tough, isn't it?"

"Yeah."

"Sorry to bother you right now. I just need to know what your show will be about tomorrow night. You said you wanted to do it but if you're not up to it, that's okay, too. We need to plan something if you aren't. I have a couple ideas I wanted to pass by you if you aren't, but they're things I'll need a day or so to get ready."

I paused for a minute. Was I really up to this? Could I hold it together for an entire hour? I didn't have any idea what to talk about. Richard was very gracious to come on my show, but I couldn't leave him hanging forever. Neither could I leave Frank and our network hanging. He needed to plan something; it was prime time. I've found that everything that's done last minute tends to look last minute. Frank was too much of a professional to let that happen.

Frank needed an answer, but I didn't know what to tell him. I looked down at my notes and saw FAVA TKY BAM 13. The answer came to me in a flash.

"We'll do it on *Beyond Revelation*."

"Come again?"

"The show will be on *Beyond Revelation*. It'll be on the power of cults. It'll be on the power of persuasion and on the need of people to be persuaded. It'll be on how sheep-like some people can be and how others are so desperate for something, anything, meaningful that they can latch onto to make sense of their lives. It'll be on a black hole in our society and how no one really knows what's going on in these places. I want to hit *Beyond Revelation* hard."

"How much do you really know about *Beyond Revelation*? I mean, really know?"

"Do you think we'll be sued?"

"Well, yeah. I think we'll be sued and the FCC could censure us for proceeding with a story such as this before we have all of our facts buttoned down. We'd be out there on the ledge, alone."

"I don't think there's any chance they'll sue us. They're up to their necks in something dirty and perhaps illegal. They won't want to expose themselves. They operate in the shadows and they need to stay that way. We may draw some attention to them, but a lawsuit would draw even more."

"Okay, but I highly recommend you talk to our lawyer before proceeding."

We didn't have a lawyer on staff but we had Stephen Askew, Esq. on retainer. He prepared and filed our incorporation papers, at which he seemed very competent. However, we had no idea if he'd have the experience or knowledge to answer questions of this type.

"That's probably good advice but lawyers always err on the side of doing nothing if there's even the minutest risk of liability. I am not doing nothing."

"Go for it, then."

Frank got up to leave, but then stopped.

"I almost forgot. Heidi and I want to invite you and the kids to our house for Thanksgiving. Emily and Frank will both be home from college. Heidi's mother will be there. I've already asked Jonas. With Eunice still in the hospital, he'd be alone. He said he'd join us. I love a big get-together."

"Richard had to remind me this Thursday is Thanksgiving. I've so lost track of time. I'll think about joining you."

"Please do. Thanksgiving is a time to be with family and you're family to me."

On the one hand, it would be therapeutic to be with other people, but then again, a quiet day at home alone with the kids might be what I needed. Then again, I knew what I needed; I needed Will, but I could never have that again.

In the meantime, I had a show to produce. I was really pushing my luck, hoping that the people I wanted on the show would be available two days before Thanksgiving. Luckily, I already had Richard and if it ended up just him and me, I could deal with that.

I called Richard and filled him in on what we would be discussing. I told him that Heather would call to brief him on the financial information she'd uncovered. While Heather could hack with the best of them and uncover the nefarious transactions and was astute enough to recognize they were significant, Richard could tell you what that significance was. He is a certified financial and economic genius. He could make sense of the information, put the pieces together and offer valuable insights.

The next person I called was The Reverend. Reverend Malcolm McKenzie could address the religious significance of an organization like *Beyond Revelation*. Also, as a former presidential candidate, he could provide insights on the political implications of groups like these. They and the evangelical lobby did play a big role in him securing his party's nomination. The Reverend said he was available and would be happy to take part. So far, so good.

The last person I'd ask to join our panel was Dr. Jorge Fernandez of New York University. He was one of my favorite professors while at NYU. He taught in the psychology department and was a leading expert in the psychology of following and followers. He could provide ideas on how these groups recruit, who they recruit, and how they keep their recruits in the fold. With this piece, we could have quite a show.

When I was at school, he tried to hit on me but, once he saw I wasn't interested, he backed off but remained friendly. We'd kept in touch over the years since I graduated, but I hadn't spoken to him in nearly a year. I wasn't sure I'd be able to convince him to take part. The show was tomorrow. He'd have absolutely no time to prepare or even think about what he'd say. He'd be setting himself up to look like a fool or a dolt. And it was two days before Thanksgiving. There probably weren't any more classes this week. If I remembered correctly, he had family in New England and would probably be heading there for the holiday. I was crazy to be hoping he'd be the last piece of my show. I dialed anyway.

"Francine! What a wonderful surprise. How have you been?"

"Not well, Jorge. My husband was murdered last week."

"I am so sorry to hear that. Your husband was an FBI agent, wasn't he?"

"He was a Special Agent, yes. He died in the line of duty."

"That is so tragic. My condolences."

"Thank you, Jorge. I was wondering if you were familiar with my weekly show?"

"I watch *Back at Ya!* every week. It's one of the best things on TV."

"I don't know if I'd go that far, but we try. This week we're moving it to tomorrow night instead of Friday this week. I know it's last minute, but I was wondering if you'd be willing and available to be on tomorrow night's show."

"Really? Me?"

"Yes, I'm doing the show on religious cults and sects in America. I thought you could provide a valuable perspective on group psychology of why some people gravitate to these, whatever you call them. You'd be joining Reverend Malcolm McKenzie and Richard Leitz and me."

"The Reverend? And Richard Leitz is the host of the second best show on TV. It was first until you left. I'd be a fool to say no."

"You're still quite the smooth talker, professor. I want to give you some background and specifics before you say yes. I will specifically focus on an organization called *Beyond Revelation*. It's a shadowy group that I believe are into some illegal activities, but there's nothing we can pin on them. I also believe they're responsible for the death of my husband and several other deaths. I also believe they have something else cooking, something bad. I want to use this show to smoke them out. I'm hoping to force them out into the open so we can get a better idea of what they're about."

"That all sounds fascinating and dangerous."

"I understand if you don't want to take part. It's a long shot on my part."

"I didn't say I wouldn't participate. I don't know if you remember me talking about my brother's son who was a fully indoctrinated member of one of these cults. My brother had to kidnap his own son and hide him away. I took part in the boy's deprogramming. It was a struggle, but we finally got through to him. The whole ordeal tore my brother and his wife, or rather former wife, apart. No one in the family was ever the same.

"After that I intensified my study of the subject and wrote several books. If I can be of any help in this endeavor, I'm in. Just tell me where and when."

"Thanks, Jorge."

I knew I'd have a good show with these three men, but there was one more piece I wanted to insert. If I didn't get him, the show wouldn't suffer, but it would be much more complete if he could join us. I dialed.

"Hello, Robert. How are you doing?"

I filled in Robert Benson on the show and the other participants.

"Robert, I wanted to have you on the show because you have a working knowledge of one of these groups. You believe in its stated core mission but can also provide some insight on how it may have gone off the tracks. You can give some information on how outside influences can permeate and change its course."

When there was no response, I added one last thought.

"I understand your reluctance. You and your family are already under security protection. Coming out publicly would expose you even more. All I know is that some terrible things have happened, including the death of my husband, that I can connect to *Beyond Revelation*. At some point in life, we all have to decide whether to take a stand or stay silently in the background."

I realized that, while I understood his reticence, I was calling him a coward if he didn't stand up against this cult. I'd had enough, however. This man was partially responsible for the success of *Beyond Revelation*. Personal guilt and introspection weren't enough now. He needed to push back along with the rest of us. In reality, I would neither understand nor forgive him if he were to be complacent on this issue.

"Okay, I'll do it," was his response.

21

"Good evening and welcome to *Back at Ya!*. I'm your host, Francine Vega-Allen."

The use of the hyphenated name produced surprised looks on the faces of my guests. Calling myself Vega-Allen wasn't planned; it just came out that way. After Will and I got married, I never even thought of changing my name. Vega was my professional name. That's how everybody knew me. Will never pressed me to change, so I kept it the way it was. I can't say I felt ashamed I didn't adopt his name, but now, looking back, I felt I disrespected him over the past couple of years. It felt right going by this name.

"I'm excited to spend some time with a most distinguished panel. With me are former Presidential candidate Reverend Malcolm McKenzie, Richard Leitz, the host and moderator of the highly acclaimed *Issues and Answers*, Dr. Jorge Fernandez, professor of psychology at New York University and Robert Benson, President and Chief Executive Officer of Benson Enterprises."

I would later find out that The Reverend and Richard and, to a much lesser extent Jorge, let their respective vast social media following know they would be on the show. As a result, the number of viewers of this show dwarfed the numbers of my other shows. In fact, the viewership of this one show exceeded the total of all my shows combined. We not only gained viewers in the New York metropolitan area but also on our website where the show was streaming live. I'm glad I didn't know this going in.

"Tonight, we will talk about religious extremism and its impact on American society, politics, race relations and other aspects of American life. As way of background, I'd like to provide you with my firsthand experiences with a religious organization called *Beyond Revelation*."

"I first became acquainted with *Beyond Revelation* when a friend of mine went missing while she was visiting relatives in a small town in Massachusetts. On the outskirts of this small town was a religious compound called *Beyond Revelation*. When I first drove past this compound, I thought it was a prison because of the high fences topped with razor wire. I had never heard of this group and, while I had no reason at the time to connect my friend's disappearance—as well as other nefarious occurrences—with this group, there seemed to be too many bad things happening to be coincidences.

"Since I knew nothing about *Beyond Revelation*, I went to my friend, Reverend McKenzie, to see if he had any knowledge of what they were about. He did. Reverend, please tell our viewers what you know."

"Thank you, Francine. Before I get into this cult—and that's what it is, pure and simple—I want to offer you my condolences, and those of my fellow panelists I'm sure, for the loss of your husband, FBI Special Agent Will Allen. Special Agent Allen was murdered in the line of duty as he was rescuing the friend you talked about. I'd met Will a few times over the past few years and you could tell from the very first encounter that he was a fine man. My deepest sympathies."

"Thank you, Reverend, and I thank everybody for the outpouring of love and support over the past week. I am doing this show in Will's honor. I'll be counting on each of you to help me keep it together throughout this hour."

"We will, Francine, we will. Now, back to *Beyond Revelation*. This group's stated mission is encapsulated in its name. It is dedicated to the Second Coming of Christ, to the end of days, to the Armageddon. Literally, the group's goal is to prepare its adherents for the aftermath of all that is foretold in the Book of Revelation."

"I noticed you referred to them as a group and a cult, but not a church. I also noticed a fair amount of skepticism in your voice about its mission, or am I imagining that?"

"I've devoted my entire life to the church, and it pains me when charlatans like this play on people's fears and insecurities in the name of religion. It makes my blood boil. So yes, I am skeptical about this cult's so-called mission. There is something going on here, and it's not good. I sincerely doubt that it will prepare people for the rapture. That much I can assure you.

"Unfortunately, they're not the anomaly. There are so many *Beyond Revelation* out there whose mission can be summed up in one word: money."

With the mention of the word money, I was about to bring Richard into the conversation, but Jorge spoke first.

"Money is a big factor but I don't think that's the entire story, Reverend. These movements attract a certain type of people. These are people who are lacking something in their lives, whether it's success, love, fulfillment or whatever, and these cults fill that basic need. I don't think these groups can be lumped together and then given a stereotypical, one-size-fits-all diagnosis."

"And neither can one gloss them up," the Reverend replied. "It's the old lipstick-on-a-pig thing. I have seen the damage they can do. I've never seen one that has changed a person for the better. They always rob from people, if not money, then definitely something more intrinsic to the individual's very being."

"I don't disagree, but the point I was making is that people are more than willing to be taken if they believe they are getting something in return."

"And I contend they get nothing in return."

"But they believe they are getting something, and in this game, perception is ninety-nine percent of reality."

I liked the exchange and sat back to let the two debate. I wanted to involve Richard but, when I looked over in his direction, he was enjoying the exchange and likewise was willing to let it play out. He'd get his say; he was in no hurry to barge in. Since Richard was a master of the talking head format, I trusted his instincts. Robert, however, didn't have any hesitation about interjecting.

"I think you're both right. I gave a lot of money supporting *Beyond Revelation* because I believed in what the order was propounding. And I truly believe it set out in good faith to help people, to give them guidance. However, somewhere along the way they and their message got perverted. Perhaps it was money or some other factor, but it changed."

I made some notes as they were talking. I knew I had to intervene if for no other reason than it was my show. I was about to re-exert myself when something popped into my mind: FAVA TKY BAM 13. What did you mean, Will? Talk to me. And then he did.

"Oh my God!" I blurted out loud.

Everybody stopped and looked at me. The professional thing would have been to beg people's pardon and continue on with the show. Instead, I excused myself and got up and left the studio. Once I exited, I pulled out my phone. I dialed.

"Hello, Jane? It's Francine."

"I was just watching you. It must be important for you to leave your broadcast like that."

"It is. Have you spoken with Broderick?"

"Not since yesterday, why?"

"He ran back out to Montana."

"He's back in Montana?"

"Yeah, he wanted to go back in the compound to investigate further. He found something Will had written on the wall, similar to when you found SLAVE in Massachusetts. It went FAVA TKY BAM 13."

"What on earth could that mean?"

I figured it out. I know what Will was telling me. He was telling me a bomb will explode on Thanksgiving at 1:00 in the afternoon."

"Really?"

"I knew Will. We'd play games like this all the time, trying to stump each other with codes. We once spent an evening making up code words for all the different holidays. TKY, or turkey, was what he threw out for Thanksgiving. He always spoke in military time so 13 would be one in the afternoon. Regarding the BAM, I'll be honest. I'm speculating, but it would fit the profile.

"He'd gotten information on *Beyond Revelation's* plans before he died. That's why they had to kill him as soon as they could, regardless of how public his execution was. But they didn't know Will; he'd always have contingencies. I bet he told Eunice, but she's not capable of communicating right now and probably won't until well after Thanksgiving. He would have left a third way to get the message out. By using Fava, he made it clear it was a message he intended to get to me."

"Assuming you're correct—which I have no reason not to—we're left with a bunch of questions. What bomb? Where is it? Who's the target? I'll definitely look into it, but we have less than two days."

"I know, but Will wouldn't have gone to such lengths to get a message to me if it weren't important."

"We'll work on it and be back in touch soon. Get back to your show."

I walked back in to find Richard leading a spirited discussion about separation of church and state in America but how that line often gets blurred. I took my seat.

"So, what did I miss?"

"Well," Richard responded, "the only thing we agree on is that each of us is 100% right."

We all laughed. We completed the show with no breakthroughs or, for lack of a better word, revelations. Neither did we accomplish my goal of smoking out *Beyond Revelation*. Still, I felt we admirably served Will.

Once the camera stopped rolling, I turned to my panelists.

"I'm so sorry for bailing on you like I did. It was rather unprofessional. Thank you all for picking up the slack."

"It's okay, Francine," The Reverend responded, "You've had a tough week. I'm surprised you held on as well as you did."

"I didn't leave because of that. I had to call the FBI. Something will happen on Thanksgiving, something bad, unless we can stop it. Probably a bomb."

There was a collective gasp.

"Will left me a coded message. The meaning came to me while we were talking. Since we're talking about two days from now, I thought it crucial that the FBI get working on it immediately."

"Do you know where and when the bomb or bombs are going to go off?" Richard asked.

"I know when, at 1:00 in the afternoon. I just don't know where or even if it's one or more."

We talked about this for a few minutes. Each of the men offered do what they could to help, but we had no details, there was nothing they could do.

Everyone left and I remained in the studio, staring off into space, not knowing what to do next. I don't know what I expected to get out of the evening broadcast, but it didn't pan out as I hoped. Now what? I kept expecting Will to speak to me from the great beyond, guiding me like he'd done so successfully for the last three years. I was sitting there when Jimmy, my show's director, stuck his head in. He spoke up, and I jumped.

"I'm heading home now."

"Okay, night, Jimmy."

"Sorry I startled you, Francine. You all right? You seemed rather zombie-like there."

"I was rather catatonic, wasn't I? Just a lot on my mind. Have a good night."

Catatonic? I realized Will wasn't the only one who may have known *Beyond Revelation*'s plans. Eunice may have overheard something. Will may have told her something. That would be like him, having backup plans and contingencies. He'd know that he might not survive, but he had to get the information out. He left me the message but he knew I might never see it. He would therefore use Eunice as a fallback.

The problem is that Eunice hadn't spoken a coherent word since her rescue. She'd been afraid and withdrawn. We should have admitted her into a hospital as soon as we found her, but we thought she'd get better care back here in New York. Even here, where she could get the best care in the world, she hadn't said a word in all this time. She subtly rocked back and forth, staring off into oblivion.

I went to visit her a few times in the hospital. I thought I detected a glimmer of recognition, but I could be deluding myself. I had to go back and see if I could break through.

I called Jonas, asking him to meet me at the hospital first thing in the morning. Perhaps with both of us there, we could get through to Eunice. Jonas was resistant. He didn't want to push Eunice too much; she'd been through so much already. I understood his call for gentleness, but too much was at stake. I knew the type of person Eunice was. For all her bluntness and bravado, she was a kind and caring person who'd want to help if she could. Finally, I put it straight to Jonas.

"What do you think Eunice will think of herself when she's better and she discovers that a tragedy occurred that she could have prevented but didn't because she stayed quiet?"

"Do you really think she'll get better?"

"I do, J.. With all my heart I do. Eunice experienced something that has rendered her mute at the moment, but she's a strong woman. And she's got a rock of a man beside her. She'll come through and, before you know it, she'll be bossing you around again like old times. Perhaps all she needs is a little push from us."

"Okay, I'll see you there at eight."

"See you then, J..."

I went back to my office to close up for the night. Passing by Heather's office, I noticed she was still there.

"Don't you ever sleep?"

"I'll sleep at one minute after one on Thursday when I hear the danger has passed."

"So, you heard."

"Jane called me with a couple questions. She needed a complete list of the states and cities that had *Beyond Revelation* branches. Since I spoke with you, I found a couple more. *The Horsemen* is not far from Fort Lauderdale and the other, *Brimstone*, is in Oregon, near Portland. A lot of money is being pumped into them simultaneously with the others."

"Which all went out shortly after a whole lot of money, most likely Russian, was deposited in the main account."

"Right."

"Any insight as to the target on Thanksgiving?"

"Nothing. Sorry."

"Keep digging. But get some sleep. You'll be no good if you're burned out. That's an order."

"An order?"

"Hey, I'm in charge here, or at least that's what I keep telling myself. Good night."

I wanted to get home to the kids, so I took a car service. It wasn't something I liked to do often. Subways and taxis were always fine with me if for no other reason than to feel the pulse of the city. I didn't have time to dawdle and, as a result, I was home in under thirty minutes. When I walked in, Emma was asleep on the couch in front of the television. I shook her gently awake.

"Hi, Emma. I'm home now. Kids all in bed?"

"Yes, but it was a struggle tonight. They're anxious."

"I don't blame them. Thank you for so much Emma, for tonight and always. You are such a part of this family."

"Thank you, Francine. I love these kids."

"And they love you. If you want to stay here tonight, you're more than welcome."

"No, that's okay. I'll walk home. It's nice tonight."

"Can you be here at seven tomorrow?"

"Yes, I can."

"Thanks."

She reached over and gave me a hug, something we're not used to doing. Emma was in her mid-fifties and never had a family. She made the Allens her family. She was always friendly enough to me, but she was fully ensconced in Will's family by the time I arrived. She exhibited Albert's reticence, seeing me as angling to take over Will's wife's place. The main difference between Albert and Emma was that she was an adult and had a social filter, so she never outwardly displayed her animosity. I constantly told her how invaluable to the family she was and how much I appreciated her help, but she never seemed to warm up to me. The gesture of a hug overjoyed me.

I went upstairs to check in on the kids and then to get ready myself for bed. I looked in on Albert, who was snoring away. I went on to Stella and Rosa's room. It's funny. When Rosa was born, Will and I offered to reconfigure things and maybe even build an addition so that Rosa could have a nursery and Stella could have her own room but Stella insisted that she and Rosa share her room. She loved the responsibility of looking after her little sister.

Both girls were sound asleep, but they were much quieter than their brother. They looked so peaceful and so untroubled that I couldn't resist trying to absorb some of that feeling. I laid down beside Stella. Even though she never woke up, she moved over a bit to accommodate me and let me lie down beside her. I held her in my arms, feeling her steady, deep breaths. Soon my breaths were in sync with hers.

The next thing I knew, light was pouring in through the slats in the blinds, awakening me. It surprised me to look down and see I was still in my work clothes. I got out of bed as slowly as I could so as not to wake Stella. I doubt she even knew I spent the night beside her, but I was so appreciative that I could borrow some of her peace for a few hours. I knew I wouldn't have any peace for some time now; it was a pleasure to ride on hers.

I looked at the clock. Emma wasn't due for forty-five minutes. I had time enough for a shower and a cup of coffee before I'd go to the hospital.

I would wake the kids before I left if they hadn't gotten up on their own by then. I didn't want them to think I hadn't been home last night. I wasn't one to provide anyone with much in the way of stability, but the little I could give the kids I had to give them. And to be perfectly honest, I needed their hugs right now before I headed off into the cold city.

As I was about ready to head downstairs, I was feeling especially vulnerable and weak. I had to force control on myself to keep from going into a full-fledged panic attack. I don't know what made me think of it, but I went over to the safe in the wall. I entered the combination, opened the door and extracted Will's reserve pistol, a Glock 19, along with a fully-loaded magazine.

I thought back to the first time Will gave me a crash course in shooting a gun. We were in Israel, attempting to stop a drone carrying a nuclear device from destroying the City of Mecca. I was shooting out the hatch of a plane in flight. I almost dropped the gun.

Since then, Will took me to a firing range several times. I'll never be a marksman or even what could pass for proficient, but I at least know which end of a handgun to hold.

I stuffed the gun into my purse. It didn't give me the instant courage I was hoping for. However, it gave me an unexpected level of reassurance.

I didn't relish the next couple of hours. Eunice had been through a great trauma and her mental state was her attempt to escape from that world. I would now try to pierce the defense she had constructed and perhaps in the process allow that world to penetrate back into her, opening the old wounds anew. Who gave me that right? Jonas was asking that very question.

I knew that, by questioning Eunice in her vulnerable state, I was jeopardizing my friendship with Jonas, especially if I pushed too hard. But if I was right about the seriousness of what Will was trying to tell me, I had to take the chance. I had to at least attempt to find out if Eunice had any information. Too much was on the line to back down now.

I arrived at the hospital at around ten of eight. When was I ever going to learn? Everybody else on earth had little or no qualms about getting to an appointment ten minutes late. Why did I feel that I was on time only if I were ten minutes early?

Jonas arrived at ten minutes after eight, making my point. Knowing my penchant for being early, he did at least apologize. Knowing what he's been going through, I didn't make a fuss. We took the elevator up to third floor. We stopped at the nurse's station to check on Eunice's status before heading to her room.

"We had a breakthrough, Mr. Clarke. She fed herself her own breakfast this morning."

I didn't realize she wasn't capable of feeding herself. Her scars had been so deep that she had to relearn even a basic behavior essential to survival. I felt worse than I had before about what I was about to do, but I would not turn back.

"That's wonderful. Did ja hear that, Frannie? At first she'd only eat if I fed her. Then she'd allow the nurses and now this. That's definite progress!"

"Yes, it is, J." I responded with as much enthusiasm I could muster.

"Can we see her?" he asked.

"Yes, that would be fine."

We walked into her room. Eunice was sitting in the chair beside her bed. She didn't seem to notice us walk in, but when Jonas spoke to her, I thought I detected a flicker of recognition in her eyes. I could have been trying to convince myself.

"Hi, hon," Jonas chirped. "You look much better today. You remember Francine, don't you? Of course, you do. Francine wanted to see how you're doing. She asks about you all the time. I tell her about how well you're getting but she wanted to see for herself. She wants to ask you a few questions. Only answer if you feel up to it."

I was sorry he said this. I didn't want her to have an 'out'. I wished he had said nothing or, even better, I wished he had coaxed her to answer my questions. But it was what it was.

"Hi Eunice. It's great to see you again. I'm glad to see you're doing better. Keep it up. We want you back with us soon. I have a few questions I need to ask you. Is that okay?"

I didn't get an answer. Nor was I expecting one, but it seemed the polite thing to do.

"Do you remember my husband, Will? He brought you back home, remember? Well, Will sent me a message that something will happen tomorrow, on Thanksgiving Day. Unfortunately, his message got kind of garbled and I don't understand what he was trying to tell me. He's not around at the moment to explain it to me and it's important that I know what he meant before tomorrow. I was wondering if he said anything to you."

Eunice appeared agitated. She wanted to respond, but nothing came out. The harder she tried, the more upset she got.

"Take your time, Eunice. You can do it. I know you can. Please tell me."

The more she tried, the more upset she got. Soon tears were streaming down from her eyes. Her eyes were pleading to tell me, but the rest of her fought it.

"Frannie," Jonas said, "I think she's had enough. She can't tell you what you need to know or she doesn't know. Let's let her rest."

I was about to protest and press her further, but then I relented.

"You're right, J. I'm sorry, Eunice. I didn't mean to upset you. We'll let you rest. I'll come back to see you soon and we'll talk about something more pleasant."

I leaned over and kissed her on the forehead. Then I turned to head for the door. Just before I left the room, I heard one word. She said 'caucus'. By the time I turned around, she had returned to her near-catatonic state. I turned to Jonas.

"Did she say caucus?"

"I think so. That's what it sounded like."

Jonas was excited that she had spoken a word, any word. He had no idea, however, what she was talking about. Neither did I.

22

We took the subway up to the office, bouncing ideas off each other of what she meant, but we were just throwing out wild guesses. Then we went on the theory that we hadn't heard her correctly. We both heard 'caucus' but maybe she said something that sounded like 'caucus' but would have more meaning to us.

The trouble is that there aren't many words that we could think of that remotely sound like 'caucus'. We were making up words and the whole exercise seemed ludicrous, so we gave up.

I went to my office, befuddled and frustrated. We'd had a breakthrough, but we weren't any further along than we were before we went to see Eunice. We had a little over twenty-four hours to figure this out. I needed to call around to see if anyone could help me unravel the mystery. Since I was dealing with a person who was having mental and emotional issues, my first call was to Jorge. He was on Route 91 heading up to Hanover, New Hampshire, when I got him.

"Jorge, it's Francine. Can you talk?"

"Sure, I have hands-free. You're not looking to drag me on TV again, are you?"

"No," I laughed, "it wasn't that painful, was it?"

"Not at all. I had a great time, but I'm not built for the life of television. I'll stick with being a snooty academic living in my ivory tower."

"Well, I'm calling you not only as a snooty academic but also as a trained psychologist."

"Ah, back in my wheelhouse. Fire away."

I described Eunice, her abduction, what I believed she must have gone through and then her subsequent rescue by Will.

"I told you last night that Will had sent a message which I believe pertains to something that's supposed to happen tomorrow. Will was always one for contingencies and back-up plans. He left me the written message but I can't believe he wouldn't try to get word out another way, especially if it's as important as I believe it is. I think he most likely told Eunice what would happen, in case he didn't make it."

Upon saying this, I choked up.

"Take your time, Francine."

I composed myself and continued on.

"I went to see Eunice this morning to see if I could get anything out of her. She was non-communicative the entire time. As I asked her questions, she got increasingly upset but still could not form any words. She was getting so upset that I left. As I was leaving, she uttered one word, 'caucus' and then she was silent again. I turned to my friend, Jonas, who is also Eunice's boyfriend, to see if he heard the same thing. He did. Neither of us could make any sense out of what she meant. I think it's important and I think it's a key to what will happen tomorrow. Since this is a person experiencing psychological trauma, I thought I'd pick your brain to see if you can offer any brilliant insights.

"You did say caucus, as in a group or discussion, right?"

"Yes."

"Now, I'm going to sound snooty and superior here, but you said Eunice had no more than a high school education, right?"

"Yes, I believe she didn't finish high school but later went back and got her GED."

"So, the word "caucus" would be an odd choice to be the sole word to come out of her mouth. It's significant and is also most likely something she recently heard. I'm thinking she was doing her best to respond to your questions, so it may have been that your husband mentioned the word to her. I have to caveat everything I've just told you since I haven't interviewed or examined the subject."

"Understood. You've been very helpful. The whole thing is one big puzzle. This is another piece put in place. Sooner or later, the picture will emerge."

"Glad I could help. Let me know what you find out. Have a Happy Thanksgiving, Francine."

"I'll try. You, too, Jorge. Bye."

I also thought it an odd word for Eunice to spout, if in fact that was the word she said. It was good to receive confirmation of this feeling, even if that confirmation was caveated and speculative. I would proceed on the assumption that Will had used the word 'caucus' and that's where she got it from. Now I had to try and decipher why he said it. I was about to dial my next source when Frank stuck his head in.

"I just wanted to remind you about Thanksgiving tomorrow. I forgot to mention it, but you should invite your sitter. What's her name, Emma? I know in the past she joined you for holidays."

Why can't I be as nice a person as Frank? I should have thought of Emma. Since her mother died a few years ago, she'd been a part of our Thanksgiving. My thoughtlessness was something else to add to my depression for the holiday season.

"Yes, I'll ask her. Thank you for thinking of her. We'll be there at noon."

Frank left. I didn't have time to brood as I dialed.

"Hi Richard. I need your help."

"Francine, nice to hear from you again. What's up?"

I went through the litany and chronology with him, including Jorge's speculation.

"Since you're the smartest person I know, I thought I would bounce it off you. Any theories why Will would use the word 'caucus'?"

"It seems like a singularly strange word for him to use in the situation he and Eunice found themselves. It must have a significance, but for the life of me I can't think of what it could be. Sorry I couldn't be smarter for you."

We talked for a little while longer, but I had to get off the line to figure this out. Time was running out. I called everyone I could think of. I asked Jonas, Frank, Heather, and anybody else who might have a clue. Nobody could shed any light.

It was mid-afternoon when my phone rang. It was Richard.

"Hi Francine, I'm about to restore your belief that I'm the smartest person you know."

"Please do, Richard."

"You ticked off a bunch of cities where *Beyond Revelation* have recently established branches. It got me thinking whether there was some commonality amongst all of them."

"Heather and I have been trying to look for a thread but we came up dry. The only thing we could think of was that perhaps someone in the order owned properties in each of these cities that they could contribute to the cause."

"I have a better reason. I started thinking of those cities in the context of the word 'caucus' and the connection became obvious. Each of those cities is the home of a member of the Congressional Black Caucus. Not just members, but the leaders of the Caucus live in those cities."

"Congressional Black Caucus?"

"Let's go through them:

o Springfield, Massachusetts – Congressman Leon Appleton, Chair of the House Appropriations Committee;

o Sacramento, California – Senator Kendall Dixon, Ranking Member Senate Judiciary Committee;

o Los Angeles, California – Congressman Alton Mapes, House Majority Whip;

o Atlanta, Georgia – Congressman William Jeffords, Chair, House Transportation and Infrastructure Committee;

o Houston, Texas – Congresswoman Manners Jefferson, Member House Intelligence Committee;

o New York, New York – Congressman Randall Adams, Member, House Energy and Commerce Committee;

o Chicago, Illinois – Congressman Wilford Pennock, Member, House Homeland Security Committee;

o Charlotte, North Carolina – Congresswoman Claire Spencer, Member, House Appropriations Committee; and,

o Baltimore, Maryland – Congressman Ezekiel Comstock, Democratic Caucus Chairman."

"Does this mean what I think it means?"

"It means that *Beyond Revelation* is looking to wipe out the country's Black legislative leadership."

"Holy shit."

"That about sums it up. And you know what else? After talking with Heather and reviewing the info she gathered, I believe Russia is behind this. Their money is funding a virtual race riot. They are out to destroy us."

"All under the guise of religion."

"Like you said, holy shit. I gotta run now."

"Thanks, Richard. I have some calls to make."

"I'll call some people myself. I know some folks on The Hill who should be able to help thwart this. It's the day before Thanksgiving, so I'm sure I'm going to get a lot of voicemails"

I hung up and dialed anew.

"Jane, it's Francine. I think I know what'll happen tomorrow. *Beyond Revelation* is looking to assassinate as many members of the Congressional Black Caucus as they can. It looks like they've been planning this for years, establishing compounds near Caucus members' homes. They've chosen Thanksgiving Day because of the higher likelihood the members will be home."

"How did you come to this conclusion that this is what they're up to?"

I described the thought process Richard and I went through.

"It's the only thing that makes sense. Even if it doesn't make sense, I don't see how it can be ignored."

"You're preaching to the choir, Francine, but I don't know what I can do."

"What do you mean?"

"What I mean is that I'm skating on very thin ice at the FBI. I was Will's person and the sharks are circling, hoping to pick off anything associated with Will since his death. They know I helped you get out of Cuba. They blame you and me and Broderick for Will's death by sending him on some fool's errand that you made up."

"I made up Eunice being kidnapped? I made up everything that's happened that can be linked to *Beyond Revelation*?"

"In a lot of minds here, the answer is yes. They see you as a publicity-seeking newshound who manufactures stories to advance your own agenda whether it's Destroy Mecca, the Zyklon Killer or *Beyond Revelation*."

"Do you believe that of me, Jane?"

I was practically in tears.

"No, not in the least. But I'm such a minor person. I'm a splattered bug on the FBI's windshield that needs to be spritzed a few times and then slapped at by the wipers until I'm gone."

"But what if I'm right? What if we do nothing and, come one o'clock tomorrow afternoon, there are 10 or more dead Members of Congress? How can we live with that?"

"The FBI will live very well, thank you. They'll look very involved and on top of things as they respond after-the-fact to this tragedy. If it comes out that they received advance warning, they'll work very hard to find someone or something to blame. It'll probably be you and me."

"What can we do? Anything?"

"Rather than work up though the chain here, I'll call the Special Agents in charge of the respective regional offices. Perhaps I can raise the threat level in their minds enough to get some agents or at least local cops to patrol the Members of Congress residences."

"Anything you can do, Jane. It's getting late."

I tried thinking of any other angle to sound the clarion, but nothing came to mind. Then I remembered John telling me about helping a Congressman get a summer place on the lake in town. It wasn't one of the Black Caucus members and I don't believe the Congressman was even in the same party as the Black Caucus members, but perhaps he could sound the alarm though a different channel. I dialed John's cell phone and got no answer. I called his home. A child answered.

"Hi, is this Marcus?"

"Yes, who's this?"

"This is Francine Vega. We met a couple of weeks ago. Remember when we had breakfast together up at the Top Hat?"

"I remember."

I expected him to be a little more excited at talking to someone he had recently met. I was sensing something was wrong.

"Marcus, is your grandfather there?"

"No."

"Who's there with you?"

"Nobody."

"Is Sara there but no adults?"

"Uh-huh."

"Did you have school today?"

"Half-day."

"How do you usually get home?"

"Grandpa picks us up, but he didn't today. We walked home. Where's Grandpa?"

Now I knew something was wrong. John would never leave his grandkids unattended, not even for a minute.

"I don't know, but we'll find him. I promise you. I want you to do something for me."

"What do you want me to do?"

"I want you to make sure all the doors and windows are locked. Can you do that? I'll wait."

I could hear him scurrying around the house. A few minutes later, he was back on the line.

"I locked everything."

"Good. Did your grandpa give you instructions on what to do in an emergency?"

"He said we should call 911."

Remembering that Chief Dumont had gone missing and that Officer Sykes might very well be on *Beyond Revelation's* payroll, I did not think this to be a good idea.

"Usually that's the correct thing to do, but in this case it might not be. Does your grandpa have a friend, maybe someone from church, who could come and pick you up until your grandpa gets home?"

"There's Mrs. Silverberg. She's very nice."

"Do you think you can find Mrs. Silverberg's number for me?"

"Sure."

He put the phone down. I could hear him clattering on the computer.

"It's (508)555-2997."

"I'll call her right now and then I'll call you right back, okay?"

"Yes, that's okay."

I dialed the number and I got a machine. It wasn't unexpected since so many people travel for Thanksgiving. I thought I would leave her a message, just in case she was around and just out shopping or something.

"Hello, Mrs. Silverberg. My name is Francine Vega. I'm a friend of John Foster's. I just spoke with his grandson, Marcus, who is alone at John's house with his sister. I've been trying to reach John but have been unsuccessful. I was wondering if you could go over to his house and pick up the kids until he gets back. Please call me back if you get this message. You can reach me at 212-555-1122. Thank you."

I wanted to get a sense of urgency across, but I didn't want to sound panicked. I called Marcus back.

"Hi Marcus, it's Francine. I couldn't reach Mrs. Silverberg. I left her a message but I don't know if she's in town or is travelling for the holiday. Is there anybody else you can think of?"

"No."

I sensed a note of stress in his voice.

"That's all right, Marcus. You're doing fine. It's understandable that you wouldn't know many people in Fairbrook since you've only lived there for a very short time. Did I tell you I have an eleven-year-old son?"

"No."

"His name is Albert. I think you'd like each other. I think you're very much alike. Albert is a very responsible young man who will do all the right things like watch out for his sisters. Are you like that?"

"I think so."

"I know so. Your grandpa told me about how proud of the fine young man you're turning into."

"He did?"

"You bet. Now he's counting on you to take care of your sister. Don't let anybody in except your grandpa, Mrs. Silverberg or me. I'll be there in a couple hours. Do you understand all that?"

"Yes."

"Good. I'll see you in not too long."

After asking Heather to get me a car service and making my 'what seemed like a daily call to Emma to see if she could stay with the kids for the night', my next call was to my new buddies Eddie and Willie.

"Hi, Eddie, this is Francine Vega. Do you remember me? You gave me the ride to Montana."

"Oh yeah, hi Francine. Did you get together with your husband?"

"He was murdered right in front of me in Montana."

"What?! I'm so sorry. Wow."

"Eddie, I need your expedited services yet again. Much shorter trip this time. I need to get up to Massachusetts as soon as possible. Little town, not far from Springfield. Can you help me out? Again, I'm willing to pay anything. I just need to get up there immediately."

"Yeah, there's a small commercial airfield just east of Springfield I fly into all the time. I got a plane all fueled up and ready to go. I gouged you last time so just going rate this go-round."

"Thanks. You know if there's a car rental service there?"

"Yeah, I'll call up there and have a car ready for you when you land. Why don't you text me your driver's license and credit card info to ease the process?"

"Speaking of credit cards, you okay with that instead of a cashier's check this time? I'm really in a hurry and can't stop at a bank."

"No problem."

"One last question. Will I be able to make phone calls while I'm airborne?"

"You bet. Nothin' but state-of-the-art in my birds."

"Eddie, you're a doll. See you in a half hour or so."

I had absolutely no idea what I would do once I got to Fairbrook. I was glad I thought to grab Will's Glock. Would I have the courage to use it on another human being if I had to? After seeing my husband gunned down in cold blood, the answer came back to me a resounding yes.

I would have loved to have had some backup. I toyed with dragging Heather along. She had a relationship with John; she'd been to Fairbrook; she was competent and could think on her feet. But it could get dangerous. I had no right to drag her into this. In the old days I would have asked Jonas to go up with me, but his hands were full with Eunice. So here I was, alone.

I called Jane to fill her in on my destination. Given our last conversation, I didn't have any hopes of her accompanying me. I just thought it prudent to let someone know where I was and what I was doing.

Jane's phone went directly to voicemail. I left a message.

"Hi Jane. Something's happened to John Foster. He's gone missing, leaving his grandkids alone. That's something he'd never do. I'm heading up to Fairbrook. Hopefully, I'll get there in time. I'd love to have you join me. We'll be taking off in a half hour from Teterboro. I'm leaving the same message for Broderick. I don't know what luck you've been having, but I have a new plan to head off tomorrow's legislative murders. I'll call you from the air to fill you in."

I had to keep reminding myself that I couldn't forget about the forest as I was staring at a tree. I was so concerned about John Foster I had to force myself to remember that the following day *Beyond Revelation* was looking to assassinate ten or more Members of Congress. Richard was making calls and Jane was doing her part, but I didn't think they were getting anywhere. I had to do more.

I arrived at Teterboro. As Eddie promised, the plane was ready to go. We boarded, and the pilots went through their takeoff procedures. Eddie gave me the phone I could use. I dialed the Reverend.

"Reverend, this is Francine."

"How are you today, my dear?"

"I need your help. Would the President take your call?"

"Yes, he would. At least I think he would."

"That sounds rather, what's the word, indefinite."

"I suppose it is. Let me explain. After the election the President and I were cordial. Then, after my brother was sacked by State, I tried calling him to give him a piece of my mind. He wouldn't take my call. I called him numerous times, but each time, he refused to talk to me.

"Then, I got word he was going to the National Prayer Breakfast. I wasn't going to take part, but once I heard he would be there, I got myself a seat. I walked up to him to confront him about my brother and he greeted me like a long-lost friend. I told him how pissed I was that he fired Edward. He claimed he knew nothing about it. He said he'd take care of it.

"I told him how pissed I was that he wouldn't take any of my calls. Again, he claimed ignorance. He said he'd look into why that happened. He gave me a number to call, a private direct line. I thought I'd try it out, so I called him a couple weeks ago to wish him a happy birthday. This time he took my call. We had a most congenial chat, after which I followed up on Edward. He repeated that he would take care of it but didn't give any details. I thought he was blowing me off. Then he said he's thinking of putting together an interfaith outreach group and thought I might be an ideal candidate. I guess I'm in good graces again, but like you said, indefinite. I'm willing to try again. What do you need?"

"I need you to call him and convince him to talk to me. He still has it out for me after last year but I'm not getting anywhere in stopping tomorrow's carnage. I need to talk to him and have him direct the FBI and other agencies to get off their asses."

"Let's try it."

He put me on hold. I sat there with the phone pressed up against my ear. Five minutes extended to ten, which extended to fifteen. I was wondering if we'd been disconnected. I was also wondering if I'd get to talk to the President before the flight ended. It was only a fifty-minute flight.

At one point, Eddie came back to see if I needed or wanted anything. He saw me looking serious, holding the phone to my ear but not saying anything.

"On hold?"

I nodded.

"You want anything?"

I shook my head.

"You look so serious. Who you waiting to talk to, the President?" he asked facetiously.

I nodded.

"You're kidding, right?"

I shook my head.

"Okay, sorry. You don't have to tell me. I'm just nosy by nature."

Just as he was saying this the line came back to life.

"Hello, Ms. Vega."

"Thank you for agreeing to take my call, Mr. President."

Eddie's eyes opened a mile wide when I said this. He hurried back to the cockpit.

"First off, I heard about your husband's death. My condolences."

"Thank you, Mr. President."

"The Reverend and I had a long chat. He gave me an overview of what you want. It all sounds far-fetched, if you ask me."

"I don't blame you for believing that, sir. If I weren't living this nightmare, I'd believe what I'm saying is outlandish. Mr. President, the way I look at it is that the worst that could happen is that, if I'm wrong, we've wasted some government resources and perhaps ruined a couple Thanksgivings. But if I'm right, we'd have prevented a national tragedy. We could have race riots on our hands. This is a calculated plot to destroy us from within. I don't want that to happen; I'm sure you don't either."

"I thought you believed me to be the spawn of a Nazi."

"A good person can have any parents. Regardless of what your father did, I never believed you had that in you. You've devoted a life to the greater good."

"The Reverend said you believed I was carrying out a vendetta against you."

"It's sure seems like it, sir."

"I'm afraid I vented my feelings about you for a period of time after the election. I have some people willing to implement what they think I want. You, unfortunately, were my Thomas à Becket."

"You weren't responsible for my station being punished and me ultimately being fired?"

"No, I didn't know about that until The Reverend advised me."

"Or firing his brother?"

"Again, no."

"Or stranding me down in Cuba?"

The President laughed.

"I wasn't responsible for that either, but that is a petty revenge worth remembering. It's a good one."

I joined in, laughing with him.

"Francine, do you know the reason I felt such animosity towards you?"

"The millions of votes I cost you?"

"Actually, I got over that right away. What I resented was that you were the last person to see my son alive. And to top it all off, I knew he loved you more than he did me. I resented you."

"I thank you for that admission, sir, and I'd like to talk with you at length about it, but for now I'd like to know whether you will order the steps to protect the legislators."

"Yes, yes I will. I'll order the Members of Congress and their families moved to secure safe locations tonight. From the way it sounds, you are still uncovering new outposts of this cult so to be safe, I'll extend this order to all members of the Black Caucus. We'll then monitor the sites and apprehend the assailants before they can hurt anyone."

"Thank you, Mr. President."

"No, thank you, Francine. I resisted even talking to you, but The Reverend is very persuasive. He reminded me how much my son valued your input. How could I not do the same? We'll be in touch."

I tried calling Jane next. She answered, but the connection was very poor. I could only understand every third word. She said "Don't", "Wait", and something about a "fool". It sounded like she was in a car. That was the total of everything I could glean from the conversation. I'd call her back when we landed.

The plane landed soon thereafter. As promised, a rental car was there waiting for me.

"Eddie, thank you so much for your help."

"You're involved in some serious shit, aren't you?"

"You better believe it."

"I hope you're on the side of the good guys."

"Yes, we're the good guys, Eddie, and so are you. Watch the news over the next day or so, you'll see what we're working on."

"I'm glad I could help. Be safe, okay?"

"Will do."

I checked my phone as I got into the car. There were a bunch of messages but only two seemed of note. The first was from Mrs. Silverberg. She said she'd picked up the kids. She was concerned about John and wanted me to call her with an update. At least I knew the kids were safe. That was one less thing I had to take care of. I'd call her when I got a chance.

The second call was from Jane.

"Francine, under no conditions are you to do anything alone. I know I can't order you, but this is an order. It's much too dangerous. Don't be stupid. Help is on the way."

I was about to heed her advice. I had my husband as a cautionary tale about going it alone. Then I reminded myself what I use to guide myself in such situations: WWRD? What Would Rosa Do? My mother went toe to toe with drug lords, slum lords and corrupt cops because it was the right thing to do. She never backed down in the face of death threats, especially when somebody needed her help.

I hope to raise my daughter, my Rosa, with the same fearlessness and goodness of heart as her namesake. But if I couldn't meet the challenge myself when a good man needed me, what kind of example would I be? John Foster might be dead, but he might be alive. I couldn't afford to hesitate. I put the car into drive and proceeded east on Route 20 toward Fairbrook. I would not stop until I got to *Beyond Revelation*.

23

It was around three in the afternoon and, at this time of year, nighttime would approach quickly. While the cover of darkness had its advantages, I would not relish wandering in the woods by myself at night. It's not an ideal place for a city girl to be. I stepped on the gas, hoping to arrive during daylight.

I arrived in Fairbrook a half hour later and drove past the razor wire-topped fence. I didn't want to park in front of the compound and give myself away. I remembered a vacant house a quarter mile down the road. I'd park my car in the driveway there and then run back.

I made my way back to the compound and then followed the fence back to where I remembered the entrance was. The place looked abandoned, but I knew—or more precisely sensed—somebody was still there.

The whole time I kept to the underbrush and trees rather than the path, hoping nobody would detect me. I kept looking over my shoulder to see if anyone was following me, but I saw no one. It made for slow going and, by the time I made my way through the gate and up to the main building, dusk had settled in.

I worked my way over to a window and peeked in. There he was. John was tied to a chair in the middle of the room. I could make out that his nose was bleeding, but that's all I could see from my vantage point. I was figuring out my next move when I felt something hard at the back of my head. I knew immediately it was a gun.

"We were just talking about you," said a Russian-accented deep male voice.

"Alexi Slatzky, I presume. We really didn't get a chance to chat when you were at my home."

There was a pause. He was trying to determine how I knew his name. Then he decided it didn't matter as he brought the barrel of the pistol down hard on my temple. All went black.

When I opened my eyes once again I was tied to a chair next to John. I didn't know how long I was out, but I'd say it was at least an hour, maybe two. I looked over at him. He was worse off than I first believed. They had beaten him badly. At first I couldn't tell if he was alive or dead, but then he coughed.

"John...John Foster, can you hear me? It's Francine."

He nodded.

"Good. Can you speak?"

"Yes, I can."

It was barely a whisper, but it was there.

"What are they after?"

"How much...you know... about tomorrow."

The door opened at that moment as two men, each holding pistols in their right hands, walked in and closed the door behind them.

"Much as I'd love to stay and get even better acquainted, we have to move on. Unfortunately, you two have to remain behind, or at least your bodies will."

"Don't you need to know how much I know?"

"Boss was worried that your husband may have said something, but we got word from our man in Montana that he died before you got to him."

"You know that for sure, do you?"

"Doesn't matter."

"Congressman William Jeffords, Congresswoman Manners Jefferson, Congressman Randall Adams, and Congressman Wilford Pennock, to name a few."

"How? It doesn't matter."

"It does to me. At least I know I still have it as a journalist."

"Glad I could make you happy in your last moments."

They both raised their guns and aimed them at our respective heads. I closed my eyes. I heard not only the sharp explosion of gunfire but the sound of glass breaking. Not feeling anything, I opened my eyes. I saw Slatzky and his accomplice crumple to the ground. A second later the door burst open as Jane and Broderick rushed in. Once they determined there was nobody else in the room, they came over and untied us.

"John needs to get to a hospital," I said, noting the obvious. He had lapsed into unconsciousness since I had my brief conversation with him.

"You should, too," Jane noted.

I had taken a hard thump to the head. It also occurred to me that for the first time in what seemed like weeks I didn't have an emergency to attend to. The President had assured me that the FBI was taking my warnings seriously. The FBI would protect the Members of Congress. *Beyond Revelation* did not know that we knew as much as we did so we'd be able to catch them at each location. Despite a throbbing headache, I felt good about things.

Broderick, Jane and I had to carry John out to the car. He wasn't a small man and he was totally non-responsive. It took a long time to get him out there, but we finally managed and laid him down on the back seat.

Jane spoke to me while Broderick punched in 'nearby hospitals' into his phone.

"I should yell at you for going in alone like you did. I'll save it for later when you're feeling better."

"I appreciate that."

"I've got to call this in and hang around to give a statement."

"I'm not leaving you here alone."

"I'll be fine. You need to get checked out."

"People have a way of dying or disappearing in this town. Until all of *Beyond Revelation* leaders are found and brought to justice, it's not safe to be out here alone."

"Ya think?"

"Ha ha, hilarious. But I'm serious. I'm not going anywhere."

"Okay. Rick, you know where you're going? I know you have to get back to the City so get Mr. Foster settled and then you can head back. Francine and I can get back on our own."

"Check. Have a Happy Thanksgiving. Ms. Vega."

He got in the car and sped off. Jane made her call to the Springfield FBI office, who referred the call to the State Police. They had a barracks in the next town and would send a trooper right over.

While we were waiting, Broderick called. He said the doctor had examined John and he would be okay. They beat him badly and had some broken bones, but he would recover completely. It would take some time. In the meantime, they heavily sedated him. He'd be out all night.

I saw my phone, purse and keys on a table off to the side. I went over to grab them.

"You can't," Jane said, "you'll be compromising the crime scene."

"Jane," I implored, "these are hardly crucial pieces of evidence. Do you know how many hoops and circles I'll have to jump through to get them back, especially in a separate state?"

She thought it over for a second.

"I'm getting soft in my old age. Okay, grab your stuff but be sure not to touch the table. Explaining how your fingerprints ended up way over here will turn into my headache."

I pulled a tissue out of my pocket and used it to pick up my belongings. I felt glad that Jane and I had developed enough of a history for her to show some flexibility regarding my request. I was especially relieved I wouldn't have to explain why I had Will's handgun in my purse.

"Right over" on Thanksgiving Eve meant that a trooper would not arrive until two hours later. In the meantime, the FBI Special Agent heading the Springfield office made his way to us. He had known Will and was very fond of him. He was also familiar with the ongoing investigation of *Beyond Revelation*. As a result, the Trooper, when he finally arrived, surveyed the scene, took our information and sent us on our way. That was it. We walked to my rental car.

"See, I told you I'd be fine. You didn't have to stay, but I appreciate that you did. I still think you should go to the hospital to get checked out."

"All I want is a night's sleep and then I'd like to get back to my family. If I'm having issues in the morning, I'll go to the hospital then."

"Let's grab a bite and find a place to stay for the night."

"I think it would offend John if we didn't stay at his house overnight; he's like that. I'd also like to go into town to explain what happened to his friend that's watching the kids."

"Sounds fine to me. I passed one of those country inns. We can eat there."

We ate at the restaurant Jane had noticed. Given all that was on my mind, I'm surprised I appreciated how wonderful a meal it was. Then we headed to a box store to get some basics for an overnight stay. I had grabbed my ever-present overnight bag before taking the flight, but Jane ran out once she got my message. The only thing she had a chance to grab was Broderick. She didn't have so much as a toothbrush.

Then it was back to John's house. He had shown me where he had hidden the key.

After we ate, I located Mrs. Silverberg's house. We went there to fill her in on John's condition. It shocked her that I arrived on her doorstep with an FBI Agent, but relieved to hear that John would be all right.

I asked if she could take care of Marcus and Sara for a couple of days until the hospital released him. She said they'd be welcome for as long as was necessary. Again, I sensed she was someone John had known his entire life. Small town life, there's nothing like it.

The guest room had two beds, so I asked Jane if she was okay with sharing the room. Even though I was positive John would find it an affront if we didn't use his place, I still had a funny feeling about taking too many liberties. Jane was fine. She looked startled when we walked in and saw all the vintage firearms on the wall.

As we were getting ready for bed, Jane got into lecture mode, admonishing me for my foolhardy solo venture which almost ended in the loss of my life. She was correct in everything she said. Still, however, I probably would do the same thing again if an identical situation arose. I thought it wiser to say nothing and just take my lumps.

I slept well that night, which is strange because I never sleep well in a new place. I slept so well, in fact, that I didn't wake up until close to ten. I guess I needed the sleep.

It took me a minute to reorient myself, but it wasn't long before I smelled coffee wafting up from downstairs. I went down to find Jane making some toast.

"I hope Mr. Foster doesn't mind that I made myself at home."

"I doubt that he would mind, considering you saved his life. I'm going to take a shower and get ready. Then I'd like to go to the hospital and check on him. Then we can head back to the city. We should be back in time to spend a chunk of Thanksgiving with our kids. I'll give Frank a call and let him know we'll be later than expected."

"Sounds like a plan. I'd like to talk with Mr. Foster, if he's up to it, to see if he has any additional light to shed on *Beyond Revelation*."

When we arrived at the hospital, they'd transferred John from the emergency room to a semi-private room. I took that as a good sign. The front desk tried barring us from seeing him since we weren't family. All

Jane had to do was flash her FBI credentials and explain that John was a witness in an ongoing criminal investigation for the gates to open.

We walked into his room and John looked at us with a dazed look, which I took to be the residual effects of the sedatives they'd given him.

"Hi John, you look better than the last time I saw you."

"I just woke up. I wanted to call you but I didn't have my phone and couldn't remember your number."

"It's a good thing I showed up then, isn't it?" I breezily asked.

"The reason I wanted to call you was I remembered something from yesterday."

"What was it?" Jane asked.

"I overheard them talking. They switched the site of the Massachusetts attack. They won't be attacking Congressman Appleton in Springfield."

"Who are they going to attack?"

"The Speaker of the House, Patricia Foley. She's having Thanksgiving with a relative in Amherst."

"Do you know where in Amherst or the timing?"

"Sorry, that's all I know."

"I'm glad you're okay but we have to run."

Jane voiced this before I could, although I would have probably put it a bit more gently. John didn't take it badly.

"Yes, go." He responded.

We hurried out.

"We have to get the Speaker out of there." I said.

"I'm not sure we can. It's quarter to twelve. We have to go on the assumption that they'll attack on the same schedule as the others at one o'clock. They'd want the maximum effect of a terrorist attack. The assailants may already be in place. I'm assuming your colleagues are laying in wait at the other sites, waiting for one o'clock to trap them. Any plan to extract the Speaker may alert them. They might speed up the attack."

"What do we do?"

"We don't do anything. I'll head up to Amherst and make some calls to alert her. You'll stay here."

"You don't even know where to go."

"And you do?"

"No, but I can find out as we head there."

She realized she was mounting a losing argument. I was coming along. She didn't have time to argue.

"Let's go."

We got in the car and headed towards Amherst. It was about a forty-five-minute drive. I pulled out my phone and dialed. As I waited for the connection, I turned to Jane.

"It's a good thing you let me take my phone, isn't it?"

She smiled.

"Heather, it's Francine."

"Hi Francine, Happy Thanksgiving. How's John?"

"Happy Thanksgiving to you, too. He's doing better. I need your help and I need it quickly."

"Sure. What do you need?"

"The Speaker of the House, Patricia Foley, has a relative in Amherst, Massachusetts. I need you to find out who it is and the address. We're on our way to Amherst right now and we'll be there in about forty minutes. We need it before then. Can you do that?"

"Shouldn't be a problem."

She hung up.

"I predict she'll have the info in seven minutes. Care to make a prediction?"

"Eleven minutes."

I looked at my watch. Five minutes later, my phone buzzed.

"I sold you short. I thought it would take you seven minutes to get the answer. Jane had absolutely no faith in you at all. She said eleven minutes."

"The Speaker's daughter, Emily Serafides, and her husband and three kids live at 8 Smith Street in Amherst. Her phone number is 413-555-7896."

"Got it. Thanks Heather. You heading over to your parents' place?"

"Yeah, I'm nervous."

"Don't be. You're a terrific person, and they love you. That's all you need. Have a good time. Give them big hugs and never let go. Have a drumstick for me."

24

Jane was already dialing the number as I hung up with Heather. A few seconds later, a woman came on the phone.

"Hello, this is FBI Agent Jane Kelly. Is the Speaker there? It's vital that I talk with her immediately."

A few seconds elapsed. I could hear only Jane's side of the conversation, but it was easy to figure out what the Speaker was saying.

"Madame Speaker? This is FBI Agent Jane Kelly. My badge number is 817437. After we hang up, I recommend you contact the FBI Headquarters to verify my identity. I'm calling to alert you to a threat to you and your family. Is the head of your security detail available?

"You what? You gave them the day off to be with their families? We can address that later, but for now have somebody make sure that all the doors and windows are closed and locked. Stay away from all windows and if there is a basement, lock yourself down there.

"No, you have to stay inside. The threat may be outside your home right now. If you try to leave, he or she may accelerate the attack. Our information points to a one o'clock attack, unless we can stop it.

"Yes, you are correct. The attack is coordinated with the attacks on the Black Caucus. I believe those threats are being addressed, but we only now received the information that you are also a target. I will be there in ten to fifteen minutes. Right after I hang up with you, I'll call the Amherst cops to help us. I would have called them earlier, but I only now got your address.

"It's immaterial how I found your address and number. I'm the FBI; it's what we do. If I found it, so can the assailant. You must take this threat seriously.

"Good, we'll see you soon."

Jane turned to me.

"I can't believe it. She gave her security detail the day off. What was she thinking? Why would she ever do such a thing? Let me see if I can raise the local cops."

I didn't respond. I knew she was talking rhetorically, using me as a sounding board. I could tell she did not relish dealing with local law enforcement. When it came to her profession, she did not suffer fools gladly, which was probably why she and Will got along so well.

Jane was driving as fast as she prudently could without getting stopped. She knew that we could get out of it in no time with a flash of her badge, but even that would have wasted time we didn't have.

Jane was having trouble getting through to the Amherst Police. At one point she was screaming into the phone that she was FBI and it was an emergency. It wasn't until we passed the huge sign announcing we were in Amherst, incorporated in 1759. She finally drummed it into a desk sergeant's head that he needed to send an armed squad over to the Speaker's daughter's house immediately. With this delay, we would beat them there. We would be on our own to handle any threats we came upon.

We made the turn onto Smith Street and there was Number 8 on the left. It was a two-story white clapboard typical house with a small, well-manicured lawn and a couple substantial maple trees in front. We parked a few houses down from the house so we could view the entire street. The street was empty. There appeared to be no threat. Maybe I was wrong. We had tried to get word on the status of the Black Caucus, but we heard nothing. For all we knew, the whole thing could have been a figment of my imagination.

The time was 12:55 and nobody had shown. That was a good thing. I'd rather the world thought me a fool for pushing this whole conspiracy than for someone who did nothing that resulted in people getting killed.

The clock turned to one, and still there was no assailant. Neither were there any local cops. Were we the only ones who didn't take Thanksgiving Day off? I was about to relax when a man came around the corner. He looked to be in his upper twenties or early thirties, but besides that, it was hard to discern anything about him. He was wearing a long, bulky overcoat even though it was rather temperate for a late November day in Massachusetts. He was also carrying a shopping bag that bulged a great deal.

He was walking directly toward 8 Smith Street with a nervous yet steady gait. As he got closer, his features became sharper to me. I pulled out my phone and scrolled through my pictures until I got to the ones Jonas had given me when I first started down this mess.

"That's Carl, Carl Rutledge. He's Eunice's cousin."

Before Jane could stop me, I got out of the car and walked towards him.

"Carl? Carl Rutledge?"

He looked in my direction but didn't say a word. He kept walking toward Number 8. I veered to intercept him.

"Carl, my name is Francine Vega. I'm Eunice's friend."

With the mention of her name, he hesitated.

"You better get away, Ms. Vega. I have to do this and I don't want you getting hurt."

"I don't want anyone getting hurt."

"If I don't do this, they'll kill Lynn. And they'll kill me as well."

He didn't know his wife was already dead.

"I'm here with an FBI agent. We'll protect you."

"You can't."

With that, he opened his coat to expose a vest packed with C-4 explosives.

"They dropped me off a couple blocks from here. They're monitoring the police bands. If they don't hear that 8 Smith Street has been blown up, they'll detonate this belt and they'll kill Lynn. I don't know who's in there and I don't care. I have to save my wife."

"But your wife is alive, Carl. My husband, who is an FBI Special Agent, rescued her. She's safe and sound. So is Eunice."

I thought it wiser to lie to him. In his state of mind, I didn't know if he'd take drastic action—including blowing himself up, and me with him—if I told him the truth straight out that they'd killed the love of his life.

"But they told me she was with them."

"They lied to you, Carl. They would do anything to get you to do what they want. And once you deliver this package, do you really think they'd let you or Lynn live?"

"I guess not."

"Let us help you."

Just then three Amherst police cruisers careened around the corner. They came to a stop strategically surrounding Carl and me. Two cops jumped out of each car with guns drawn as they hunched down behind the doors of their vehicles. One of the cops had a bullhorn and began barking orders at us to lie on the ground with our arms spread. Instead, I instinctively jumped between the cops and Carl. Perhaps it was the mother in me as my protective instincts came to play. Perhaps I figured they'd be less likely to shoot a Black man if they saw a white woman in the way. I hated thinking that way, but I also thought it was a realistic appraisal of the situation.

Jane jumped out of the car and pulled out her badge as she strode purposely toward the squad cars.

"FBI! FBI! FBI!" she kept screaming. "Stand down, you morons. Who's in charge here?"

I was worried one of the cops would turn on this ranting woman and start firing. Luckily, cooler heads prevailed as the officer with the bullhorn ordered his men to stand down. The officer who gave the orders walked over to Jane. They shook hands and talked for a bit as Jane looked over at me. Then she called to me.

"What's the situation, Francine?"

I told Carl to stay where he was and I walked over and spoke with Jane and the officer, James Jenkins. I laid out what had happened. Jenkins looked petrified when I mentioned about Carl both holding a bomb and being strapped into one,. Jane took the facts in and showed no outward reaction.

"Stay here," she ordered as she headed over to Carl. Jenkins and I readily complied.

She chatted with Carl and then carefully took the bag from him. She looked inside and then reached in. Next she carefully opened the front of Carl's coat and examined the vest. I thought I could see a smile crease her lips as she shook her head. She pulled a wire and then a second one. After that, she unbuttoned the vest and took it off Carl. She put the vest on top of the bag. Then she walked Carl over to us.

"Boy, are they amateurs."

"I didn't realize you had bomb defusing experience." I noted.

"One of my many talents."

She turned to Officer Jenkins.

"We've minimized the threat, but those are still real explosives and should be removed by your bomb squad."

"We'll get the State Troopers for that, but my guys can keep it isolated until they get here. What now? Shouldn't we take this man into custody? He threatened a Member of Congress and endangered other people who wander onto this street."

"He's a victim," I interjected. "He was kidnapped along with his wife. He was coerced into doing this. They threatened to kill his wife if he didn't comply."

Jane looked at me and was about to say something, but I shook my head to tell her not to say anything. Carl was still in earshot and we needed to be tactful in how we told him his wife was dead.

"I agree," Jane said, "we'll take Mr. Rutledge into FBI custody, but he should be taken to a hospital. Can you take care of that, Officer Jenkins? Great. We should let the Speaker know that the danger has passed."

"Before we do that," I suggested, "I was wondering if we could do something. Carl mentioned to me that his captors were monitoring police broadcasts. Is there a way to let them think Carl was successful? We want to catch these guys and if they think they were successful, maybe they'll become complacent. But we have to do it soon."

Jenkins thought about it for a second and then got on his phone to his superiors to see if there was a way to transmit a distress message over their radios without setting off a panic. While he was trying to work this out, Jane called the Speaker to let her know there was longer any danger. Then she called back to the New York office to alert them that, if *Beyond Revelation* used the same modus operandi in all the planned attacks, there should be people of color approaching the houses of Members of Congress. She wanted the agents at each of these locations to know that these people are innocent victims and not to shoot until there was absolutely no other alternative.

While she was making these calls, I had nothing to do. While I was standing there, Carl approached me.

"Can I talk with Lynn now?"

I'd nearly forgotten that I'd lied to him. Now I had to break the truth to him.

"Carl, I'm sorry but I had to lie to you. Lynn's dead. I'm so sorry."

"She, she can't be. No, I don't believe it."

"It's true, Carl. I'm telling you the truth. She's dead."

"What happened?"

"She was found in the woods in Fairbrook. She took a severe blow to her head."

"I see. Do you know if she suffered?"

I wanted to tell him she didn't suffer, that she died instantly and felt no pain. However, I couldn't lie to him again.

"I don't know, Carl. We couldn't get a straight answer from the coroner. Once this is over, we'll get you an honest answer. I'm sorry I can't tell you any more than that."

"Why did you lie to me?"

"I didn't know what you'd do. I was afraid you'd hurt yourself if you found out with a bomb strapped around you. I was considering my own safety. I was very close to you. I'm sorry."

He considered what I said for a moment.

"You're right. I would have blown myself up. Do you know if Eunice is alive?"

"Yes, she's alive."

"Well, that's good."

He sat down right there in the street and cried. I let him. He needed it. A female paramedic, who I hadn't even seen arrive, came over to Carl, put a blanket around him. We both helped him up and led him off to an ambulance. He was still crying as the ambulance drove away.

The Speaker had asked Jane to come in. She wanted to thank her in person for her actions. Jane told her she had a phone call to make and then she'd come in. As soon as she hung up, she turned to me.

"Speaker Foley wants to meet the person who helped save her life. Since you're even more responsible than I am, let's both go in."

We walked up to the door and introduced ourselves. The Speaker invited us to join her for Thanksgiving dinner. I originally wanted to get back to my kids for the holiday but when Jane said she wanted to stay in the area for the next day or two to take part in questioning Carl, I agreed to stay. I remembered Will telling me that we owed it to our children to be everything we could be, to see things through to the end. I couldn't cut and run at this point. After calling the kids to talk with them and checking with Emma to see if she could stay with them for a day or two more, we agreed to have dinner with her and her family.

I have to say that the journalist in me was pleased to be cultivating a contact as powerful as the Speaker of the United States House of Representatives. Take that, Allied Broadcasting, I thought.

25

Over the next few days, Carl recovered enough to tell his story. I asked Jane if I could participate in the questioning and his deposition. My request was denied, but Jane promised to keep me apprised of what he said and perhaps slip me a copy of his transcript. She thought I deserved that much.

Confirming Karen Gagnon's account, four men roused Carl, Lynn and Eunice from their sleep at around two in the morning. After a brief struggle, the three were injected with a drug. He woke up on the floor in a room at *Beyond Revelation*. His ankles were shackled to the wall. Lynn and Eunice lay on the floor beside him, likewise in shackles. He had no idea what time it was or even what day it was.

Over the subsequent days, the three of them were threatened, beaten, debased and ordered to perform whatever services the members of the order asked of them. In short, they were slaves.

They separated Carl and Lynn the second day into their captivity. He never saw her again.

There were two additional African-Americans there: one man, Kendrick, and one woman, Frieda. They likewise were kept as slaves. Carl did not know what happened to them.

Every minute of every day, their captors fed them a constant diet of white supremacy. They were told they were inferior, and that idea was continually reinforced. They were confined to one building, every minute of every day. They were threatened with severe punishments, including death, if they even attempted to escape or contact the outside world.

It was only two days before Thanksgiving when Carl learned *Beyond Revelation* had a specific purpose for him. They were sending him to Springfield to deliver his explosives, but then one of the leaders rushed in with exciting news. There was a change in plans. They were heading to Amherst.

Carl had no idea who were to be the targets in either city. All he knew was he had to deliver the package. Otherwise, they'd kill Lynn and Eunice. He had no way of knowing that they'd killed Lynn weeks earlier or that they had shipped Eunice out to Montana. It was unclear what intentions they had for Eunice, but they had no purpose for her in Massachusetts. Perhaps she would be useful down the road. In the end, she'd be murdered as well.

Jane questioned Carl whether he was aware of any Russian involvement in *Beyond Revelation*. He said he had heard some men talking in a foreign language. It may have been Russian, but he couldn't swear to it.

They also asked him if there was any talk about the Second Coming, Revelation, The End of Days, etc. Carl said he didn't hear any talk of that sort, but he wasn't particularly listening for it so it wouldn't have made much of an impression if he had heard it. The only message that resonated was the message of white supremacy.

By Saturday, Carl had told them everything he could. Jane thought we could head back home. She'd keep in touch with the local FBI office if anything new came up, but it was time to head back.

John was being released from the hospital that morning and we hung around until he got back home before we left. His friend had to help him out of the car. My heart ached for him and all he went through. We walked out his front door to greet him.

"Francine! Jane! I'm so glad you're still here. I can't thank you enough for looking out for my grandkids. Esther Silverberg told me about your help in getting them over to her. Thank you."

"I just recognized you would never leave them unattended."

"Oh, and while I'm at it. Thanks for saving me."

As usual, John Foster had his priorities straight.

"So, fill me in on what happened. Was *Beyond Revelation* successful in killing any Members of Congress? There hasn't been any news on it one way or another."

"Because it's an ongoing investigation, we've released nothing publicly, but you have a right to know the details," Jane responded. "We thwarted every attack. They were unsuccessful and no Members of Congress were hurt. Unfortunately, four of the people coerced into delivering the bombs were killed. I sent out word that these people were victims but some units didn't receive this notice until it was too late. They were viewed as terroristic threats.

"In two of the cases, local law enforcement shot them dead. They didn't have a Francine Vega to recognize the man and save the day. In the other two, *Beyond Revelation* sensed something had gone awry and set off the vests. Luckily, nobody else was in the vicinity when they blew."

"Do you have the names of all the messengers?"

"Yes, I believe I do."

I scanned down the list and then I came on the name I was looking for, Vernon Boyd. I nervously looked to see if he made it or not. There were no notations next to his name. He's alive. His father will be so happy. I made a note to give him a call once I got back to New York. Odds are the authorities would have called him, but I've seen too many communication gaps to make that assumption. Mr. Boyd and I had a personal connection, so it seemed the right thing to call him.

After making sure John was settled in, we headed back. Jane dropped me at home. I was eager to spend time with the kids.

26

Albert was back to being a little standoffish when I got back home. I didn't blame him. Emma had done her best to make a proper Thanksgiving for the kids, but they missed their father. They resented me for not being there for them. I can only imagine how tough Christmas was going to be.

We all did our best to settle back into the rhythms of our lives over the next few weeks. Albert and Stella were back in school. I made their lives as normal as possible. I devoted time and energy to fulfilling my long-neglected duties at the station. What killed me the most was not picking up the phone every once in a while to see how Will was doing or to get one of his pep talks or advice. Every so often, I'd close my door and have a good cry. I'd feel somewhat better afterwards, but it wouldn't last.

I wasn't sure how long Westbrook Broadcasting could last but every time I sat down with Frank over the next couple of weeks, he advised me of new things that were happening and new stories we were working on. The station was turning somewhat of a corner. A large part of the success was Frank's dogged determination. The man was tireless and was always coming up with new, fresh ideas. I also found that we were getting new leads for stories from the most unlikely of sources. I couldn't figure out why we were so lucky but then I realized what was happening. My new friend, Speaker Foley, was referring her contacts my way.

When we had Thanksgiving dinner with her, I chatted about my career and the new network I had to create because I'd been blacklisted. I told her how the US Government had stranded me in Cuba. I told her about my conversation with the President, who revealed that the entire affair had a bit of a Thomas à Becket air to it with the President's aides viewing me as the "meddlesome priest". She said she had come to know and like President Kent in the short time he'd been in office. She said she'd put in a good word with him for me.

She asked many probing questions about Westbrook Broadcasting. I thought we were simply making conversation, but now I understand she was figuring out how she could best help me and the network. Her paying me back for protecting her and her family was to refer news sources my way. I was now getting leads before the networks on many stories out of Washington. Some nights we had so many breaking stories it was difficult fitting them all on the air. This is a problem we'd love to have all the time.

Jane showed her cynical side when I told her about the Speaker's help.

"The Speaker has a reputation for being a smart, cautious person. She probably doesn't want you blabbing about how she dismissed her security detail. Her opponents would characterize it as a bonehead move. If she's that lax with her own security, they'd say, guess how lax she'd be with the country's security."

I thought Jane was going a little too far, but then again sometimes I have a tendency to give people a little too much credit and discount ulterior motives. The truth, as usual, is probably somewhere in the middle.

Jane kept me apprised of the progress in bringing *Beyond Revelation* to justice. I wanted justice for Will but apprehending Caleb Smith would not bring my husband back. I would go on with my life either way.

The FBI had captured a number of *Beyond Revelation* members, but not anybody they could definitively say was a ringleader. They couldn't pin any crimes on the people in custody. These people all had the same story: they joined for religious reasons. They were awaiting the Second Coming. They wanted their souls prepared as the end approached. There was no way to tell whether they were sincere or lying.

The authorities needed to capture Caleb Smith, but he was elusive. Nobody even knew what he looked like. The only existing pictures of him were decades old. He'd appear before his congregants only via video. No one could swear they'd met him or that the person on the monitor was Smith. In addition, the man in front of the camera sported a long beard. Whether it was real or fake was anybody's guess.

It took time, but the FBI and all of law enforcement woke up to the fact that *Beyond Revelation* was a real threat to the safety and security of the country. Smith was on the run now. Even if he assumed another identity— as a chameleon like Smith does—he had lost his base. Anything that was left of the entire operation was underground now.

I would severely doubt that the Russians were thinking too fondly of Caleb Smith right now. They had poured a lot of money into his venture hoping to disrupt America and all it stands for. He failed and now the FBI, and probably the CIA, were investigating the Russian connection.

Caleb Smith was a wounded animal, not a dead one. He could still be dangerous. I was sure he had connections and influence. I never discount the power of charisma. The Reverend had only met him once many years ago, but he spoke in awe of Smith's abilities and magnetism.

Personally, though, I had to move on. The kids had to move on. I couldn't consume myself with a desire for revenge. And, since I'd already done all the damage I could to him and his cause, I had to proceed as if he was no longer a threat to me and mine.

27

I had to plan my next segment of *Back at Ya!* and I didn't really have any ideas on what to talk about or who the guests would be. I went into Frank's office to brainstorm with him. Neither of us had any brilliant ideas. We hadn't left ourselves a lot of time for research or to develop ideas, so we decided to go with something basic. We went with a year-end recap of the first year of the Kent Administration.

President Kent had gotten a few major pieces of legislation through Congress. He'd proven especially adept at working constructively with the opposing party. Legislation to address climate change, to update federal sentencing guidelines and to improve roads and bridges throughout the country, to name a few, had been enacted. It seemed like a safe show that could be put together relatively easily.

I needed to line up a few guests. I called Richard. He'd analyze the financial and economic implications of Kent's policies. I knew I was pressing my luck since he was just on and I didn't know what sort of repercussions he faced from that appearance. Nothing ventured, as they say, so I called him. To my surprise, he agreed! Also, he asked if I would consider being on his show sometime early in the new year. I said a resounding yes.

Next I wanted someone from the social justice realm. Given my heritage and my mother's constant quest for justice and opportunity for the less fortunate members of society, I wanted to include a spokesman from that arena. The name that popped into my mind was Diane Marrow. Diane was a well-known—and controversial—affordable housing advocate and organizer. I met her the previous year at a presidential fund raiser. She was dynamic and funny, all the while being totally committed to her cause. Plus, she professed to have been in awe of my mother. How could I not include her? I called her and she said she'd love to participate. I was on a roll now.

I could have gone with the three of us but there was one more call I wanted to make. I called the White House Communications Office. I would love to have someone from the Administration participate, especially since I expected it to be positive to the President. I had to hope I was no longer the persona non grata I once was. After my conversation with the President, I hoped that was the case, but you never know whether the word had trickled down.

I spoke with a relatively low-level staffer in the office. He took down all the information and logistics. I made it clear that, while we'd love to have someone in person, we could do a video or even just an audio hookup if that was more convenient to whoever took part. I could hear him tapping away on his computer as I spoke. He said he would discuss it with his superiors and get back to me. Oh well, I thought. At least I tried.

Confident I had set up my weekly show, I went to work concentrating on today's lineup and broadcast. We had had our daily meeting first thing in the morning to set everything up for the day and to discuss the content of the day's shows and the evening news broadcast. However, news is a constantly morphing beast, and we always had to keep our eyes and ears open for any breaking news that would throw the entire schedule out the window.

My phone buzzed about an hour after I called the White House. I was heavily into my preparations and I toyed with letting the call go to voicemail, but I glanced at the screen. It was a 202 number. I didn't think it could be the White House getting back to me since I had called them on the office land line, and that was the number I gave them. This call was coming in on my cell. I answered it anyway.

"Please hold for President Kent."

A second later, the President got on the line.

"Francine, the Speaker told me how you saved her butt."

"The FBI did, anyway."

"Don't be modest."

"Well, thank you, Mr. President."

"I understand you're doing your upcoming show to give me a first-year report card."

"That's as good a summary as any."

"And you were looking for someone from my Administration to take part?"

"Yes, sir."

"And when is it?"

"Tomorrow night, Tuesday, at nine."

"Okay, it's on my calendar."

"Your calendar, Mr. President?"

"Would you rather have somebody else from my office?"

"No, I'm just a little stunned, that's all. We'd love to have you."

"That's good to hear. I'm afraid I must do it remotely. We'll set up a camera feed. I hate doing phone call-ins. I'll have my Communications Director call you to work out the logistics. Who else will be on?"

"Richard Leitz and a community organizer from here in the City, Diane Marrow."

"I'm not familiar with Ms. Marrow but I know Richard. I was on his show a couple times over the years. He's intimidating, but fair. It all sounds good. Until then, bye Francine."

I hung up stunned. I walked down to Frank's office. He was immersed in some programming issues so I only had half his attention.

"Hey Frank, I got the participants for tomorrow's show all locked down."

"Shoot. I'm listening."

"Richard Leitz will be here."

"Richard. Good."

"Then I asked Diane Marrow. She's a housing and community organizer from here in the City. I met her last year. She's very dynamic and will be strong on social issues that we get into."

"Don't know her. I'll trust you on that one. Anybody else?"

Frank was typing this whole time. Anybody else, I would have been offended but I knew Frank well enough to know that he could multi-task very well and was taking in everything I was saying.

"The last person will operate remotely."

"If we have to."

Frank was never a fan of remote tie-ins. It was essential in our business, but he'd seen too many times when the audio has not worked or some other glitch ruined the continuity of a program.

"The participant's name is Peter Kent."

Without looking up, Frank responded.

"Name sounds familiar. He's with a think tank, right?"

"Not exactly. His work address is 1600 Pennsylvania Avenue."

That was enough to get Frank's total attention as he stopped his typing.

"You got THE Peter Kent?"

"The THE himself. I called hoping to get a White House official to take part. An hour after I called, Kent called back, telling me he'd be happy to take part. I can tell you're as stunned as I am."

"Who's next for you, the Queen?"

"Don't count me out!" I retorted as I retreated from his office.

I went back to my office to compose myself. My little cable show would have the President of the United States on it, I kept telling myself. I was on such a high and then it crashed around me as I instinctively grabbed my phone to call Will to share my excitement. I wondered when I would stop doing that. I also wondered if I would ever get to where it didn't tear out my guts whenever I made that mistake.

I was about to head home when Jonas stuck his head in.

"Got a minute, Frannie?"

"Sure, J., have a seat."

"I got good news and bad news."

"Bad news first."

"Eunice's cousin Carl tried to kill himself last night."

"Oh my God."

"He couldn't take the loss of Lynn. He took a bottleful of pills. His neighbor happened by and found him. They got him to the hospital just in time. He'll be okay, but he's in a psych ward now. He's got a long haul to go."

"I guess anything would be good news after that. What is the good news?"

"They're sending Eunice home tomorrow. She's improved so much since you saw her. She's talking again. At first it was halting, but now she's almost back to the old Eunice. I can't shut her up."

"And you sound like you're loving it."

"You bet. She's talking with a therapist. She's even told me what happened to her."

Jonas paused for a second.

"You don't have to go on, J. As long as I know she's getting better; that's enough for me."

"Frannie, they raped her. They beat her. Then they lynched a man in front of her. That was when she snapped. How does anybody recover from that, Frannie? How can she ever recover?"

"I don't know, J. But if anyone can help her heal, it's you."

"Well, one thing's for sure."

He pulled a little black box out of his pocket. He opened it to show me the ring.

"As soon as she's better, I'm going to ask her to marry me. I've dragged my feet for too many years."

"It's about time!"

"Oh, one more thing. You already know this, but your husband was an absolute hero. He was just monitoring *Beyond Revelation*, but then when he saw Eunice, he let himself get captured so he could get her out of there. He didn't want to go in without backup, but he couldn't wait. Eunice was in trouble, and he acted without hesitation. Just thought you should know."

I went home and asked the kids if they wanted to go out for dinner. There was a little diner around the corner that the kids loved. Will and I would take them there at least once a month. This would be the first time we ate out together since Will died and I was nervous. What if they associated the diner with their father and didn't want to go there with just me?

They were excited to go to the diner. I had to smile when Albert ordered a grilled cheese sandwich. I thought back to John's grandson who wanted a grilled cheese for breakfast. Initially, the waitress refused because it wasn't on the breakfast menu but the owner overruled and the grilled cheese appeared.

We all had a great time together. I was relieved. Albert was animated as he talked about a new classmate who had just moved into the neighborhood. The spirit of Will hovered over, around and through us, but we were learning to move on, just as he would want us to do.

We walked back home from the diner. Rosa was asleep and I carried her home. Stella was ready to sleep and couldn't wait to get into her pajamas. Still, she helped me put Rosa in her pajamas and get tucked her in. Then she got herself ready for bed. I kissed them both goodnight.

Albert was still somewhat wired and wanted to stay up. I relented and told him he could stay up for another hour watching videos or playing games in his room. The only stipulation was that he had to be quiet to not disturb his sisters' sleep. He readily agreed.

I went to my room. Totally exhausted, I needed a good night's sleep. I had a busy day coming up. I walked in, threw my purse on the bed, turned on the light and closed the door behind me. As I turned, I jumped. There was a man sitting in the chair at the desk by the window. He had a sawed-off shotgun on his lap.

"Good evening, Ms. Vega. Got the kiddies all tucked in, I see."

I gradually regained my composure.

"Officer Sykes, this is a surprise. Or, outside of Fairbrook, do you prefer to go by the name Caleb Smith?"

"You are a clever girl, aren't you?"

"I try."

"We all try; you succeed."

"I used to date a man who did nothing but quote movie lines. It was my job to guess the movie. It was rather tiresome, if you ask me."

"Well, your cleverness has ruined everything, for the moment anyway."

"I don't know. We've thwarted all of *Beyond Revelation's* plots. You're a wanted man by the FBI and I can't imagine the Russians are too thrilled with you. Any way you look at it, you're screwed."

A sly smile appeared on his face.

"We'll see."

He saw me glancing around the room. He brought his shotgun to a more ready position.

"Don't even think it, Francine."

I fixed my gaze back on him.

"So, we're on a first name basis now. That's nice. Tell me, Caleb, what's next?"

"After I'm done here, I have to get back up to New England to oversee some unfinished business. Oh, Caleb isn't my real name either. Frankly, I've gone by so many names, it's getting difficult to remember my given name, but that's no never mind."

" 'After you're done here' I suppose means killing me. You've left quite a trail of bodies—Karen Gagnon, Lynn Rutledge, my husband, to name a few—haven't you? And whatever happened to Chief Dumont? For what, Russian money?"

"The rubles were nice, but they were to support of the cause. It was always for the cause. Those unfortunate people, and you, were just in the way."

"The cause. You mean preparing people for the Rapture?"

He chuckled.

"That was a brilliant ruse, if I say so myself. We had some people at each of our compounds who believed they were preparing themselves for the Second Coming. There are so many gullible people, aren't there? We needed them for authenticity but kept them segregated from the real purpose of the order. I was so convincing that this was the true purpose of *Beyond Revelation* I got my IRS non-profit status. That allowed me to stockpile without the fear of government intrusion."

"What is your 'cause', if you don't mind me asking?"

"I thought it obvious and I don't mind telling you since you won't be around much longer. It's White America, an America you could only be a part of as a menial servant, I'm afraid. Your Cuban blood must have some inferior races mixed in there. We need to return to our roots where everyone knew their proper places and stayed there. I would have liked to accomplish my ends through a more peaceful approach, but we were born in a bloody revolution. We shall be reborn in a bloody revolution."

"The Reverend said you had a charisma and could turn a phrase with the best of them. I see now he was correct."

"Ah yes, The Reverend. He had such promise, but he's betrayed us of late. Pity."

Caleb Smith raised his shotgun.

"I could really use John's father about now."

"What the hell are you talking about?"

"John Foster told me about how his father saved his life. John was about to be killed when his father came out of nowhere and shot John's attacker in the back of the head."

"That's not going to happen," Smith laughed.

The door flew open. Standing in the doorway was Albert. He was holding an old hunting rifle I didn't know Will owned. He was trying to aim the gun at Smith, but it was too heavy for his eleven-year-old arms as it shook and wavered.

Smith turned when the door opened. Startled at first, he smiled as he surveyed Albert.

"That's way too much gun for you, boy."

As he was saying this, I jumped on the bed, grabbed my purse and pulled out Will's Glock. While I rolled over to be on my back, I flicked the safety off. Sensing my movement, Smith turned back to me to fire, but he was too late. I leveled the Glock at him and pulled the trigger twice. Both bullets struck him squarely in the chest. He staggered back and fired once, but the shot went wild, shattering the window. He banged against the bureau and fell to the floor.

I lay there for a second as my adrenaline levels receded. I then jumped out of the bed and ran over to Albert. He was still standing there, staring straight ahead, attempting to raise the rifle. I pried the gun from his hand and let it drop to the floor. I held him tight.

"My brave boy. My brave, brave boy. Your Dad did such a fine job with you."

I kept my hands on his shoulders as I held him away from me so I could look in his eyes.

"There's no more danger. He can never hurt us again. You've had to endure so much in your young life. You should be worried about your next Pop Warner game or a social studies test or wondering why your opinion of girls is changing. Instead, you've had to become a man much too quickly. I'll try to do a better job of protecting you so you can just be a boy for a little while longer. Would that be okay?"

He numbly nodded. I pulled him close to me. I walked him back to his room and tucked him into bed. I sat by his side until he fell asleep. I checked on the girls. Despite three gunshots, neither had awakened. I felt silly for admonishing Albert earlier that he had to be quiet so he wouldn't disturb their sleep. These two could sleep through anything.

I went down to the kitchen. I poured myself a glass of red wine. Then I sat down and dialed Jane's number.

"Hi Jane, it's me. Can you get over here right away? I just shot Caleb Smith."

"You what? Where? How?"

"In my bedroom. He was waiting for me when we got back home from dinner."

"Are you okay? The kids?"

"Albert's pretty shaken up. He saw it happen. Otherwise, we're all fine."

"I'll be right over."

"Should I call the NYPD?"

"No, I'll do it. I know who to call."

"Okay, see you soon."

The doorbell rang forty minutes later. I walked Jane up to my bedroom. She kneeled down to examine the body. Will's Glock was on the bed and his hunting rifle was on the floor where I had pried it from Albert's grip.

"Should I tell you what happened?"

"Why don't we wait until Detective Martinez arrives. He should be here any minute. Let's go back downstairs."

"There is one thing I feel I should tell you now."

"That is?"

"I think there'll be another attack."

"What makes you say that?"

"Caleb Smith was so certain he would kill me he felt he could reveal his plans to me. I think he wanted to rub it in. He wanted the last thing on my mind to be I failed, I hadn't stopped him after all. He told me that after he killed me he—and I quote here—still had to get back up to New England to oversee some unfinished business. And he said I had—and again I quote—ruined everything, for the moment anyway. He seemed confident that whatever he was about to do would put him back in the Russians' good graces. He didn't seem at all concerned about the FBI or any other domestic law enforcement."

"Do you have any idea what he was looking to do or where or when he was going to do it?"

"That's all I have. Somewhere in New England."

"Is there still a danger? Will someone else carry on in his absence?"

"I don't know."

"Not much to go on."

"Sorry."

There was a knock on the door. I opened it and Detective Martinez walked in and introduced himself. We sat down and I went through the events of the evening along with my history with Caleb Smith/Andy Sykes or whatever his real name was. Jane offered her insights and concurrences where she could.

Martinez examined the body and the crime scene. A short while later the coroner's office and forensic team arrived to process the crime scene. I don't know if it was because we were dealing with a detective rather than a beat cop, but I was much more impressed with the NYPD than the previous time when Alexi Slatzky broke in.

Martinez took my statement, asking an occasional question to clarify a certain point, but otherwise he just let me talk. Again, Jane interjected points on Smith's background and his being a fugitive from justice.

The forensic team said they were through, as did the coroner's assistant. An ambulance had arrived in the meantime. Smith's body was placed on a stretcher and taken away. Martinez said his report would reflect that this was a home invasion and the killing was justified self-defense. He said the ultimate charge would be in the hands of the District Attorney's Office, but he didn't see any reason why they wouldn't accept his recommendation. We shook hands, and he departed.

"Jane, thanks...again."

"My life was a lot more boring before I met you."

"Would you like a drink?"

"I could use one. Thanks."

We went back to discussing Caleb Smith's last words. Perhaps he just wanted to scare me before he killed me. Perhaps I could be over-analyzing what he said. Perhaps he was blowing smoke; there was nothing more planned. Perhaps the final *Beyond Revelation* scheme died with Caleb Smith. However, we both believed that *Beyond Revelation* had one last big event planned for us. The problem was the where, when and what of the attack. Nor did we know who the target was. We agreed that we would think about it overnight and then talk again the following day when we were fresh.

Jane left, and I got ready for bed. I grabbed clothes and headed for the guest room. If nothing else, the window in my bedroom had been blown wide open by Smith's blast and it had gotten cold outside. There was also Smith's blood on the floor. I just didn't have the inclination or energy to clean it up. It would have to wait until tomorrow.

28

Despite being so exhausted, I woke up before any of the kids. I was nervous about Albert's mental state, both when he woke up and long-term. I wanted to be awake when he got up to assess him. The boy had gone through so much already and then, last night he witnessed a man being killed.

It relieved me when he came downstairs and the first thing he asked was whether he could have pancakes for breakfast. I agreed but then got nervous. Given how little I'd been home lately, I was worried whether we had the ingredients. Thank goodness for Emma. Left to me, there wouldn't be an egg or as much as a glass of milk in the house. I made up the batter.

Albert appeared to be normal; kids were so resilient. To be sure he was okay, I made a note to set up an appointment with the therapist affiliated with his school.

After I fed Albert and Stella and sent them off to school, Emma showed up to take care of Rosa. I headed off to work. I still had no brilliant insights as to when and where any attack might occur. My first task was to set Heather to work on the problem.

I wanted her to dig up everything she could on Andy Sykes. We had always had somewhat of an interest in Sykes because there appeared to be some level of linkage between *Beyond Revelation* and him, but we never saw him as a key player. Now that we know he was Caleb Smith, we sharpened our focus on him.

Per my discussion with Jane, the FBI looked into Smith, but my money was on Heather to come up with answers. Her skills are that great, but it's not just that. Details such as obtaining a warrant have never constrained Heather or kept her from doing what she needed to do. Also, the FBI was more likely to focus its resources to pursue hard leads, not hunches. Jane and I were giving the Bureau's analysts nothing but speculation. Heather, on the other hand, would dive deeply into anything I asked her to do, speculative or real.

Caleb Smith had always been very careful to preserve his anonymity, thus remaining elusive. I hoped Andy Sykes was not as careful. In this persona, which he was assuming would be a temporary stopover that could be erased as quickly as it was established, perhaps he left more of a trail than he did as Caleb Smith.

One burning question I had is how he got his job in the Fairbrook Police Department. In my brief exposure to Andy Sykes as a police officer, he did not have much in the way of experience although he was in his forties. Nor did he have any kind of rapport with Chief Dumont. Somebody foisted Sykes on the town and its police department from outside. Who was it that put the pressure on? Was that person connected to *Beyond Revelation*?

Heather left my office with her usual committed zeal. She would not rest until she got answers to my questions. Hopefully, her answers would provide a key to what they had in mind and where they planned to act. I only wished we knew how much time we had.

There was nothing more I could do. The case was in the hands of Heather and Jane, at least for now. I had to concentrate on my show. We had our daily lineup meeting and then I sat down with Frank to go over some questions I'd be asking the President.

We did not dare do much to promote having the President of the United States on our talk show. There was too big a risk that his appearance would fall through. Even though we did not advertise it, word spread when The White House included the President's participation on his official calendar. Once his calendar was released, word spread like proverbial wildfire. Our *Back at Ya!* website received over 300,000 hits in two hours. Our site nearly crashed, but it was worth it. My show was finally on the map.

Heather came in with news.

"I dug up how Sykes got his job. There's a letter scanned into the Fairbrook personnel database from Captain Michael Parker to Chief Dumont. Captain Parker is Deputy Director of the Massachusetts State Police. He ordered the town to hire Sykes. There's nothing overt in his threat, but there's enough there to read between the lines. Sprinkled throughout the letter were strong hints of things like withholding funding to the town for State training and equipment if they didn't hire Sykes.

"I then checked Parker's financials and found a recent purchase that is very curious."

I gave Heather one of my looks. One of these days she was going to get caught hacking into places she shouldn't legally be.

"Don't worry. I always cover my tracks. Anyway, a month ago Parker purchased three dozen detonators, the kind that can be set off remotely via a radio or cell phone."

"Three dozen?"

"Yes, my reaction exactly. I'm no expert, but I bet that many detonators could blow up a lot of C4. Since this guy's a high muckety-muck in the State Police, this purchase wouldn't come under much scrutiny."

"No, it probably wouldn't. Anything else of note?"

"Not really. He took the ferry from Woods Hole to Martha's Vineyard over the Thanksgiving weekend."

"I'm reading something into everything I hear, but I know people who like to go to places like the Vineyard over the holidays to get away from the crowds. Holy shit, I'm on the air in two minutes. I better run."

I thought about having Heather call Jane to tell her about the detonators, but I reconsidered. Jane will want to know how she came across this information and I didn't want Heather incriminating herself. I'd call her after my show.

Back at Ya! exceeded my wildest expectations. The one thing I was worried about was that the President would intimidate the show's participants, myself included. My worries were unfounded. While Richard, Diane and I were all supportive of President Kent's policies, we weren't shy about expressing ideas about areas where we felt those policies fell short.

The President welcomed the criticism. He acknowledged the shortcomings but offered valid political and practical reasons he could not go as far as he would like. In others, he gave a strong counterargument, pointing out flaws in the points being made. I lost track of the issues we discussed. Gun control, climate change, foreign trade, the Middle East, manufacturing jobs were some of the topics that came out. By the end, we were all exhausted but exhilarated.

"Our show is coming to an end, I'm afraid. I want to thank President Kent, Richard Leitz and Diane Marrow for participating. I don't think I'm overstating it when I say that this was one of the most informative shows I've ever had. Nobody here will contradict me if I state that each one of us will walk away much more informed than when we walked in. Now, each of you is welcome to make some final remarks before we close out. Diane, why don't you start us off."

Diane reiterated my thoughts and gave a nice recap of the night along with a promise to keep working hard. Richard said the same things.

"Mr. President, do you have any parting words for us to ponder?"

"Have you ever met a politician who didn't want to have the last word? Thank you, Francine for the opportunity to talk with you and Diane and Richard. You and Richard I knew from a previous life, but it was a revelation talking with Diane. Hearing what she does every day to improve peoples' lives was a real eye-opener for me. All too often, politicians get cloud-level observations of the world and its issues, but we forget there are people attached to and impacted by those issues. Taking part in forums like this should be a requirement for all political leaders. Abraham Lincoln used to hold what he claimed were his 'public opinion baths' where the doors would be open to anybody who could come in and give the President a piece of their mind. While many of these people were there to land a government patronage job, Lincoln also got to hear firsthand the concerns of the people. That's what tonight was for me. I hope for more in the future. Before I leave, I want to give a shout out to the former first lady, Michelle Harris, whose birthday is tomorrow. Make sure that husband of yours gives you something good!"

And that's how the show ended. President Kent had a few parting off-camera pleasantries to each of us, after which his feed went blank. Richard and Diane stayed around for twenty minutes, still on a sugar high from the show, just like I was. After they left I wrapped up a few things and then headed home.

I gave Jane a call while walking to the subway. I told her about the detonators. I was glad she didn't inquire how I got that information. She trusted the information I gave her. She'd worry about its provenance later if it were to be used in a trial.

Like me, the purchase of all these detonators and their possible use concerned her, but neither of us had a clue as to the when and where. We agreed to talk again in the morning.

When I got home, Albert was watching a movie while Stella and Rosa were playing some nonsense game together. Technically, they were all up well past their bedtimes but, on nights I worked late, I was a little more lenient. I was being selfish. I liked to see my children before they went to sleep.

Emma headed home. I worked on getting the kids to bed. Albert surprised me by asking me what the President was like.

"You watched my show?" I asked him with surprise in my voice.

"Yeah."

"Well, the President is a good man. We had our differences in the past, but that seems to be behind us now. Perhaps someday you'll meet him."

He was very excited at the prospect.

We all finally went to bed. My mind was still racing from the day and from not being able to figure out when and where *Beyond Revelation* last strike would occur. Finally, I fell asleep.

I woke with a start and looked at the clock. It was 2:37AM. I grabbed my phone and dialed. After six rings, I was afraid the phone would go to voicemail. A groggy voice answered.

"Francine, I know we said we'd talk in the morning, but this is ridiculous."

"Jane, I know who the target is. I know when and where will happen."

Jane still had cobwebs in her head.

"What are you talking about?"

"*Beyond Revelation*. The detonators. The attack will happen today, on Martha's Vineyard. It's big."

Jane was finally awake and alert.

"Start from the beginning."

"In closing the show, the President wished the former first lady a happy birthday. It's today. When he was President, the Harris family would often spend special occasions on Martha's Vineyard, in the Oak Bluffs section. One thing I didn't mention to you because I didn't think it relevant at the time was that Parker took the ferry over to the Vineyard over Thanksgiving weekend. He wasn't there to celebrate the holiday. He was there to plant bombs."

"Plant bombs?"

"He knew that the Harris family would be there on her birthday. Think about it. President Harris is still the strongest symbol the Black community has. Plus, Oak Bluffs is a thriving, predominantly African-American neighborhood on the island. Having a conflagration there would send quite a message to White Nationalists everywhere."

"We have to get the former President and first lady out of there."

"It might be like the Speaker. They may be watching the neighborhood and if they see them leaving, they might detonate the bombs."

"You're right. Let me get on the horn. We have to warn them about not going out. Then what we need to do is get some heavy-duty frequency jammers there and some dogs to sniff out the bombs. I'll get back to you."

I couldn't go back to sleep after that. I tried to read a book but I couldn't concentrate so I threw an old movie DVD into the machine. I watched that movie for a half hour. I was more tired than I thought. The next thing I knew, I heard the kids milling about. It was seven thirty.

I called Jane to see if there were any updates. The call went to voice mail. I got myself ready for work.

By the time I got to the office, I still hadn't heard from Jane. I put national news on. Thankfully, there were no major stories, nothing from Martha's Vineyard. It wasn't until two in the afternoon that Jane called.

"We did it, Francine, we did it! I called my boss after I spoke with you. Boy was he pissed hearing from me at three in the morning, but thanks to you, my track record's good of late, so he heard me out. I laid it all out for him. After he took it all in, he got the former President on the phone. Then he got some agents and dogs to the Vineyard. It was a bit of a logistical nightmare, but he was able to get a military transport.

"The first thing they did was to jam all radio and cellular transmissions in the Oak Bluffs neighborhood. Then they walked around with the dogs. Those hounds sniffed out thirty bombs. Bomb disposal experts disarmed each one. From what they could determine, the detonators were all set to the same frequency. Once they sent the signal, there would be explosions all over Oak Bluffs. Hundreds of people could have been killed.

"They could then home in on the origination of the signal. It was coming from a house about a mile away. There'd been a small camera placed across from where the former president and first lady were staying so the guy could monitor their comings and goings.

"We got a warrant and busted in, arresting the man. His name's Jay Watson. He lawyered up right away, so got nothing out of him. My superiors asked where I got my information. I've played it coy, but you have to help me out here. I know of Heather's hacking prowess. I know she was the one responsible for dredging up financial information on Parker."

I was about to offer a response, but Jane beat me to the punch.

"Don't bother trying to deny it. I'm not looking to get her in trouble, but we need to get something on Parker that can stick. He's second in line at the State Police; whatever we get has to be rock solid. What Heather gathered was instrumental in stopping this insanity, but there's nothing here that we could admit in court.

"I need her to help me back into the case here. The FBI is tickled pink being able to stop all the carnage we did. Now we want to catch the people responsible. Caleb Smith is dead, but Parker is still out there. I need Heather to walk me through how she found Parker's connection to Andy Sykes, his purchase of the detonators, his trip to Martha's Vineyard and anything else she got. Using this info, we'll come up with a probable cause to get a warrant. We'll get the same info she gathered but it will be legal and admissible."

"Thanks, Jane, for not throwing the book at her."

"Throw the book? Hell, we may want to hire her away from you."

"Good luck with that." I chuckled.

29

I did not look forward to the upcoming holidays. It would be my first Christmas in nearly four years without Will. For the kids, it would be their first ever. It looked to be a long, dreary winter.

I was trying to think of something special for the kids, something that would take their minds away from their reality. I remembered that last year we stayed in Frank's cabin up in the Adirondacks and the kids had such a great time. Albert especially had a wonderful experience fishing. I even went out on the boat to fish. I had fun, provided I didn't have to bait a hook. Maybe we could do it again.

I then reconsidered that idea because I thought it would dredge up fresh memories of Will. The reason the trip last year was so much fun was because of him. He showed how to do many things us city dwellers had never done. While I was game, I was no replacement. I ran the risk of the kids either spending their time bemoaning the fact that their father wasn't there or being bored out of their minds.

I was wracking my brains, trying to come up with ideas when my phone rang. It was John.

"John, how are you doing?"

"So much better. I'm back home with the kids. I have to take it easy for a bit, but definitely on the mend."

"When are you finally heading for Singapore?"

"Given all that's happened, my son and I decided to wait until the summer. The kids like the school here and Nathan's trying to get himself settled in his new job. The doctors said it would be okay for me to fly, but they said waiting a few months might be better for that long a flight. All in all, it's working out well for all of us. How are you doing? You holding up all right?"

"As well as can be expected. I was just going to call you. We were both right about Andy Sykes. He was bad news. In fact, he was Caleb Smith, the founder of *Beyond Revelation*."

"Well, that explains a lot. You said he was Caleb Smith, in the past tense."

"He's dead. I killed him."

"I'm sorry you had to go through something like that. It's never pleasant to witness a death, no matter who's it was."

"But at least this nightmare is all over."

I filled him in on the attempts on the lives of the Speaker and the former President. I didn't mention Parker's name or his involvement since that was an ongoing investigation and Jane probably did not want too much information out there.

"Wow, sounds like you've been busy of late."

"I was just thinking I needed of a place to decompress with the kids. It'll be a tough holiday season without their father. Perhaps I could lessen the pain if we got away for a few nights and did something different."

"Why don't you come up here to Fairbrook? I feel I owe it to my town to present it to you in a better light. It's beautiful this time of year, especially with all the Christmas lights around town. You and the kids can stay down in the cottage at the lake. My family has owned it since the 1930s. I totally renovated it about a decade ago. It'll be a perfect place to get away from it all. Also, your kids are about the same age as Marcus and Sara so they'll have someone to pal around with. We're supposed to get some snow over the weekend, so Marcus and Albert maybe can get some sledding in. This is looking better and better the more I describe it."

"Mr. Foster, are you trying to play me?"

"Yes, I believe I am."

"Okay, I'm played. When do you want us?"

"Give me a week to get the place ready, so weekend after next? Come up next Friday?"

"That would be perfect."

The kids were excited to go on a trip to a new place. The thought of living in a cottage beside a lake added to their excitement. We packed up the car and set off at ten in the morning.

Unlike my previous trips up there, I was in no hurry. We drove on local roads through New York and Connecticut to enjoy the scenery. By the time we reached Hartford, there was a coating of snow on the ground. It was lovely. There was a forecast for additional snow that evening, but not a significant amount. It would be just enough to be beautiful.

We arrived at John's at three. Marcus and Sara had just gotten off from school, so they were all there to greet us. The kids all hit it off immediately. Albert and Marcus were about the same age. Stella was a year or two older than Sara, but since Stella was used to playing with Rosa, that wasn't an issue. The four of them went out to play in the side yard. Rosa stayed with John and me in the house and contentedly amused herself.

We all had a late lunch together and then we proceeded to the cottage on the lake, about a mile away. It looked very quaint, but it had three bedrooms and a huge porch that overlooked the small lake. In the middle was a huge fireplace. Once we put our bags in our respective rooms, John directed us back outside to the huge pile of firewood logs. He handed out gloves to each of us and then started handing us logs to carry inside. Our respective size and strength determined the number and weight of the logs we carried. Even Rosa got some kindling to carry in so she would feel included.

Once we brought in a stack of wood, John made a roaring fire for us. The temperature had dropped into the thirties and the heat felt good.

"Have you ever cooked your own popcorn over an open fire?" John asked.

We all responded no, we hadn't.

"Then you're in for a treat."

He pulled out a wire rectangular basket with a long handle on it and then went and got the popcorn.

"Before we get this going, let's make some caramel sauce to go over it. Stella, why don't you help me with this."

Stella dutifully but somewhat skeptically followed John into the kitchen. It wasn't long before we heard Stella giggling away. Soon, they returned to us.

"I put Stella in charge of finding the appropriate goo factor for the sauce. I think we now have the perfect amount of goo, don't we?"

Stella vigorously nodded her head.

"Now, the popcorn. No offense, ladies, but this step takes a man's touch. Albert, it's all yours. Hold it over the fire, but not too close. And shake it around and around. At some point you'll see and hear them pop. Take it away, Albert."

Albert took the basket and very studiously shook it over the fire. Occasionally, John would reach in to help Albert hold the basket to keep it from wavering. I thought of him trying to steady Will's hunting rifle in the face of Andy Sykes. I pushed the thought away.

Albert was getting frustrated but then the first kernel popped, and then a second. Albert's face lit up. He looked over at me with pride.

"Okay, raise it higher but keep it over the heat and keep shaking it. You're doing magnificently."

Soon, the entire basket was filled with popped popcorn.

"Okay, let's take it away and put it into these bowls. This one will be for the caramel sauce expertly prepared for by our own Stella Allen and this one will be for the more traditional butter and salt."

We sat around savoring the popcorn.

"John, I can't thank you enough for this weekend. It's exactly what we needed."

"You're welcome, Francine. I wouldn't be here if it weren't for you. It's my pleasure."

Even though it was dark when we got there, there was a full moon so the view over the lake was idyllic. I told Albert we were staying on a lake, but I don't think it had sunk in until he saw it. He then excitedly announced he wanted to go fishing the next day.

"Isn't it a little cold to be out there fishing?"

"No," he firmly stated.

John spoke up.

"I'll be happy to take him out to fish. Marcus, you want to join us? But we have to get out there early to catch the big ones."

I wasn't sure Marcus wanted to fish, but a chance to do something like fishing with his grandpa was too irresistible to turn down. It made me a little sad that my kids didn't have any grandparents to show them things like this. I stifled the thought they now didn't have a father, either.

"Okay, we'll come back here at 7:00 in the morning."

John and his kids left and went back home. We settled in for the evening. It was so peaceful and serene. I lived most of my life in Manhattan and sometimes I find Queens a little too quiet for my taste. This solitude was jarring, but after a short while I found it blissful and fell into a deep sleep.

We woke up the next morning to find it had snowed overnight, but only enough to apply a fresh new coat of white on the ground and trees. It was gorgeous and magical. As promised, John and Marcus were there to take Albert out fishing promptly at seven. What was surprising was that Albert was ready. In fact, he'd been up for an hour.

John gave Stella and Sara the opportunity to go along, but they turned up their noses at the idea. John pulled the aluminum rowboat out from under the tarp and grabbed the fishing poles, life preserver jackets and oars from the garage and they were off. We women folk worked on breakfast, which would include a healthy dose of hot chocolate, prepared in anticipation of their return.

An hour and a half later John rowed them back in. They'd caught eight fish—an assortment of perch and bluegills and one pickerel—none of which could by any stretch of the imagination be considered legal but John wasn't about to tell either of the boys they couldn't keep their bounty.

I announced I was about to make up some pancakes, but John asked me to hold off for a few minutes. He would filet the meager fish, dredge them in egg and breadcrumbs and fry them up as the boys' contribution to the breakfast menu. I wasn't sure how well fried fish would pair with pancakes and syrup, but I wasn't about to be the one to rain on the boys' parade.

Throughout the day, we traipsed around town. It was a beautiful, brisk and sunny New England day. The whole time, John kept up a running commentary on the town's, as well as his own personal, history. He was especially animated when he described the old cemetery down the street from his house. Eight early settlers were buried in this graveyard. They'd been killed by Indians. The monument to them spoke of their glory and valor, although John was more than a little dubious about the veracity of the account. He thought the settlers were either in the wrong place at the wrong time or that they were the aggressors, not the Native Americans.

We had a light lunch at the Top Hat. Everyone took Marcus's lead and ordered grilled cheese. I had a cup of tomato soup with mine.

John had something to attend to in the afternoon, so he asked if I would mind looking after the kids for a few hours. He'd return to the cottage at six to bring us all to dinner at a local restaurant called the Pilgrim's Bounty. He had to prove to me that Fairbrook had a more to offer, culinary-wise, than just the Top Hat.

We went back to the cottage and rested up some. The kids played some games together. When five-thirty rolled around, I corralled all of them and got them cleaned up for dinner. John picked us up precisely at six.

The restaurant was about three miles away. Along the way, I recognized the Rutledges' house. A sense of sadness settled over me. John sensed my mood.

"I went to visit Carl the other day. He's doing much better. He fully admitted he tried to do a stupid thing, but he's in therapy now and feeling better. I'll keep an eye on him."

We pulled into the restaurant's parking lot. There were many out-of-state cars in the parking lot. Somewhere as beautiful as this much get tourists all times of the year, I thought.

We entered the restaurant and a tall, graying man came over.

"John, great to see you."

"Dickie, this is my friend, Francine Vega and her family. This is Albert. That's Stella, and the little one is Rosa. You've met my grandkids, Marcus and Sara, before, haven't you?"

"But of course. Great to see all of you. If you will follow me."

The man, who was the restaurant's owner, led us through the restaurant toward a room in the back. Along the way, I leaned over to John and whispered to him.

"So, is he a lifelong friend or someone you helped get out of a legal jam?"

John laughed.

"Both actually. I've known Dickie since first grade and a couple years ago I helped him through a lawsuit."

Dickie led us to the back room and then opened the door. The lights were out as we walked in. Once we were in, the lights came to life and we were greeted with a huge "Surprise!"

I looked around the room. Frank and his wife, Heidi, were there. Emma was there. Heather was there. Jane was there with her son and daughter. Broderick was there. Richard was there with his wife. Reverend McKenzie was there. And Jonas was there.

"I can't believe this. What are you all doing here?"

John answered.

"This was all Heather's idea. She knew you didn't get much of a family Thanksgiving so, after you told her you were coming up here for the weekend, she called me and set all of this up. Now, this place is famous for its prime rib, but you'll have to order that on a subsequent trip because I spoke with Dickie and he agreed to pull out all stops and do his traditional Thanksgiving turkey dinner. I've had everyone here sign releases holding me harmless for forcing them to have two turkey dinners so close to each other."

"I don't know what to say."

Frank responded. "That's a first."

We all laughed. John suggested we all sit down to eat. A waiter brought in a huge, beautifully roasted turkey. He carved as we watched. We were asked our preference, white or dark, which was promptly delivered. Other waiters brought out the side dishes.

I chatted with everybody. Jonas told me that Eunice wanted to come, but he thought it too soon for her to return up here. I told him he was probably right, noting how tough it was for me passing by Carl and Lynn's house.

I had trouble holding back tears the entire meal. Finally, I clinked my glass and stood up.

"I still can't believe all of you are here. Thank you Heather, and you too John, for pulling this together."

I breathed in deep.

"This has been a horrific year. Albert, Stella, Rosa and I never would have made it through if it weren't for the people in this room. You're the ones who kept me going. My friends and colleagues always have my back. No, let me correct that. You're more than friends and colleagues, you're my family."

"We're Fava's Army!" Jonas shouted out. The crowd applauded in response.

"While I appreciate the title, each one of you is an army, a formidable force, in yourselves. I can look at each one of you and think of all the courageous and resourceful things you do daily. But there's something else.

"In the businesses represented here—journalism, politics, law enforcement, even religion—we encounter some of the worst people on earth. This year, we encountered the absolute worst people one could ever imagine, but they never imagined they'd run up against the likes of Heather or Jane or Jonas or John or any of you. They couldn't stand up to my young man, Albert.

"I look out on a sea of goodness. I know I'll never be alone. Now, you better stop me before I break into Henry Fonda's speech at the end of The Grapes of Wrath. Let me just say thank you from the bottom of my heart for this evening, and for always."

I raised my glass.

"Here's to all of us."

"To us!"

NOTE FROM THE AUTHOR

Word-of-mouth is crucial for any author to succeed. If you enjoyed *Beyond Revelation*, please leave a review online—anywhere you are able. Even if it's just a sentence or two. It would make all the difference and would be very much appreciated.

Thanks!
John

ABOUT THE AUTHOR

John Hazen lives with his wife, Lynn, in Florida and spends his days writing novels that reflect and illuminate the issues and events of today. When he's not writing, he's reading, practicing his clarinet, playing the occasional game of tennis and enjoying the Florida sun. John grew up in Massachusetts but spent the bulk of his life in the New Jersey/New York City area.

Thank you so much for reading one of **John Hazen's** novels.
If you enjoyed the experience, please check out our recommended
title for your next great read!

Fava by John Hazen

"18 Best FBI Thrillers Books" of All-Time

— *BEST THRILLERS*